Underclyff

Mark Brend

HORNET BOOKS®
PUBLISHING TALENT

Undercliff
Published 2019 by Hornet Books
Text © Mark Brend
This work © Hornet Books Ltd
Paperback ISBN 978-0-9957658-6-3

Editor: David Roberts
Proofreader: Suzannah Young
Cover design and photography: David Roberts
and Adrian Arnett

Hornet Books
Ground Floor, 2B Vantage Park, Washingley Road,
Huntingdon, PE29 6SR
www.hornetbooks.com
info@hornetbooks.com

Printed and bound in Great Britain by Clays Ltd, Elcograf S.p.A

*For there shall arise false Christs, and
false prophets, and shall shew great signs
and wonders; insomuch that, if it were possible,
they shall deceive the very elect.*

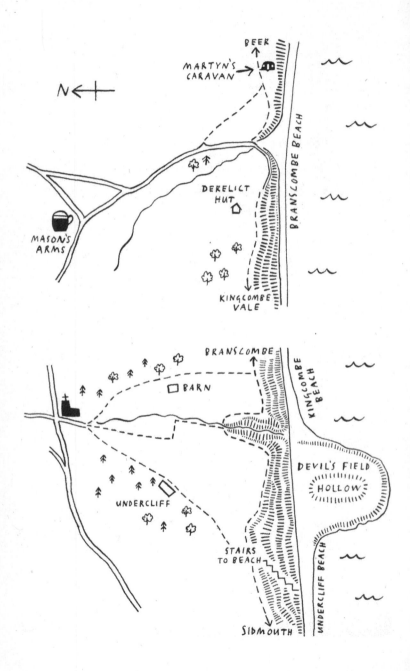

Prologue

The day after reading the news of my death I went for a walk. It was clear and I could see the long arm of Portland Bill stretching into the sea miles ahead.

The words meant nothing to him. He closed the manuscript he had opened at random, put it down and picked up the letter that came with it.

October 31st, 2015

Dear Adam

The enclosed arrived in the office the day after you left for your break. It was addressed to you, but there was no accompanying letter. I have left it in the packaging in which it arrived. As you can see, it has a British stamp and a London postmark. I assume it is something you are expecting, possibly in relation to your research, so I am forwarding it to you.

I hope you have a productive sabbatical.

Best regards

Julia.

He picked up the manuscript again. Not only was there no covering letter, there was no author's name, and no other identifying marks. He flicked through the pages again. It was not something he was expecting. It seemed to have nothing to do with his research. But grateful for a reason to put off writing his thesis, he sat down in his chair by the window overlooking the garden and began to read.

CHAPTER 1

August 1972

I was 36 when I came back to London, after nine years away. Those years had been spent, happily enough at first, in Leicester. I'd moved there with Lillian from a basement flat in Archway, where we'd spent the first 18 months of our marriage. We'd met in London in 1961 when I was a cub reporter on the *South London Press*, and she was at teacher-training college. It was cheap in Leicester and she had family nearby, and we could get a terraced house for less than the sale price of the flat. We both found jobs that were a little dull, but which paid adequately without being too onerous. I'm writing this because I want you to know that my life was straightforward. There was nothing odd about it. I was a sub-editor on a local newspaper nurturing, like many sub-editors, a plan to write a novel. Lillian was a primary school teacher.

She loved children, and that's where things started to go wrong for us. We both wanted to start a family, she more than me, I suppose. And we tried, but nothing happened. We had tests that revealed no problems and tried again, but still nothing happened. Gradually, imperceptibly, what began as a common cause binding us together became a simmering resentment that drove us apart. In my mind we weren't old enough to be desperate. But she interpreted my attempts to express this as excuses. "You don't really want this baby," she'd say, as if it existed somewhere and I was refusing to go through the necessary procedure to claim it. She was one of those people who would withdraw when angry, go silent rather than shout. I can remember a faint tremor in her jaw that was a sign of something wrong. Very slight, yet giving the impression of a powerful mechanism working loose. Rows weren't our style, but I remember a howling one just after Christmas, which was a sign of how bad things had become.

After that it all started to unravel quite quickly. I can't really remember any more crucial, defining events or conversations, just a mutual acceptance that the marriage had failed. I was somewhat dazed, but still functioning. For a little while it was as if a flimsy, opaque gauze separated me from the rest of life, but I soon brushed it away. I wasn't distressed particularly. Things had simply ground to a halt. We put the house on the market and accepted an offer on it in a week at a considerable profit. This was luck, not judgement. We set a divorce in motion, one of the few things we could agree on.

When my parents died I saw the gulf between my present and past for what it was – unbridgeable. I knew that I had entered a new phase. When Lillian and I separated I had no such sense of the tectonic plates of life shifting. It was as if something that had been happening to me had simply stopped. I knew then that I had never loved her. Now, so many years later, I struggle to conjure up an image of her face.

With more money in the bank than I'd ever had before, and nothing to keep me in Leicester except a job I wasn't that interested in, I resigned and returned to London. It wasn't that I wanted to, particularly. Just that there didn't seem to be anywhere else to go. My parents were gone, and with them any lingering attachment to the town in which I had grown up. At least back in London I knew a few names and had a few threads to pick up.

It was August 1972 when I returned, staying at first, rather grandly, in a small hotel in Bloomsbury. The 60s hadn't really happened in Leicester and though I was in my mid-30s I felt like a gauche and awkward teenager amidst an unfamiliar sophistication: Habitat, vegetarian restaurants, Compendium Books, clothes and hairstyles I'd until then seen only in magazines or on television. I picked up once again the novel I'd tinkered with when we'd first moved to Leicester, which I had set aside when things with Lillian had deteriorated. I can see now my plan was a fantasy, the sort of dream you cherish when you want to escape a situation you don't like. In this dream I'd find a cheap flat and live off the profit from the house. I even caught myself thinking of the flat as 'rooms'. I'll take cheap rooms and write, I thought. The hotel, which was clean and functional but devoid of what people call character, fed these notions for a day or two. The view from the window took in the iron railings around the British Museum. I managed to persuade myself that I was in the heart of thinking, literary London. But it was a delusion easily dispelled by a week of desultory scribbling in the museum café. Truth is, I was a bit short on self-motivation then. I needed a framework, people around me, and I had enough self-awareness to recognise my limitations. Perceptive enough but short on imagination. I put the book aside and signed up with a few agencies, and soon found myself with a temporary sub-editor's job covering someone's maternity leave at a travel publisher. It was about as boring as the job I'd left behind in Leicester, but I could handle the work easily enough and it felt like the beginning of a fresh start. I told myself I'd continue working on my novel in the evenings and weekends, but I rarely did.

Even though I now had a regular income the hotel was eating a big hole in my wallet. I set about looking for a flat. I felt I was too old for a house share. And anyway, I wanted to live alone. I enjoyed the comfortable solitude of the hotel, so I looked for something that would replicate that feature at a fraction of the cost. I imagined a spacious studio in an Edwardian mansion block. On polite nodding terms with neighbours passed on the stairs, all of us discreetly coming and going. Somewhere near the river. Wandsworth? I could see myself strolling around the park on Sunday morning. I had so thoroughly entered into this idyll that I was deflated when a Saturday morning tour of estate agents left me in no doubt that although the studio in the parkside mansion block did indeed exist, there would be no buying it on a temporary contract and a half share of a few years' profit on a house in Leicester. There would be no renting it either, not in Wandsworth or Putney, or Battersea or Clapham for that matter, all on the rise in those days. I had been away too long.

Sitting in the café in Wandsworth Park I considered my options. South of the river, anywhere beyond Clapham was off the map as far as I was concerned, and I didn't want to go north as that was where I'd lived with Lillian. The memories weren't that painful, but I wasn't inclined to revisit the scene of previous failure at my stage in life. Divorce wasn't unusual then, but it wasn't as common as it is now. A sense of defeat clung to me, even though I had wanted the marriage to end. So I looked south again, flicking through the tattered A–Z that survived from my previous spell of London living. Brixton, Stockwell, Elephant and Castle, Bermondsey. I'd only travelled through these places, and in my mind they retained a sense of menace. They were rough areas, where gangsters came from in TV programmes. Peckham, Camberwell, East Dulwich, Nunhead. I knew nothing about Nunhead save for one fact: it had a Victorian cemetery that almost matched Highgate for crumbling, overgrown appeal, which I had visited one Sunday afternoon in a London history phase years before. With this single faintly positive association, and no immediately negative ones, I caught a bus to Nunhead that Saturday afternoon. Now, it seems, as if pulled by invisible strings. I didn't really have a plan, except that I'd wander around the area and see what it was like. There was a row of shops on the main street, interrupted by still un-reclaimed bombsites. I learned later a V1 had hit a corset factory and killed women working inside. Had the allotments that bordered the cemetery extended a few hundred yards further they'd have connected with the tip of Peckham Rye. Pubs. No tube station but an overground line that ran into London Bridge. A mixed, obviously poor area that fell short of deprivation. It was one of those places that felt like a secret, and I decided there was enough there to make it at least an option. Then, at about 3.30pm one of those life-changing things happened, which seemed at the time nothing more than a convenient coincidence.

I walked into the one estate agent I could see and said to the receptionist that I was looking for a one-bedroom flat to rent in the area. A woman sitting in the lobby behind me interjected. I hadn't noticed her. She was sorry to appear nosy, but she herself had a one bedroom flat to let and was just waiting for the agent to sign the relevant papers. Twenty minutes later I was standing with the woman in her flat, the estate agent brimming with eagerness behind us. The place was untidy as the woman was packing to leave, but I could see at once it was right. One large living room with a galley kitchen off it, a decent-sized bedroom and an adequate, if cramped, shower room. Neutral décor and comfortable furniture, according to the agent's notes. The price was about two-thirds what I had been quoted for something smaller in Wandsworth that morning. I accepted there and then, and agreed a moving in date of the following weekend, pending formalities.

As we walked down the stairs I realised that I had yet to register any information about the building. So I asked the owner and looked around as we walked and she talked. "I think it is late Victorian. There are eight flats and an office in the ground floor, in what used to be a hairdresser's." She said this as we exited the front door onto the pavement and I saw, to my right, a large frosted glass window and a glass door. Etched in to the glass was a logo. Slender branches and little leaves formed a sort of wreath around the words, *The Olive Grove*, and underneath in a smaller, swirly script, *together in power*.

"What's The Olive Grove?" I asked.

"Some sort of free church, I think you'd call it. That's the office. They meet in the old bingo hall on the high street. They seem nice enough, but you hardly ever see them. No noise, which is the main thing."

We filled the short walk back to the office with small talk. She worked for the Foreign Office and had been posted overseas at short notice, for a year at least. I wondered if she did something classified. Ms J Wilkinson. I remember forwarding some post. She was a few years older than me. Quite attractive in a severe, academic sort of way. I realised I was looking at her with faint longing, and then I realised I was lonely.

CHAPTER 2

August to November 1972

I'd been in the flat about a week when I bumped into a couple about my age coming out of the Olive Grove office as I was returning from work on Friday evening. They said hello, asked if I was new, and we got chatting. I liked them immediately – earnest, open-faced people so clearly devoted to each other they had begun to look alike. They, it turned out, were not employees of the church, just enthusiastic members who helped out as much as they could. They gave me a card decorated with the Olive Grove leaves design and invited me along to what they called a newcomers' night in the office the following Tuesday. I thanked them and went up to my flat, not imagining for a minute that I'd actually go. I put down my briefcase, left the card on the coffee table and forgot about it.

The following Tuesday after work I was at a loose end. I picked up the *Radio Times* from the coffee table to see if there was anything worth watching that evening. There was the card where I had left it. Although I hadn't been to church since coming back to London, and indeed for some time before that, I wasn't entirely unsympathetic. There was nothing I wanted to watch on TV so I thought I might as well give it a try. After all, I only had to walk down some stairs. If I didn't like it I could make my excuses and walk back up again. I had nothing else to do.

It turned out to be a pleasant evening. There were half a dozen of us newcomers, plus the couple I'd met the week before, Neil and Kath. Most of the time we just sat around chatting. Wine, coffee and a few snacks were served, and Kath spoke about the Olive Grove for ten minutes. She said it was very relaxed and informal – no pressure – and on this showing I believed her. I went for a stroll afterwards to get some air, and bumped into a younger man who I'd seen there but hadn't spoken to. "Jesus freaks", was all he said when I asked him what he thought of it. Maybe they are, I thought, but I liked them.

I went along to a meeting the following Sunday evening. As promised, it was relaxed and informal. Coffee was served before the service and people strolled to their seats clutching plastic cups. Just that one modest little break with church tradition felt liberating. There was no protocol about standing up or sitting down at certain points in the service either. You just did whatever you felt like doing. I remember wondering at the time if all of this apparent casualness was carefully orchestrated, contrived even, but at the same time not caring if it was. Straight away I felt at ease, and as the weeks went by I found that most members of the Olive Grove – and I soon considered myself one – had been attracted to it because of the prevailing atmosphere of relaxed informality. We'd all talk amongst ourselves about how good it was that the Two didn't have control issues. Control issues. That was the phrase.

I've just realised I've mentioned the Two but haven't explained who they are. Or were. Magnus Eves and Simon Hill: the two main leaders of the Olive Grove. There was a team of elders too, men and women, but the Two steered the ship.

Conspicuous casualness aside, services at the Olive Grove were conventional. We sang songs, there were prayers, a talk, then we were encouraged to pray for each other where we sat or stood. The talks were usually delivered by one of the Two, occasionally by an elder. Once every couple of months, though, the Two would preach together. Standing at two lecterns mounted on a stage about 15 feet apart, they would hold forth without notes. Swapping lines, then occasionally emphasising a point by joining their voices in perfect unison. It was impressive, and when first witnessed, eerie. You soon got used to it, though.

Whether speaking separately or together, the content of their talks was orthodox. As far as I could tell, anyway, and I wasn't a novice. There was a lot about self-sacrifice, and how eternal life was something to be experienced now, not some vague hope of future regeneration. Unlike a lot of evangelicals, though, they made a point of saying that all religions had something to teach us. They said we should not look for the day or the hour, but even so the end times were another recurring theme. The books of Daniel and Revelation were quoted often, as was an American writer named Hal Lindsey, who was forever seeing intimations of coming judgement in current world events. Culturally they seemed quite broad-minded. They quoted from contemporary books and songs and were open to analysis and therapy – unusual for church leaders in my experience. They came across as being very mildly counter-cultural, in a 60s hippy, polytechnic lecturer sort of way. But even allowing for that the whole thing was resolutely normal. I can't think of a better word for it. It was comfortable and easy. Magnus was about 5 foot 8, olive-skinned with thinning dark hair cropped short, which was unusual at the time. I wouldn't call him black, but he looked like he might have had some North African or Arab blood in him. Simon was white, taller, with neat, longish grey hair in a side parting, and a silvery beard. They were both in early middle age, with Simon probably the slightly older. Both slim almost to the point of thinness. They dressed casually.

I never saw either of them wear a tie. Think of geography teachers who run marathons. They liked football, or said they did. Magnus, I remember, supported Charlton Athletic, Simon Crystal Palace.

Their speech was informal and scattered with Americanisms – "you guys", "we're going to do our thing now", "oh man", "wow" – and they had little catchphrases. "You start to live when you learn to give" was a sort of overarching principle, that your own life would be enriched in proportion to the extent in which you gave of it. Then there was 'telling'. This was when a group of people, usually led by at least one of the Two, would gather round someone and make affirming, aspirational statements to them. "You're coming into a season of blessing", "you've got a heart for peace", "I see a new strength in you", "believe what you were made for". After a month or so I experienced my first telling, led by Simon after a Sunday night service. I don't recall a word they said to me, but I do remember leaving the building in a state close to euphoria, which lasted well into the following week.

We sang a mix of conventional hymns to piano accompaniment, and folky worship songs in a sort of acoustic soft-rock style, backed by guitars, bass, electric organ, drums, and usually flute. The group of musicians responsible called themselves The Flock. They'd sometimes get bookings in folk clubs and pubs in South London, where they'd sell cassettes of an album they'd self-recorded in the Olive Grove's main building.

The Two seemed open and approachable. They hugged you or slapped you on the back rather than shaking hands. Both were single and I never saw any sign that either had any intimate relationships. Each spoke easily with men and women of all ages, and children. The one time I saw something that might have been anger sticks in my mind because it was so unusual. I was helping pack up the band's equipment after a Sunday gathering. We used to lock it all in a store-room to the side of the stage. I wasn't really concentrating and tried the handle of another door marked *STRICTLY NO ADMITTANCE* by mistake. It was locked, of course, as it always was.

"Martyn! No!"

Magnus's voice in my ear was quiet but so urgent and unexpected that I started. Within a second or two Simon was at my other side, a hand on my shoulder, emollient. "Sorry Martyn," he said, and explained that the heating system was housed behind the door, that it was old and could be dangerous. "Got to think of the children, you see. Safety first. It's the one rule we've got." His voice was easy as he turned me toward the other door, the one I had meant to open. Magnus was walking away from me, across the room. I didn't think much of it at the time.

It was generally known that he, Magnus, who was a little more reserved than Simon, had once been married but that his wife had died, though I never heard him speak about her. I went to their homes. Simon lived in a small terrace in Peckham, Magnus a flat in East Dulwich. Both homes were comfortable, but thinking about it now they lacked the stamp of personality. Everything was new. There were books and records, but they were the sort of books and records anyone might have had at the time. No family photos that I can recall, apart from a faded snap on Magnus's mantelpiece of a woman with long curly hair, presumably his late wife. No old furniture handed down from parents, no artwork by a niece or nephew stuck to the fridge. I don't think I ever heard a specific reference to earlier lives. Just "when I was younger...", or "I once met someone...", or "when I worked in the Midlands...", or "when I was at university..."

Much later I did some research and found a few press cuttings. The information was scant. Certainly no scandal, but the biographical specifics were thin. A feature in *New Life!* – a magazine I remember as an attempt to harness some of the style and language of contemporary youth culture for younger Christians – revealed that Simon spent some time travelling in the East in the 1960s before becoming ordained. Magnus had worked in insurance. You were left with a sketchy outline that only acquired colour and detail about three years earlier. Simon was a curate in an Anglican church in East London. He met Magnus at a retreat centre in Norfolk where Magnus was working as the catering manager, having given up insurance a few years before, following the death of his wife. The move to Nunhead to start the Olive Grove had been a step of faith in response, they said, to various dreams and prophetic visions. They arrived in the area in 1969, buying the bingo hall with a trust fund in Simon's name. He left the Anglican Church, though still professed respect for it. At the very first meeting of the Olive Grove just one homeless man joined Simon and Magnus in the hall. That became a cherished part of the church's creation myth. The place became quite well-known for a while in radical Christian circles. They self-published a book about it, written by a single mother who sang in The Flock. It had a cover with a design of vivid, multi-coloured leaves woven into the shape of a cross, but I haven't seen a copy in decades. Google 'the Two' or 'the Olive Grove' now and there's nothing at all. It's as if they've exercised their right to be forgotten.

During the week we met in small groups in each other's houses. There was something of the commune in how we gathered together, although most of us had jobs and lived ordinary lives. We'd sit on the floor, eat vegetarian food we prepared in turn, listen to obscure Christian rock made by Jesus people in San Francisco. Many of the men were bearded and hirsute, and I, though a little older than most of them, grew my hair to my collar. The women wore long skirts and cheesecloth blouses. In hindsight we were an anachronism, a 60s throwback. But in church circles, Christians being what they are – forever two steps off the cultural pace – we were alternative, radical and new.

I volunteered to host one of the gatherings at my flat, and every Wednesday half a dozen of us sat and pored over a Bible passage, sometimes with the help of guidance notes from the Two. It was here that I met Amelia.

Neil, who led the group with Kath, phoned me one Monday early in October, when I'd been at the Olive Grove for about two months:

"Martyn, hello. We've got someone new coming this week. A woman called Amelia. Met her yet? She's just joined."

"Don't think so, but good. It'll be a bit cosy if we've got a full house. Are you leading?"

"It's Kath this week. Hebrews again. Melchizedek."

"Sounds good," I said, and it did. I had become fascinated by the Bible.

I suppose I underwent some sort of conversion in those first few months at the Olive Grove. I'd been an intermittent churchgoer since before National Service, though even more intermittent than usual over the previous few years when things were going wrong with Lillian. As a teenager I'd attended a youth group run by a skiffle-loving curate who rode a motorbike, and I'd have called myself a believer if pushed. But there was something that clicked for me around that time. Though what that means now, I've no idea.

Amelia came early. Neil and Kath had been there for 20 minutes and we'd shared our usual pre-meeting prayer, but she was next after them. I first heard her voice on the intercom. A faint hint of an accent that turned out to be more pronounced when not mediated through the receiver's tinny speaker. French? I opened the door and stood by it, waiting as she walked up the stairs. A few seconds later she appeared at the end of the short hall, a question in her smile as she tucked her dark fringe behind her left ear. She looked different from the other young women at the Olive Grove. Her clothes were neat and modest, but chic somehow. A plain, dark skirt. A fitted, short corduroy jacket. Flat shoes of the sort you didn't see in high street shops. There was an elegant precision in her facial features, a clean jawline, and wide-set eyes. She dipped her head a little as she spoke, like the beginning of a bow, an unintentional gesture that became familiar to me.

As she walked into the flat I stood aside, but the space was too small and she brushed against me as she passed. Our first touch. I ushered her into the lounge and she greeted Neil and Kath with kisses. I walked past her, careful not to bump her arm, and went into the kitchen. "Drink?" I called over my shoulder.

"Do you have any herb tea?"

"I've got green tea?"

"That's fine – thanks."

Neil and Kath began to talk about something they hoped to discuss later in the meeting, leaving me to speak to Amelia. Rather too obviously, I thought.

"So you're new?"

"Yes. I came to London about two months ago."

"Me too. And what brings you here?"

"I'm temping in a translation agency at the moment."

"She's writing a book!" interjected Kath from across the room, prompting another duck of the head from Amelia. She coloured slightly.

"Oh yes? What sort of book?" I could see common ground just ahead, but I didn't get the chance to explore it. Amelia was half a reluctant sentence into an answer when the buzzer rang again. The rest of the group came streaming in.

***

"Well, nice to meet you. Hope you'll come again," I said.

"I will," she answered, and I thought I saw a flicker in her eyes.

And she did come the following week, though I didn't see her on the Sunday in between. Then the following Saturday I ran into her on Nunhead Lane. It turned out that she lived just on the other side of the road, into Peckham. We talked politely for a minute or two, me feeling shyer than I could remember feeling since I was seventeen. I asked if she wanted to go for a coffee. She said she couldn't as she was having her hair cut in ten minutes. There was a pause before we both spoke at once. She said "maybe another time" and I said "what about a drink later?" We both laughed, she pushed the fringe that would soon be a little shorter behind her ear, and we agreed to meet at 5.30pm, at the Clockhouse, on the other side of Peckham Rye.

It was a warm, clear October evening. I arrived ten minutes early and sat outside. I didn't know how she'd get to the pub and so from what direction she'd come. I learned that evening that she didn't have a car, but I didn't know that as I waited. As it happened she surprised me, coming down Barry Road on the near side, while I looked straight across the flat, grassed area at the bottom of the Rye. Before I noticed her she was at my side.

"Looking for angels?"

"Sorry? I didn't see you. How are you?"

"Oh, fine. You were daydreaming. Looking for angels. Isn't William Blake supposed to have seen one in a tree on Peckham Rye? Can we go inside? I think it might get cold soon."

We settled in a booth at the back of the pub and she took out a packet of cigarettes and offered one to me. My surprise must have shown. I said something like "no thanks, doesn't agree with me," as she said "everyone smokes where I come from." She'd had her hair cut short at the nape of her neck. I'd never seen that on a woman before.

We spoke for an hour and a half that evening, then she had to go to meet friends for dinner. I could give an account of every one of those 90 minutes. I swear I could, even after all these years. They passed with a slow-moving, dreamlike quality, as if clock time had been suspended and replaced by something less mechanical and more fluid, and yet my senses were sharpened to an acute, penetrating point. What did I learn about her? She was 29, the longed-for only child of a mother and father both into their 40s when she was born, French-speaking Belgians from a hamlet near Charleroi. They had died within nine months of each other, her father succumbing last about 18 months previously, leaving her a modest cottage, now sold, and a little money. She was bright, academically. Her accented English was impeccable. When her parents were still alive she had studied for an Eng. Lit. MA in London, and had fostered an interest then in Dorothy L. Sayers. She'd always hoped to return, and once she'd dealt with her parents' estate and sold the house – which had taken longer than she would have wished – she had made her way back. Her idea was to eke out her inheritance with temporary work while writing a study of Sayers. Something to do with the theology of her detective stories.

She was friendly in an introverted way. A Catholic frustrated by Rome and exploring alternatives. She gave the impression of setting aside a percentage of herself for some other purpose that remained obscure.

After that meeting we spent what was left of autumn circling each other. She had to go back to Belgium for a few weeks to sort out some final details of her parents' affairs, and I had a holiday, so for about a month over late October into November we didn't see each other. I recall a sense of relief when I returned and saw her again, and she thanked me for my postcard. There were no dates, but I always looked out for her at church, and we'd generally find ourselves sitting together. I was pretty sure she liked me and I knew I liked her, but she was reserved and I surprised myself when I realised I'd lost a bit of confidence with women.

Later in November we were both invited on a weekend away, along with about 15 other members of the church. The Olive Grove had acquired a big old house in Devon, close to a seaside village called Branscombe. The name seemed familiar, and I remembered after a while that a cargo ship had run aground nearby a few years before, and the press had enjoyed itself with stories of locals reverting to type – torch-lit midnight processions to the beach recovering cargo washed up from the broken vessel.

The house was in some disrepair, and most weekends

parties from the church would drive down for a couple of days of DIY interspersed with prayer. Our group left in the Olive Grove's Ford Transit minibus and two cars at about 6pm on a late November Friday. I sat in the front seat of one of the cars, an elderly blue Vauxhall estate driven by Harry, a plumber from Bermondsey who took pleasure in making a caricature of himself, always ready with a joke about jellied eels or Millwall football club. I found him rather trying. He was the foreman for the weekend's working party, though that turned out to be a nominal role. Neil and Kath were in the back. I started the journey frustrated that I hadn't been able to engineer it so that I was sitting next to Amelia, but a woman called Pam had diverted her into the minibus. She was one of the big personalities at the church. Shrill voice, and a mass of tightly-curled, copper-coloured hair. One of those people who feels that circumstances around her will descend into chaos unless she tells everyone what to do. She had acquired a measure of fame and status in the Olive Grove when the Two had apparently healed her of psoriasis. It was a dry, clear night, and getting cold. The intention to drive in convoy was rendered meaningless by the London traffic. By the time we'd reached the South Circular we'd lost sight of our friends, so we all made our own way to Devon.

Progress west on the M4 was slow. The traffic was heavy and we stopped once. The engine hum, the headlights passing like meteorites and anticipation of a weekend in close proximity to Amelia conspired to lull me into a protracted daydream of romantic imaginings. We sat in silence for most of the drive. It took us three hours to reach Bristol, where we turned south and I saw a sign for Exeter. 73 miles. We'll be there by 10pm, I thought, and indeed we did get to Exeter not long after my estimate. But I hadn't appreciated that the journey from there to the house, though not much more than ten miles, would be a slow one. Our meandering drive along the road that ran inland parallel to the coast was unhurried, slackening to a crawl in Newton Poppleford and Sidford. From here we climbed a steep hill into woodland, where an unsigned, unlit right turn I would not have noticed took us briefly on an even steeper zigzag climb, which the Vauxhall took in a straining second gear. Abruptly we reached a peak, the road overhung with dense trees, and began a descent toward what I sensed must be the sea. The trees thinned out and we turned left, past some sort of memorial in a fork in the road. The descent became steeper at this point. We passed a few dwellings and on our left, a church. A little further on and the metalled road curved away down to the left while we carried straight on to a mud track. We bumped along at 5 mph for about 100 yards before bearing right around the top of a small copse, and there before us was the house.

I could see, even in the moonlight, that it was big, and in some disrepair. It presented a plain, almost symmetrical frontage, with two sets of four windows of equal size, two on the ground floor and two on the first floor, flanking the porch. Above this was a slightly larger window, which was boarded up. The building was coated in a pale render – crumbling in places – which, daylight later revealed, was once powder blue. I learned over the weekend that the house dated from the late 1920s, which accounted for the rusting metal window frames. An architect in thrall to art deco had built it for a gentleman scholar who wanted a Georgian-style country retreat with modern amenities. The result was a hybrid that was not unpleasing. What had once been a sweeping drive was overgrown with weeds and a few small shrubs. At the far, seaward end of the house some roof tiles had slipped and a drainpipe had broken away from the gutter and stood at an angle from the wall. In the wind it waved like a reed.

We pulled up in front of the house, next to a Land Rover and the other car from our party. The minibus had not yet arrived. We got out of the car and stood in the still darkness for a moment, stretching, listening to waves breaking onto a beach I later discovered was just over half a mile away. The night was clear, and a crescent moon stood brilliant in the sky. It had been some time since I had been outside a big city, and I'd forgotten how dark the night was, how bright the stars. It was one of those vivid moments that felt like insight.

As we were unloading our bags from the boot the front door of the house opened, casting light over us from inside. A middle-aged woman with long, greying hair tied back in a loose ponytail stood in the doorway and called out a welcome. Harry, Neil and Kath had visited the house many times before and obviously knew her well. Kisses were exchanged. I stood to one side waiting my turn until the woman turned to me and introduced herself:

"Martyn? Jenny Cummings. My husband Tim and I are what you'd call caretakers." For a moment I wondered how she knew who I was without being introduced.

"Make that gardeners, farmers, builders, hosts, interior designers, cooks and a lot more too," added Neil, as we walked into the hallway. It was square, with a staircase rising from it, which divided into two arms that doubled back and up to a galleried landing. There were four doors from the hallway, one to the right, one to the left, and one on each side of the staircase. The door on the right was open into a lit room, providing the hallway's only source of light. Everywhere there were floorboards. No carpet.

"You'll have to feel your way around half the house, I'm afraid. We're on the mains again, but only the rooms on this side have safe wiring. so everything over there isn't connected yet," said Jenny, waving behind her as she led us through the open door into the light.

CHAPTER 3

November 1972

The room was at least 30 feet long and 20 feet deep, and incorporated the two ground floor windows to the right of the front door. A fire was burning in a stone fireplace in the middle of the wall facing the windows, but apart from that there were few comforts. A door to the left of the fireplace was closed. Two standard lamps with tattered shades, plugged into those old round pin sockets you don't see anymore, joined with the fire to cast an irregular light around the room. Another closed door in the far corner of the room, this one glazed, reflected the flickering of the fire. The windows themselves were hung with ragged curtains. The floor was bare to the boards, the walls partially covered by fading wallpaper, though in several places around the windows this had been torn away, the plaster beneath stained and crumbling. But for a selection of faded-green canvas camping chairs drawn into a wide arc around the fire, there was no furniture. On some of these sat the others from our group who had already arrived, and Tim, Jenny's husband, a tall bald man I judged to be in his late 50s, dressed in the sort of green sleeveless quilted jacket you get in country outfitters. He had an upright, formal bearing that seemed at odds with our mild counter-cultural affectations. As if realising this and wanting to compensate, he wore sandals and a vivid, patterned shirt. He was more reserved than Jenny, but welcoming nonetheless. "Come and sit down and have a drink," he said, ushering us to vacant camping chairs with one hand, an unlabelled green bottle in the other.

"It's our first batch. Home-made blackberry. The garden

is overrun with the things so we thought we might as well make use of them. We've got pots and pots of jam too."

I sat back in my chair and sipped the sweet, syrupy drink. It was strong, and I could follow a point of contentment as it crept through my body. The sense of passive well-being was spiced with the anticipation of Amelia's arrival, which surely couldn't be long. I was wanting to ask if they'd heard when the Transit would arrive, when Tim said:

"No idea when the others will be here. The phone isn't reconnected yet. It's getting on so just in case they're going to be a while yet, how about if I do some introductions?"

Without waiting for an answer he gestured to his wife, who was standing to the left of the fireplace, half in darkness. "Jenny and Tim Cummings. We look after this place. We've been here just over a year, and with the help of fine people like you we're slowly getting it into shape. We used to go to the Olive Grove in London, and when the opportunity came up we moved here as we're country folk at heart, and our circumstances had changed and it felt like time for a fresh start. Why don't we go round the room and everyone say who they are? You might all know each other, but we don't know you."

We all spoke though I barely listened, even when I was speaking myself. I knew everyone anyway, and the wine was having an effect. I don't think I actually dozed off, but I came out of my reverie when I realised Tim was speaking again:

"...called Undercliff. Built in 1927 or thereabouts. The original owner was Sir Arthur Handley. He'd made his money in the Great War when the family agricultural implements factory converted to munitions – ploughshares to swords, you could say. His younger brother was killed in action and poor Arthur was wracked with grief and maybe a bit of survivor's guilt. He sold up and devoted the rest of his life to God, building this place and spending his days in prayer, meditation and spiritual research. He left to travel just before the War and didn't return. There is talk that he went to North Africa with a couple of assistants to research the religious rituals of indigenous peoples. Other people say he was spying for Germany, but no one knows what happened really. All we know is he never came back. The house remained in the care of a solitary retainer for decades. As he aged he became increasingly reclusive, and the place deteriorated around him. He died at a great age about ten years ago, after which the house stood empty. The Two bought it last year. Simon had been on holiday in the area several times when he was younger, and remembered it in its better days. He came back to this part of the world for a break and noticed the house was empty. The Two were looking for somewhere to use as a retreat centre, so – well, to cut a long story short, enquiries were made and now it belongs to the Olive Grove. That was just over a year ago. Since then we've been bringing it back to life. Slow but rewarding work. Which is why you're here. This room was once a drawing room. It's the biggest in the house, so it is where we meet. That door there leads to what was once a library. The floor is rotten so we don't use it. That glass one over there leads to the orangery, which we'll probably have to pull down as the frame is so rusty. For safety reasons, those two rooms are out of bounds."

Jenny took over, in what was obviously a well-rehearsed routine. Parties from the Olive Grove came here almost every weekend. She began to talk about the work of restoring the house and reclaiming the garden, what they'd already done and what was planned for the weekend, when a knock on the door interrupted her. It was the Transit, and Amelia. Tim went to answer while we all stood up to welcome the rest of our weekend companions. They came in, the driver telling Tim about a wrong turning that accounted for their tardiness. We all exchanged kisses and embraces, Amelia and I both going to the same side for our kiss, and me forgetting it was both cheeks. I always got that wrong. "How was your journey?" I asked. Amelia shrugged, a gleam in her eye.

"Pam?" I whispered. She didn't answer, but pursed her lips to one side and raised her eyebrows.

"I suggest the blackberry wine."

"I'd love a cigarette."

"I'm not sure that's approved of."

"Oh no, it's fine. Tim smokes a pipe. But I can wait."

"I didn't know you'd been here before."

"Yes, just once. Just after we met, actually. It's a beautiful place."

Our conversation stalled, as it sometimes did, and we both looked around the room. The group began to settle again and we all found canvas chairs. Tim gave a précis of his earlier speech for the benefit of the latecomers, before Jenny took over and explained again the weekend's routine. We went upstairs after midnight, the men in an improvised dormitory in what had once been the master bedroom, with camp beds in a row along one wall. I later discovered that the women's dormitory was a little more comfortable, with a selection of second-hand beds, but I never saw it. There was a tacit acceptance that men and women didn't go into each other's rooms, but it was never expressed as a rule. Tim and Jenny had their own flat in the attic, which again I never saw.

I passed a disturbed night, though not an unhappy one. I had not slept communally since the Army, and found I'd lost the knack of filtering out the background noise of a group of men asleep together in one room. But as I lay awake thinking of Amelia and watching the sky lighten through the sheets serving as makeshift curtains I felt content. For as long as I've been conscious of myself I've had this persistent sense of living conditionally, as if waiting for the game to start. As if the gears were not fully engaged. As if waiting for a set of preliminary conditions to be fulfilled, or a sequence of events completed, before the real business could begin. Very occasionally that falls away and I feel like I am occupying the moment. Very occasionally, but I did then. I just lay in that cold, damp, smelly room listening to the snores of my companions and felt more alive and at ease than I had for years. This, I thought, was life as it was meant to be lived.

There was an optional prayer meeting at 7am, which everyone went to. I got up at 6am and crept out of the dormitory without waking the others, my clothes under my arm. I washed as best I could in one of two operational cold-water bathrooms and went downstairs, wondering if anyone was up.

I found Tim in the kitchen, a square, single-storey room at the back of the house. Windows looked onto a tangle of blackberry bushes. He was wearing a short-sleeved khaki shirt tucked into jeans belted high at the waist. I noticed again how upright he was. I imagined a spartan outdoor life of discipline, physical activity, and plain food.

He was standing at a table smoking his pipe while waiting for an urn to heat up water for morning coffee. He remembered my name.

"I hope you don't mind, Martyn," he said, waving his pipe, then nodding to the window and continuing before I could answer. "That's where the wine comes from. We think it was some kind of fruit and vegetable garden once, as there's a wall around it and a couple of old apple trees, though you can't really see either because of the weeds. Anyway, even if it wasn't, that's what we plan to make it into. As Jenny mentioned, clearing it out forms part of this weekend's duties."

He stood up and began spooning instant coffee from a catering tin into an assortment of chipped mugs. I made to help him, asking how he and Jenny had come to join the Olive Grove.

"Well, it was about two and a half years ago. We'd had some ... um ... difficult times, and it helped us. We jumped at the chance to come here. We needed a fresh start, and we've got a real vision for it. What about you?"

"I was back in London after some years away and I was newly ... well, my marriage broke up, to be honest, and I moved into a flat in the building that happens to house the Olive Grove office, and I met Neil and Kath one day. And that's it."

"A lot of us at the Olive Grove joined after difficult experiences," Tim said.

"The love and acceptance in the place is a great healer. So many church leaders imply disapproval of our chequered pasts, even when they talk of forgiveness. The Two aren't like that, though. They just accept that where you are is your starting point on a journey back to God. It's the direction you're facing that counts – not how far along the road you've travelled."

"We'll have a testimony time later. Always good to hear people's stories and how they've changed. What do you do for work?"

"I'm a writer, though not in any exciting sense. A copywriter and sub-editor, rather than an author." I never liked those sorts of questions so asked "What did you do before moving here?"

"Well, RAF in the War. North Africa and Italy, mainly. Then I went to Cambridge in 1946 and married Jenny. After coming down I qualified as a teacher and we spent 25 years in a succession of minor public schools. In this part of the world, actually – Exeter, Taunton, Tiverton. Then we moved to London when I took up a position in Wimbledon."

He asked me where I'd grown up and what my parents did, and it was apparent that the life of an electrician's son, a grammar school boy in a small Midlands town, was beyond his experience. Even so, we chatted on for a while, comfortably enough. Churches do that to you. It's an odd mix of intimacy and distance. You end up talking quite openly with people you'd never otherwise have even encountered.

***

Neil led the 7am prayer meeting. It was short and quietly reflective. By 7.30am we were sitting down to breakfast at trestle tables in another large, bare room off the kitchen. The food was basic and plentiful – porridge, blackberry jam, dense wholemeal rolls Jenny had baked herself, apples, hard-boiled eggs, all served in mismatched crockery. By 8.45am we had finished, cleared up and gathered in the drawing room to be allocated our duties. We were to split into two parties, one working in the house and one in the garden. We'd work for four hours until lunch, and then another three hours afterwards. Then, after a tea break we'd meet back in the drawing room for testimony time before dinner. I was assigned to the garden party, the first name to be called out. So, thankfully, was Amelia.

Fifteen minutes later we were back in the kitchen. Tim, who was leading our group, ushered us out of the back door onto an area of cracked paving, and explained that our task was to continue to clear the walled vegetable garden that he had mentioned to me earlier. Neil was in the group, and four others, but I wasn't interested in anyone else. Harry the plumber led the indoor party, assigned a task that required more technical skill.

"You can't even see the wall it is so overrun with weeds, apart from here where it joins the house," Tim said, pointing to what I'd taken to be a steep bank that formed three sides of an area roughly 60 feet by 40 feet, the house itself forming the fourth, shorter side of the rectangle. "But it is there, and we need to cut everything back so that we've got an area of clear ground that we can replant. All we'll leave are the existing fruit trees, though they'll need pruning." With that he began to hand out tools – archaic shears, loppers, saws, scythes, their rusted blades oiled and sharpened back to life – and directed us to work our way through a patch of dense undergrowth about 20 feet wide. We advanced in a line, like native bearers hacking through jungle in some colonial hunting expedition. Tim and Neil, each with a wheelbarrow, gathered up our cuttings and wheeled them through a gate in the wall, near the house, and around a corner to add to an already impressive pile. This Tim planned to burn at some celebration or other. Looking at the confusion of sycamore, ivy, bindweed, brambles, stinging nettles, hawthorn and much else I couldn't identify, I turned to Amelia and said I had my doubts. She smiled an agreement, but we entered into it with vigour. I was entranced by her slender back and the nape of her neck as she bent to the task. The clearness of the night had continued into the day, and the sun shone on us as we joked, and chatted and worked.

After two hours Tim disappeared for five minutes, before reappearing with a wobbly two-tier trolley, loaded with lemonade and flapjack and apples. We sat wherever we could in the decimated garden, admiring what even I had to admit was impressive progress. We'd cleared an area about 15 feet by 20 feet, with everything that had been at least six feet high now cut back to a few inches of stubble and root. Beneath this the remains of a network of brick paths was visible. We ate and drank, and in the fresh autumn air, pleasantly exerted, I once again felt an immense sense of well-being.

Someone asked Tim why the house was called Undercliff.

"Undercliffs are a feature of this coast, here in Devon and up through Dorset. They're formed when a patch of land breaks off from a cliff and sinks down to a lower level. Imagine if that field over there just split off and sank a hundred feet. There'd be a new cliff down to the fallen field, with another step down from that field onto the beach. It's something to do with the rock and soil in these areas, and coastal erosion, but don't ask me about that – I'm no geologist. I just know that every year this bit of England shrinks foot by foot and there's nothing we can do about it. Still, I think we're far enough back here to be OK for a few thousand years, though the way things are going I doubt we'll have that long to wait."

At this last remark there were smiles, nods and murmurs of approval. Though we never put a date on it, there was a general acceptance in the Olive Grove that we were in the end times. It was liberating in a way. We felt we had nothing to lose.

"There's an area of undercliff just down from here next to our beach, called Devil's Field," Tim continued. "A legend says that the Devil himself split the earth with a massive lightning bolt as punishment on the inhabitants of a little village by the sea who'd forsaken their heathen ways and converted to Christianity back in the Dark Ages. There's another area called Hooken along the coast between Branscombe and Beer. Apparently a slip in 1840 at Lyme Regis took a field sown with wheat completely undamaged, down to a lower level. The farmer charged spectators to watch him harvest the wheat later in the summer. They've got a character all of their own, those places. They tend to be very thickly overgrown – a bit like this garden – and there's a stillness. It feels like you are between two worlds when you are down there. It's not the beach but it's not properly inland either. We'll go for a walk tomorrow and take a look. Now let's see if we can get this back to bare earth by lunchtime."

We got up and reclaimed our tools. Most of us, unused to physical work, took a few minutes to shake out the stiffness in our arms, backs and shoulders. Falling back into the same loose formation we began work again, a little quieter this time. After maybe 15 minutes, during which progress was considerably slower than before the break, Amelia, who was next to me, stopped, straightened up and stood a few paces back.

"Look at that," she said, scanning the ground in front of us.

I stared for a moment and, not noticing anything of particular interest, asked her what she was looking at.

"Doesn't that look like some sort of pattern? There."

Then I could see what she meant. As we'd advanced a few feet further through the undergrowth it became apparent that the brick paths we'd uncovered before the break – three of them – were converging on a central paved area, itself made of leaf-shaped terracotta tiles that overlapped each other. We'd only uncovered a fragment of the design, but it looked like it might be circular. Tim, who had wheeled a barrow of cuttings around the corner, returned to take a look.

"Let's all work on that area and see what we can find," he said. "Looks like there might some nice features under this lot."

With that we grouped closer together and worked around the perimeter of the paved area, soon confirming that it was indeed circular, about ten feet in diameter. Once we had reclaimed the outline of the circle we worked to clear its centre, and after another 30 minutes we stood back to survey the whole shape. The leaf-shaped tiles emanated from a small, central disc. The tiles themselves had a rough-edged, home-made look to them, and a number were damaged, but the effect remained pleasing to the eye. It was clear that five other paths joined the circle at intervals, making eight in total: one from each corner of the rectangular walled garden, the other four between the corners, equally spaced.

"It looks like a flower," someone said.

"Or the sun, with the paths its rays," said Amelia. "Did you know it was here, Tim?"

"No. We've got a couple of old photos that we found in a cupboard when we moved in, but none of them give a clear view of this part of the garden."

"I'd love to see those sometime," I said, to murmurs of agreement.

"I'll have a look for them later," said Tim. "Now, let's get on. One big push before lunch."

CHAPTER 4

November 1972

When the morning's work was done the other group joined us in the garden. They had been ripping out lead pipework in rooms around the house. Jenny brought out a picnic lunch, taking several trips with the wheeled trolley. We sat where we could, on tree stumps, sections of retaining wall and on the ground, leaning against the house. The conversation was good-humoured and inconsequential. We remained like that for maybe 40 minutes before Tim called us back to our duties. We were all beginning to relax after what had for most of us been a morning of strenuous exertion. The afternoon shift was not as productive as the morning one, and we accepted with some relief Tim's instruction to down tools and take 30 minutes to freshen up before convening in the main room. Freshening up involved little more than splashing our faces with cold water, and changing into clean clothes. Then we all trailed into the room with its semi-circle of camping chairs, weary of limb and with faces flushed. A few people chatted quietly. I sat in silence, disgruntled that I'd been unable to position myself next to Amelia, who had come down before me and was flanked by Pam and another woman whose name escapes me now. But she smiled at me across the room.

After five minutes Tim walked into the middle of the semi-circle holding two small objects that I couldn't at first identify. He held them up – a tuning fork and a little metal hammer to hit it with.

"We haven't a guitarist with us this weekend, but we can all raise our voices to the heavens," said Tim over the murmur of scattered conversation. The room fell silent and he hit the fork.

A pure, sweet note rang out and hovered in the air. Then Jenny, who had walked to the front next to Tim, began to sing:

"My life is a sacrifice, my life is a sacrifice, my life is a sacrifice, my life is a sacrifice," ascending in pitch and intensity through the first three repetitions, before falling away on the last. We all knew the refrain and joined in, some hesitantly at first, our modal unison singing stark in the bare room. I looked around as I sang. I was the only one with my eyes open. After a few minutes, by which time the singing had gone beyond restraint or inhibition, someone (a woman, I'm not sure who) broke off and began to sing exactly the same part, but starting on the third beat of the first bar, after the word "is". A few others joined her and we sang on like this for some time, a billowing rise and fall of voices. Eventually the singing died away, a slow fading in volume and intensity as if a hidden hand was adjusting a rotary control. Then near-silence reigned, broken only by the faint rustle of wind in the trees outside, and the indeterminate creaks old houses make. Finally, Tim spoke:

"It's become something of a tradition on these weekends that we all tell our stories, and then pray for each other. I know it can be a little daunting to talk about ourselves in front of people, but we are all friends here. This is a safe place. We'll start, to get the ball rolling."

With this Tim looked at Jenny, who, after a moment's hesitation, began speaking. She stood upright and her voice was measured and clear, but there was a sense of effort, of holding herself, in her bearing.

"Tim and I both came from well-off families. Not rich, but comfortable. I grew up in a Kent village where my father was the local GP, Tim in the Cotswolds where his father was a solicitor. It was a life of boarding schools, tennis clubs, horse riding, maids and nannies, gardeners, church on Sunday. I had no other expectations from life than that I would meet a man, get married, have children and continue in the same vein. Tim was bright at school, destined for a foreign office career or something of the sort."

"But the war made a mockery of our generation's cosy plans and assumptions," continued Tim. "I joined the RAF at the age of 18, in 1940, and became a navigator on Wellingtons. My elder brother Andrew was already flying Spitfires. He was lost over the channel in 1941. Jenny joined the WAAF and we were stationed together in East Anglia. Only for a short while, but we kept in touch as best we could when I was posted to North Africa and then Italy. Ours was a romance mostly conducted in minute handwriting on Air Mail Letter Cards, but we were married within weeks of meeting again in late 1945.

"The war knocked ambition out of me and all I wanted was a quiet life in a backwater of the England I'd fought to preserve. So I went up to Cambridge as a mature student, while Jenny supported us with office work. Then I became a Classics teacher and we set up as house parents in a succession of private schools around here. Our son, who we named Andrew after my brother, was born in 1949 when I was still at Cambridge. We assumed he'd have brothers and sisters in due course, but that never happened. Jenny."

"Thank you, Tim. For fifteen years or so we lived the life we wanted. Term times were spent in small houses in the grounds of whatever school Tim was working at, which Andrew attended when he was old enough, then in the holidays we'd go to a little cottage we'd bought in

Cornwall." There was a tremor in her voice as she talked of meandering journeys to this retreat.

"Andrew was an unusual boy. Creative, but he tended to get very absorbed with things and cross when his attention was interrupted. Single-minded. He had lots of friends when he was little but by his mid-teens he'd become somewhat solitary. We worried about him, but he seemed happy enough as long as he could pursue his interests. By the time he was 17, his main thing was rock music. He became quite proficient on the bass guitar and wrote songs, but whenever he joined bands it wouldn't last. He went to the London School of Economics in September 1967 and we'd only hear from him once a week, when he phoned from his hall of residence. At first he came home in the holidays and for odd weekends, but as time went on he tended to stay more in London. In the summer of 1968 he moved into a shared house and we were pleased that he seemed to have some new friends. We never met any of them but a few names cropped up regularly when we spoke to him.

"During that next academic year we only saw him once, for a week at Christmas. We wanted to be closer to him, but lots of friends said that when their children first left home there was a period when they seemed quite distant, so we tried not to seem concerned. And we weren't concerned, really, we just wished we could see a little more of him. When we did see him he seemed well enough. His hair was very long, and his clothes a little – well, outlandish – but that was normal for young men at university by then. He'd lost his interest in music by this time, and instead was reading a lot of esoteric books. He agreed that Christmas to spend a week with us at the cottage in the summer, but at the beginning of June 1969 he telephoned us to say he wouldn't be visiting after all. Instead, he planned to spend the summer at a monastery in India. He was vague about exactly what and where this place was. We were disappointed and a little worried, but we couldn't stop him. That was the last time we spoke to him."

Then Tim said: "We had one postcard from India, which arrived in early July. It said, simply:

Arrived safely. All well here, despite the heat and inevitable stomach trouble. Hope you enjoy Cornwall.

Love Andrew.

"In the first week in September, the day before school term was due to start, a policeman came to our door early in the morning to tell us that Andrew had died in India, and that his body would be repatriated in due course, following an official investigation. He could tell us very little else, and we didn't learn much more once the investigation was complete. Andrew has been found by the side of a road near a beach on the east coast. His rucksack was torn open and his passport and money taken. There were no signs of injury, and no obvious cause of death. We still don't know what happened and we probably never will. Maybe he got ill and died naturally, and someone robbed his body.

"The school gave me compassionate leave but I knew I could not go back, so we left as soon as we could. We spent the winter in the cottage in Cornwall with thoughts of early retirement, but it was a desolate, lonely time and we agreed we'd be better off keeping busy. In the spring I got a job in a small prep school in London and we moved there for the summer term. It was a change for us and we thought it would do us good, but truth be told we barely functioned. A fellow teacher at the school went to the Olive Grove and invited us along one Sunday. We were wary at first, as church for us had meant not much more than weddings, funerals and school chapel for years. But the Olive Grove didn't really seem like church. And we slowly settled, and we found healing." Tim delivered those last words with a faint hint of a question in his intonation. "And as we explained yesterday, now we are here."

Tim and Jenny stopped speaking and looked slowly around the semi-circle, wordlessly asking who would be the next to speak. They both displayed a reserve that you could easily have mistaken for serenity. The room was quiet, dead still, and I could feel my heart beat. After a minute Neil stood and, with a formality incongruous among the camp chairs and peeling wallpaper, took Kath by the hand and led her to the front. Tim and Jenny walked back to their chairs, Jenny touching Kath on the shoulder as she passed. As if taking this as a cue, Kath made one step forward and, with a nervous laugh, began speaking, her voice more clipped than it was in conversation.

"Hello everyone. Neil and I met at Oxford. We're both beneficiaries of the grammar school system. Like a lot of people from modest backgrounds we felt the need to prove ourselves and worked incredibly hard. We hardly socialised at all and we'd never have met if it weren't for the fact that we both frequented the Bodleian Law Library, which had just opened. I won't say it was love at first sight, but after three years we were engaged. Our plan was to marry the summer after graduating, then move to London and go to Bar School. But the best laid plans … The evening after we finished our final exams we went out for a meal together and stayed up talking through the night. We were quite insular as a couple, really, and we didn't join in with the revelry, but we did drink a couple of bottles of wine that night. That might have been part of it. I wasn't used to it. We planned to have lunch next day in a country pub but I was tired so at about 8am I decided to go home to sleep for a few hours – I remember stepping out onto the pavement feeling a little woozy, and then nothing – next thing I was waking up in hospital days later not knowing who or where I was." These last sentences Kath spoke at an increment faster than normal pace. She was bent forward a little from the waist.

"She'd been hit by a car," Neil said. "The first inkling I had that something was wrong was when I went to her room to pick her up for lunch. I was worried when she wasn't there, and when I asked around and no one had seen her I had a sort of premonition that something very bad had happened. I walked around Oxford, anywhere she might have been, and by late afternoon I was panicking. I went to the police station and asked if they knew anything. I recall being hugely frustrated by the bureaucracy. It was obvious that they did know something but they wouldn't tell me because I wasn't next of kin and I had no way of proving the nature of my relationship with Kath. They even seemed suspicious of me. In the end I had to get a professor to come along to the station and declare that Kath and I were engaged. That was enough, and I was led into a side room to be told that Kath had been hit by a car and was gravely injured. When I eventually got to hospital I wasn't allowed to see her."

"I had fractured my skull and pelvis, damaged three vertebrae, my right arm was smashed and I'd lost a lot of blood. As for internal injuries it was less a case of what was damaged, and more what wasn't. I was in a coma and not expected to survive. But I did."

Neil and Kath spoke on for ten minutes, sharing a precision witness statement to the impact of the accident on their lives, and Kath's recovery. The gist of it was that she was in a wheelchair for most of the next three years, in considerable discomfort and unable to work. Neil finished training and abandoned the Bar, instead practising as a solicitor. They married and tried to get on with their lives, but both became depressed. They were at a low ebb when a client of Neil's mentioned the Olive Grove in passing, and Neil and Kath went along to a service.

"Something amazing happened, and we weren't even looking for it. I was sitting in my chair when I felt my bones realigning inside me, and a hot, tingly sensation wash through me. I walked unaided that night for the first time since the accident."

At this the room murmured its approval. I had heard the story twice before and suspected that everyone else had too, but we never tired of it.

" ... so the doctors tell us we can't have children," added Neil, "but we don't listen. After all, they told us she'd never walk unaided again, and now look at her."

We clapped. The rest of the testimonies, mine included, were brief, and none so dramatic.

Pam recounted how she'd been healed of psoriasis. She was, it turned out, a recovering alcoholic. There was someone else who had contracted polio as an eight year old and spent two years in an iron lung. A couple had followed the hippy trail to Morocco, where they claimed to have spent time with Brian Jones of the Rolling Stones. There was a university lecturer, a former Marxist. Harry had simply liked the feel of the place when he'd come to do some plumbing work at the bingo hall. Amelia was the last to speak, facing the group with that dip of the head. I knew her story, or at least thought I did, so concentrated less on the words and more on her neat, composed features. She got to the bit about a broken engagement when she was

21. I knew about this. A boy from the village. They wanted different things from life. Then this:

"After that I spent maybe six months seriously considering if I had a calling to become a nun. I spoke to a Sister at an Abbey nearby, and went on silent retreat there several times. In the end I decided against it, but there was something in the total, absolute abandonment of oneself to the Divine that appealed to me. It still does."

When Amelia had finished Tim directed us to get into pairs so that we could pray for each other. I teamed up with the former Marxist. "Pray for your stories, that they may continue to unfold in the sight of God," Tim said.

This and the public telling of our stories unblocked something in the group, and we filed into dinner fifteen minutes later talking volubly, laughing and embracing. We sat down at the trestle tables where we had eaten breakfast, now lined with candles, and drank blackberry wine while Jenny and Tim busied themselves in the kitchen with dinner. This time I managed to sit next to Amelia, and though we talked little as Pam, on her other side, spoke loudly and almost continuously, her nearness and the occasional brush of her leg against mine were enough. In a brief but welcome break in Pam's monologue, I said:

"I didn't know you'd thought about being a nun. You never mentioned it."

"Well, I hadn't thought much about it for some time, but coming to the Olive Grove and here, it's almost as if … well, maybe I did hear a call, but somehow misinterpreted it. I could only see it in the context of the culture I lived in at the time. I don't know …"

But Pam began again, and we didn't get any further with that line of conversation.

The next morning, after breakfast and a morning

service, Tim led a walking party down to the beach, while Jenny and Kath prepared lunch. This was the first time I had strayed beyond the overgrown garden, and I began to get a sense of the wider location. Undercliff was on the west side of a valley that ran down to the coastline about half a mile away. The ground between the house and the sea belonged to us. A public footpath ran along our boundary, near the bottom of the valley. On the eastern slope of the valley stood a farmhouse, the fulcrum of a network of small fields grazing cattle and sheep. Apart from a derelict cottage on the same side of the valley as the farmhouse, there were no more dwellings to be seen. The few houses I had noticed as we had driven in on Friday lay behind us, obscured by trees, from which the church tower peeped.

Undercliff itself stood on a terrace levelled from the slopes, at a 45-degree angle to the coastline, so that, when the gardens were cleared and trees cut back, the rooms at the front would look over both the valley and the sea. The rising ground behind the house was thickly wooded. It required little imagination to understand why Sir Arthur Handley had chosen the spot as his retreat, combining as it did seclusion and a wide-open vista. I had a picture of him gazing ruminatively down the valley from his garden.

The path we followed to the coast was through our grounds, parallel to the public footpath lower down. It had, Tim said, become overgrown and rarely used until the Olive Grove had arrived to reclaim the house. It was an easy walk down a gentle slope until it crossed the more clearly-defined coast path, itself just a few feet from the cliffs. Tim took us straight over this path as if he intended that we should all simply step off into mid-air, but when we reached the edge of the cliff we saw that a gated iron staircase, marked 'Private', zigzagged down to the beach.

This, Tim, explained, belonged to Undercliff, constructed by Handley to allow access to his own section of the English coast, which lay 150 feet below. Those of us without a head for heights – me included – felt uncertain, but Tim assured us that the staircase had been repaired and declared safe by a party from the Olive Grove led by a structural engineer. Even so, I stepped onto the pebbled beach a few minutes later with some relief. It was about 200 yards wide, ending on the western side just to the right of the staircase where the cliff turned sharply seaward. Tim pointed up the beach to the east:

"Devil's Field. It's not ours but you can only really get onto it from our beach. Let's walk along and explore."

We spread out across the otherwise deserted beach, some gazing at the sea, abstracted in thought, others ambling along staring up at the cliffs, or scanning the pebbles for driftwood and jetsam. Apart from us, the place was deserted. Amelia and I walked in silence close to the foot of the cliff, sometimes clambering over boulders and mounds of rubble that had once been embedded 20, 30, 100 feet above. I saw to my right a mass of knots of thick green rope like a beached leviathan. After a few minutes we came to a bigger pile of rocks, soil, and smashed vegetation still green, evidence of a recent landslip. It projected about 25 feet into the beach, and being too high and crumbling and loose to climb over we walked around it, looking up at the cliff that it had once been a part of. A battered shrub, still growing, stuck out of the newly-disturbed ground at a 45-degree angle. About halfway up a neat indent in the cliff's contour revealed the source of the landslip. It was as if a segment had been cut out of the top slice of a sponge cake and thrown onto the ground. A wire fence was strung between posts along the top of the cliff, to deter walkers on the coast path from straying too near the edge. The slip had occurred between two of the fence posts, which stood intact. The wire itself, undisturbed, stretched in mid-air across the newly-formed absence.

Devil's Field, when we reached it, turned out to be a plateau 20 feet higher than the beach. It projected about 30 yards out from the cliff, and was about the same width again as Undercliff beach. When the tide was out a narrow ribbon of shingle ran between it and the sea. We scrambled in single file up a rough-stepped track, emerging one by one into a clearing in the knotted shrubs and stunted hawthorns that seemed to cover the whole area. You could see these from the beach as you approached, but even so there was something disorientating about the abrupt transition from pebbled shoreline to verdant thicket. Two paths disappeared from the clearing into the undergrowth. These, we discovered, gave access to a network of tracks that criss-crossed the whole area, occasionally broken up with open areas of various sizes, usually around one or more large rocks. Although from the beach Devil's Field looked level, as you explored it you became aware of a gentle descent into a hollow in the middle, where the shrubs and trees thinned out and rough grass took hold. We all explored the field for 20 minutes, gradually converging on this open area. Here, with the cliffs behind and the higher seaward part of Devil's Field in front, a concentrated stillness prevailed that wasn't silence but had some of its quality. In fact, you could hear the sea quite clearly, though by a quirk of acoustics the sound seemed to be coming from the cliffs.

Pam spoke, and I noticed in her voice a trace of worked-up enthusiasm that I'd been conscious of at dinner the night before. She reminded me of a children's TV presenter. "Tell us about the legend again, Tim," she said. He responded readily. It was clearly a favourite subject of his.

"Well, there are several versions of it I've seen in various folklore collections. They all tell of a clifftop fishing settlement that converted to Christianity when the first missionaries came through sometime in the 4th century. The Devil, it's said, enraged that they'd abandoned their pagan ways, struck the ground with a lightning bolt so fierce that there was a landslip, which created the field. Most versions say the entire village perished but one has the villagers surviving the landslip and defiantly singing hymns to their new God in this very hollow, where they built their first church. Handley carried out an archaeological dig here looking for evidence of that church. He didn't find anything, but sometimes, when I've sat here, it's almost as if I could hear those villagers singing to their new God."

We sat in silence for some time. Even Pam. There was something about the place that demanded quiet, like a library or a monastery. Eventually Tim broke the spell, suggesting that if we didn't get moving we'd be late for lunch. As we walked back Amelia and I fell into pace with him and he told us about the birds he'd seen on the cliffs, and the odd objects he'd found washed up on the shore. Once, he'd come across a photo album, higher than the tide line. It wasn't clear if it had been in the sea or just left on the beach. Its vinyl cover was preserved, he said, but the photos, still fixed to the sodden pages by those little corner triangles, were unknowable smudges. It reminded me of the old photos of Undercliff he had mentioned yesterday, and I asked him if he'd found them. He said he couldn't lay his hands on them at the moment. There was so much old stuff in the place it was easy to lose things.

As we got close to the staircase I noticed that beyond it

a steeply-sloping field ran down to the cliff edge. There, on that precipitous incline cows stood grazing, impassive and at ease. From time to time one lifted its head and ambled unevenly a few yards on to another grazing spot.

"Do they ever fall?" I asked Tim.

"Apparently hardly ever. I've never seen a carcass or bones at the foot of the cliff in my time, and if one did fall it would lie there for a long time as the tide doesn't get up that far. Seems they can sense danger. They never go too close to the edge and when the wind or rain get up they all walk up to level ground."

CHAPTER 5

November 1972 to January 1973

That weekend marked the beginning of my relationship with Amelia. At least, it felt at the time that we had entered into some sort of attachment, though looking back now it seems like a tenuous thing. On the walk back to the house from Devil's Field she took my arm. Nothing was said, but I knew that we arrived at Undercliff single, and believed that we left a couple. We never formalised that tacit agreement in conversation, but Amelia seemed to share my assumption of a chaste connection, asking, before we left, when she would next see me. Others noticed, and we began to be invited to events as a pair.

Amelia went to Undercliff again for a women-only retreat in early December, and then we went together for a longer spell shortly after Christmas, into the first few days of the New Year. There were more of us this time, maybe 30, including the Two. There weren't enough habitable rooms to accommodate a larger group so a handful – me included – slept in two small caravans parked in front of the house. That disappointed me. My caravan was cold, damp and cramped. And even though I was in every other sense fully involved in proceedings – eating, working and praying with the others – I felt like I didn't quite belong, the few paces from the front door of the house to my sleeping quarters at the end of the evening somehow placing me in exile, outside the main flow of events. Was that deliberate? Amelia slept in the house.

One morning I woke early. Chilly and uncomfortable in my caravan bed I decided to get up and go into the house. It was just past 6am but I thought a few people would be up already. Even if there was no one around I could go into the kitchen, the warmest room in the house, and make myself a cup of coffee. The front door into Undercliff was left unlocked overnight so that those of us in the caravans could come and go as we pleased. It was warped and a little stiff. Generally we slammed it shut, but I didn't want to risk waking people so instead I leant my weight against it while holding the handle and pushed it gently but firmly back into its frame.

The door into the main room was closed. As the front door latch clicked into position I thought I heard someone moving around in there. I looked in. The room was dark, the fire unlit. There was nobody about but the door to the left of the fireplace, which led to the old library, was open a crack, showing a dim light. It was usually locked because, Tim said, the floors were rotten. I walked toward it feeling a little uneasy, wondering if a burglar had taken advantage of the unlocked front door. I paused when I got to the threshold. Then I pushed the door open.

The library was about two-thirds the size of the main room. Bookcases, some glass-fronted and all full of books, covered three walls floor to ceiling. On the third there were two large, shuttered windows and a closed door that must have led into the orangery. There were rugs on the floor and two leather club chairs, each with a standard lamp standing guard behind. One of these was switched on. I couldn't see any sign of a rotten floor, but maybe it lay hidden under the rugs. Simon was standing on one of those stepladders you see in libraries with something like a lectern at the top to stack books. He had his back to me as he scanned the shelves. I was tempted to noiselessly push the door shut and leave him to it, but that would have left me feeling that I was spying on him. So I spoke:

"Found anything interesting?"

I saw the hint of a start, but he recovered immediately and turned to face me, smiling.

"Not really. Old science textbooks, most of them. I was up early and thought I'd take a look." Climbing down the ladder, he continued: "Cosy in here, isn't it? Actually, we ought to lock up. Best not to mention we were in here. Tim says the floor's dangerous and he's the boss."

With that he ushered me out of the room, took a key from his pocket and locked the door. We went together into the kitchen.

I mentioned just now that we worked during this visit. We did, but not much. It was more like a holiday. We spent a lot of time eating, drinking, sitting in front of the fire and walking on the beach. By that time some progress had been made on the house. The main room had been painted, the floors varnished and laid with rugs, and an idiosyncratic collection of second-hand armchairs and sofas now augmented the camping chairs. The walls were hung with artwork made by Olive Grove members, and a record player stood in the corner, next to a Christmas tree at least nine feet tall that Tim had found growing in the garden. There were two meetings each day, in the morning and early evening, but these were short and low-key. We sang and prayed but there were no talks. It was as if everyone, even the Two, were off duty. For me, in spite of my dissatisfaction with the sleeping arrangements, it was a happy holiday. I spent a lot of time walking with Amelia down to the beach and over to the hollow on Devil's Field, where we'd sit in companionable silence. I began to hope that things might develop further, but I said nothing. There was a reserve about her, emotional and physical, which placed invisible boundaries around my expectations. We would hold hands and lightly kiss, and talk of faith and life, but never anything more. Though I was a little frustrated at times I liked the atmosphere of restraint in which we interacted. I felt there was something pure and unsullied about it.

By now I knew that Undercliff lay on the fringes of Kingcombe Vale, between Sidmouth and Branscombe. It was a tiny place, no school, shops or pub, just a scattering of houses around a church. We knew from Tim and Jenny that there was some unease in the village about the Olive Grove's occupation of Undercliff, with locals worried that a cranky hippy sect had set up in its midst. The Two wanted to dispel those fears, and suggested we all attend a church service to demonstrate that we were keen to play a part in village life. This was a mistake. We rarely saw or spoke to anyone local, apart from the odd stilted greeting when we were out walking. So when nearly 30 of us turned up on the last Sunday of the year – at a stroke more than doubling the size of the regular congregation – there was a tangible sense of defensive awkwardness on both sides. This despite the polite handshakes and the vicar's welcome of "our friends from London." As we walked down the aisle to find vacant pews, I noticed a memorial on the wall to a woman from the village who'd died at over a hundred years old.

After the service, as the vicar, a hesitant, thin-necked man, conducted conversations of strained bonhomie in the church porch, a number of us strolled around the graveyard. It was a cold, bright late morning, traces of frost crisping the grass. The sun picked out intricate detail in the texture of the lichen on the gravestones, most a hundred or more years old.

I was drifting around on my own, reading the inscriptions, when a voice behind me asked:

"Morning. Have you come across our resident scientific celebrity yet?"

It was an old voice, cultured, polite, a little weakened by time. I turned to see a short, wiry, upright man who must have been in his 80s, immaculately turned out in a heavy tweed coat, maroon silk scarf, and brown brogues polished to a mirror-like shine. Neatly-cut, snowy hair framed an outdoor face. He reached out his hand:

"Sorry to interrupt your reverie. I'm John Muir. I was wondering if you'd seen Fleming's grave yet. Sir John Ambrose Fleming. Eminent Victorian scientist who retired to Sidmouth. Still around when I arrived. Do you know him? He was an electrical engineer – invented the first valve or something of that sort."

"I don't think so, no. I'm Martyn, by the way," I said, shaking the old man's hand.

"It's over here, look. I only ask because he was friends for a while with Handley, the chap who built the place you are doing up. He wrote about him in his autobiography."

We stood looking at a gravestone.

Sacred To The Memory of
Sir John Ambrose Fleming KT MA DSc FRS.
Born Lancaster November 29th 1849.
Died Sidmouth April 18th 1945.
RESURGAM.

"Latin for 'I shall rise again'," said Muir.

I was worried that I had been cornered by a lonely, elderly soul short on opportunities for conversation, and I made several attempts to move on. But John Muir turned out to be a genial, interesting man. He told me he had retired to the district from the Army to farm, arriving in the mid-1930s. He'd been worshipping at the church for 40 years. His wife had died some years before but he remained active and still kept chickens, hunted, grew vegetables. I'd never heard of Fleming, but I asked what Handley was like.

"To be frank, rather grand and absorbed in himself. He came to church every week and you'd run into him when he was out walking, always wearing a very wide-brimmed hat. He was polite but a bit distant and standoffish. Withdrawn, you might say. Never really felt like he was a part of the village. In fairness, most of the people in the area were a little narrow-minded and suspicious of him, though. He had an interest in Eastern religions and spiritualism. From time to time he'd have foreign-looking visitors down for weekends, and most here had never seen a brown face. I'd served in India, though. You'd hear gossip about ceremonies in the garden. Chanting and standing in circles at full moon – that sort of thing. All greatly exaggerated, I expect."

I wondered if this was a sly dig at us, the Olive Grove. Maybe, but Muir had an open face. It was hard to imagine any deviousness in him. We chatted for a little longer before the old man declared that he was "motoring into Sidmouth for lunch at the Victoria," and with that he turned and walked back through the graves.

By this time most of the Olive Grove people had escaped their painful exchanges with the vicar and were gathered in a group near a lower gate from the churchyard, which opened into a car park just off the road. I joined them and we ambled back to Undercliff, a few laughing about what they called 'traditional Christians'. I felt a shiver of pride as I found myself in step with Magnus. I've already said that the Two were not aloof, but even so there was something about the dynamic in the Olive Grove that meant that when you spoke personally with one or both of them you felt you were being granted a privileged audience. Magnus had the capacity to appear to be giving you his rapt, undivided attention. As if nothing was more interesting to him at that moment than you and what you were saying.

He asked me what I thought of the service, then said he'd noticed me talking to the old man in the graveyard.

"John Muir, yes. Seems like a nice man. He's been in the village since the 1930s. He actually remembers Arthur Handley, who built Undercliff."

"Yes, I'd gathered that."

"Oh, so you've spoken to him as well?"

"I think I might have, yes, but it was a while back. Did he have anything interesting to say?"

"Well, he indicated that Arthur Handley was always viewed with some suspicion in the village, on account of his esoteric interests and exotic friends. I wondered if that was a wry reference to us."

Magnus smiled. "Esoteric and exotic. Might have been, yes."

"Do you know much about Handley?"

"Well, not much. A little. He was one of a type that's all but disappeared now, but wasn't uncommon back then. A sort of gentleman dilettante with a private income who could afford to stand back from the concerns of everyday life and lose himself in his pursuits. Hence the eccentrically-stocked library we've inherited. Not a bad life in some ways, but perhaps a little self-indulgent."

"He vanished, didn't he?"

"So I'm told, yes. All a long time ago. The world was a turbulent place then. A lot of people went missing."

With that we arrived at Undercliff where Jenny was waiting, ushering us straight in for lunch. Magnus ended the conversation with a smile and a nod.

It was a traditional meal by Olive Grove standards.
Tim had got hold of several turkeys from the farm over
the valley. I volunteered to help wash up after the meal, a
time-consuming business as hot water was limited. I was
put on drying duties, and Jenny asked me to ensure that
all the blue-and-white enamelled metal plates and cups,
which I hadn't seen before, were piled together on a table.
These, I learned, were a reserve supply, army surplus, that
we only used when larger groups came to stay. When the
drying was finished she asked me to take the dishes into a
small room off the kitchen. It was empty apart from a large
pale green dresser against one wall, which was where the
reserve crockery was stored. I carried it all into the room
and rested it on the work surface of the dresser, opening
the cupboard door below. Bending to slide plates onto the
shelf I noticed, toward the back, a black ring-binder folder.
Taking it out to make room for the plates I laid it on the
floor next me, intending to put it back in again when the
cupboard was full. The ring-binder appeared to be empty,
but when I picked it up to return it the covers fell open, and
I saw inside a handful of small photos the size of postcards,
in little plastic wallets punched with holes to slip over the
binder rings. I flicked through them. They were, surely, the
old photos of Undercliff that Tim had mentioned. There
was the house, looking neat and new, a black, boxy saloon
car parked on the drive. And a view of the valley down to
the sea. Then several formally-composed group portraits
taken in the garden. All men. Men in tweeds, the occasional
darker-skinned face, a turban. A man in a wide-brimmed
hat in their midst, presumably Handley himself. The last
of these caught my attention. There were five men in two
rows, the first row of three sitting on chairs, Handley in the
middle, resting one arm on a stick with an ornate carved

handle in the shape of some animal's head. Two other older men flanked him. Standing in the second row were two middle-aged men, one in a dark suit, the other in light linen. I gazed at it for a while, and feeling an irrational twinge of guilt that I was looking at something private, closed the folder and put it back where I had found it.

That afternoon the weather closed in. It remained cold. Dark clouds promised rain and the wind was up. Most people elected to stay indoors, many playing board games and listening to music in the main room. Amelia said she was tired and was going upstairs for a nap. I sat in a chair in an alcove under the staircase, a good place to read. I'd been there about ten minutes when I heard footsteps and voices on the landing. Simon and Magnus began descending the stairs. I heard Magnus say my name but I didn't catch the context. When they got to the bottom they turned to go into the main room and saw me. "Miserable outside," Simon said, smiling.

I was pleased when Amelia came down and suggested another walk to Devil's Field. She was more animated than usual, talking and joking, taking my arm and leaning into my shoulder as we walked toward the cliff. By the time we got to the staircase down to the beach the wind was blowing hard off the sea, and it was with some difficulty that I conquered my unease during the descent. In contrast Amelia was enjoying herself, shrieking with delight when a sudden gust almost unbalanced her. As we stepped onto the beach the rain began, and we ran toward Devil's Field in search of shelter. Climbing the rough steps onto the plateau I grabbed Amelia's arm and pulled her toward a thicket of stubby trees.

"No," she said, "we can't go there. What if there's lightning? Follow me, I noticed a place up here once."

She led me through one of the lesser-used paths off the main clearing, in places the vegetation on each side entwining above us to form a tunnel. It led us on a gentle climb around the back of the hollow toward the cliff, opening into a clearing on higher ground screened by a dense hedge. If you stood at the hedge you could look down onto the main clearing in the hollow and probably not be seen by anyone who might be standing there. The higher clearing was no more than 20 feet across and half that in depth, the bare, sandy earth patched with tufts of grass and a few scattered boulders. It seemed unusually dark and, looking to the sky expecting even greyer, thicker clouds, I saw the cliff loom over us in a massive overhang, deflecting both rain and light.

"I found this on my first visit. Seemed like a good smoking spot," she said, sitting down on a rock and taking a packet of cigarettes from her coat pocket.

"It's quite a vantage point. It's like looking down on a maze," I replied, seeing the network of paths. "Yes. Definitely the place to hide if ever you need a hiding place."

I sat beside her and she put an arm over my shoulder. "Would you have carried on smoking if you'd gone into a convent?" I asked.

"Mmm. Good question. I don't know. The mystery of the smoking nun."

Amelia's buoyant mood subsided as we sat beneath the overhang for 30 minutes or so, looking out over the sea and barely saying a word while the rain grew first heavier and then eased off as the wind died away. We remained dry, sheltered by the cliff. "One more and then shall we go back?" she said, pulling out the cigarette packet again.

"OK," I replied. "You know Tim once mentioned some old photos of Undercliff? I think I came across them earlier when I was tidying up. They were in a folder in that room off the kitchen."

"Oh really? What were they like?"

"Not that interesting. Mainly groups of men sitting around a man with a stick and a wide brimmed hat, who I assume was Sir Arthur Handley, who built the house."

"I'd like to see them. Can you show me when we get back?"

"I guess so. I feel we ought to ask Tim though, or at least tell him we've found them. They're not ours, after all."

"OK, but there's nothing, well, private about them, is there?"

"No, but even so, they're not ours."

"OK, well, why don't you ask him when we get back? I'm just intrigued to see what Handley looked like. You know I love that period anyway." With that she stubbed out her cigarette in the bare earth, yawned, and stretched her arms and legs in front of her. "We ought to be getting back. I don't want to be climbing those steps in the dark."

The path to Undercliff was steep in places, even after you'd ascended the steps back up the cliff. We returned at a pace, a little out of breath and hardly speaking. The wind was beginning to blow again and it was cold. The fire in the drawing room was a comforting prospect. As we turned into the drive of the house Tim opened the front door and began walking toward his Land Rover. He stopped when he saw us and asked if we'd been caught in the rain. We told him where we'd found shelter and he said he knew the spot. Amelia caught my eye and I mentioned to Tim that I'd come across the photos while putting the dishes away. Were they the ones he had mentioned? He said they sounded like it, and Amelia asked if she could see them.

"I'll see if I can dig them out when I get back. Jenny was

sorting out that cupboard earlier so she might have put them upstairs somewhere. Anyway, see you later. I've got to go and get some milk."

He opened the Land Rover door and drove off up the hill, heading, we knew, for a garage on the outskirts of Sidmouth with a small convenience shop attached. It was the only shop in the vicinity open all day on Sundays.

Leaving our boots in the hall by the door, we walked into the main room. Pam, unusually quiet, was sitting by the record player listening to music. A few people were reading, others dozing. A small group were playing a board game. Magnus and Simon were standing near the fire talking with the couple who'd been to Morocco. Simon turned to the door as we walked in and beckoned us over.

"Nice walk? You must have got soaked," he said, offering us cups of coffee from a tray.

"Not really, we sheltered under an overhang at the back of Devil's Field," Amelia replied.

"I think I know where you mean, yes. Are you ready for tonight?"

We talked a little about the planned party to see in the New Year, which, weather permitting, would culminate in a bonfire. Amelia said she was tired and was going to have a rest. The Morocco couple moved to a vacant sofa. Magnus put his hand on my shoulder and steered me around so that we were both facing the fire. "We've been wanting to speak to you," he said. Simon stood to my side at right angles to the grate, looking at the side of my face. They began to talk, taking it in turns, so fluent you couldn't see the joins. Like one person. Their voices a little lower than normal conversational volume. Not whispers, not conspiratorial, but I had to lean in to hear.

"You've got a gift, Martyn. You see things. Your gift is

to write down what you see. You are a reporter. You will report inner things, things hidden."

They continued like that for some time. The fire warmed me. I felt a surge, something like bliss. I had barely mentioned my writing at the Olive Grove. It had all but ground to a halt, anyway. But it felt like a failure and they – somehow – had seen this secret frustrated longing and affirmed it and released it.

Then Neil joined us.

"I heard on the radio earlier that 1972 is going to be the longest year in human history. They're adding another leap second on the end – apparently there's already been one. It's something to do with coordinating universal time with solar time. Don't ask me – I didn't even know there was such a thing as a leap second, but we all get an extra one right at the end of the year."

"A nice thought," replied Simon. "We could all do with a little extra time."

Early in the evening, Tim, who had returned from his errand with bags of supplies and a can of petrol, came into the main room and asked for volunteers to help clear it for the party. While most people went upstairs to get ready I stayed with Tim and a couple of others, moving all the chairs to the walls, and setting up an amplifier, speakers and a few microphones next to the fireplace, in front of the door into the out-of-bounds library. Then we plugged in a selection of table and desk lamps around the room and turned off the main lights. We carried one of the trestle tables in from the dining room and placed it next to the main door. Jenny began loading it with bowls of nuts, dates, crisps, bottles of wine and lemonade, plastic cups and paper plates.

Tim said we could go and get ready. I went upstairs to wash and change at about 7.30pm and when I returned

30 minutes later most people had already gathered in the room. Everyone seemed to have made an effort, many of the women in long skirts, scarves, strings of wooden beads, the men in wide ties and big-collared shirts. The former Marxist was wearing a corduroy suit. An LP of old festive songs – Bing Crosby, Nat King Cole – was on the record player. The fire, newly stocked, was flaring and spitting. A row of candles burned on the mantelpiece.

I poured myself a cup of wine and as I stood looking around the room I felt a sense of companionship and belonging, rare for me. I would have been content to stand there watching for a while, but Pam came and talked at me. She asked me if I'd be dancing. I must have shown some reserve because she gushed, "Oh, Martyn, you mean you haven't experienced an Undercliff folk dance extravaganza? You're in for a treat. Tim and Jenny do the music and frankly, participation is compulsory. Join in or leave. Wallflowers will be picked. It doesn't matter if you don't know the steps, you'll soon pick it up."

I hadn't experienced folk dancing at Undercliff. Indeed I don't think I'd attempted anything of the sort since primary school. Not a natural dancer, I felt a little uncomfortable, but it soon became apparent that the only way to get out of it was to leave the party, and I didn't want to do that. I saw Tim and Jenny positioning themselves behind the rudimentary sound system I'd helped set up earlier. Tim was holding a concertina in one hand while adjusting a microphone stand with another. Jenny took a fiddle from a case. They both played a few notes to check the sound, Jenny attempting to play along with Bing Crosby, before somebody turned off the record player and she spoke into her microphone: "Hello, are we ready?" She got a cheer and applause in response, and people began putting drinks and plates down wherever they could find space. "Take your partners, please!"

In spite of myself I quite enjoyed it. As Pam said, there was really no escape, especially as she grabbed me as her partner for the first dance. Tim and Jenny were obviously old hands and played effortlessly, Tim stamping his foot to keep time while Jenny called instructions. I learned later that they had first met at some folk dance society event. The proximity of the Sidmouth Folk Festival had been an additional factor pulling them to Undercliff. It was all new to me but almost everyone else seemed to know what they were doing. I found myself propelled around the room in their midst. Writing that now, it seems like a metaphor, but that's hindsight for you. I got to dance with Amelia, but then so did everyone else. But that didn't matter. Those of us with inhibitions shed them. The room wasn't quite big enough to comfortably accommodate us and we all brushed up against each other. Simon and Magnus were in the thick of it. I remember the former Marxist – normally a stiff, cerebral type – corduroy suit jacket abandoned, face shiny with sweat, laughing as he careered into me.

I don't know how long we carried on. It seemed like a long time. Eventually Jenny announced the last dance, she and Tim finishing with a flourish, Tim holding the concertina above his head. We all clapped and, reclaiming our drinks, collapsed into chairs. Later, cans of beer, sausage rolls, turkey sandwiches and trifle appeared from the kitchen. Amelia, red-faced, came to sit next to me. Someone put the record player on again. We sat like that for a long time, as happy as I ever was at Undercliff.

"Not long to go, everyone. Why don't we all get our coats and assemble round the back." It was Simon speaking at the microphone. I looked at my watch and saw that it was a quarter to midnight. A few minutes later I was standing in the garden huddled against the cold in my duffel coat, Amelia hanging onto my arm. We all formed an arc around the bonfire. It had been piling up for months, and stood at least 15 feet tall. I'd seen Tim the day before standing on the top rung of a stepladder throwing things onto it.

"Stand back, everyone," Tim said. "With all the rain, this is going to need a bit of help." He stuffed rolled-up balls of newspaper and dry kindling from the house into the base of the bonfire, and then walked around it splashing petrol on the damp pile of wood.

"Further, everyone," he said, ushering us back 20 feet or more. He then walked around the side of the house, returning with a long, thin rod, the sort of thing people use to unblock drains. To the end of this he tied a rag that he splashed with petrol. He lit the rag and held the pole above his head. Magnus shouted,

"Remember everyone, we've got an extra second this year, so we'll count down from 11."

He looked at his watch and waited for what seemed like a long time, then began:

"Eleven, ten, nine …"

We all joined in. Tim approached the woodpile holding the burning rag as far in front of him as the pole allowed. When he judged that the kindling and paper had caught sufficiently he dropped the pole and jumped back into our midst.

"Four, three, two, one!"

With a rushing sound like a wind the flames took hold.

CHAPTER 6

January to February 1973

When we returned to London I found it hard to get back into the routine of day-to-day life. It was miserable January weather and my mood dipped, as it often did then at that time of year. Work seemed an irrelevance, and a boring one at that, and I had to remind myself daily that it was necessary. In theory I was still working on my book, but on the rare occasions when I sat down with the manuscript I was dogged by a sense of futility. The Olive Grove and Amelia seemed big and important and real and vivid, and everything else looked grey and limp in comparison. Through January and into early February my life was dull routine brightened by Sundays and midweek Olive Grove meetings, and occasional dates with Amelia. Like walking down a dreary street of identical terraced houses, anticipating the sweetshop or ornate street lamp you knew was just ahead. I met Amelia maybe once a week – a meal out, a gallery, a walk by the river – usual London things.

One Wednesday we both took the afternoon off work and went to a screening at the National Film Theatre of an old black-and-white film based on a Sayers book. It was part of a season about English crime fiction. I doubt there were more than a dozen people there. A group of students, and a few old men who might have remembered the film from its original release, or might just have wanted somewhere warm to spend the afternoon. And us, huddled together in the dark. It wasn't much of a film, but the best of afternoons even so.

"Apparently she hated it," Amelia said.

"Don't blame her," I replied. It was one of those rare moments when real life coincided with the better one I imagined.

I would have liked to see more of Amelia, but she was often busy. Sometimes she was working on her book. Other times she mentioned going to meetings at the Olive Grove of which I knew nothing, and I had a sense again of not quite belonging to an inner circle.

One wet Saturday morning right at the beginning of February we met for coffee on Charing Cross Road. She only had an hour as she had an appointment at the British Library to see a rare Sayers pamphlet. She asked me if I was doing anything that evening.

"The Flock are playing at a pub. They're short of people to help them set up so I said I'd go along. Do you want to come?"

The people in The Flock were all at least ten years younger than me and I wasn't particularly interested in their music, so I hadn't ever seen them play apart from at services. But it was a chance to spend an evening with Amelia.

"OK. Why not? Where and when?"

"The pub is called the Half Moon in Herne Hill. I think it is near a railway bridge. We need to get there at about 5.30."

I knew the place from my time as a reporter on the *South London Press*. A big, beery Victorian hotel with a wooden-panelled interior and lots of mirrors. A room at the back where they put on live music most nights. When I got there that evening it didn't look as if it had changed at all in nearly 15 years. Most of The Flock had arrived just before me in a newish-looking red minibus and an assortment of shabby cars. Amelia was with them. The back doors of the minibus were already open and men were lifting out drum cases and amplifiers. I joined in. Feeling a little awkward, I cast around for conversation openers with the heavily-bearded youth next to me. New van? No, same old one reborn courtesy of Harry's respraying skills. He's a handy boy, that Harry. Within 20 minutes we had all the band's equipment piled up on the greasy stage in the pub's back room.

While the musicians set up and sound-checked I hung around at the back of the room. The music, semi-improvised I imagine, was insufficiently structured for my tastes but I could tell the musicianship was proficient. A woman called Angie did most of the singing. She wrote the book about the Olive Grove I mentioned before. Short and slight, she looked fragile, almost transparent, her wispy blond hair appearing to float above the shoulders of a long-sleeved, green velvet dress. I'd heard she was a drug casualty who'd got pregnant at 18 and wound up at the Olive Grove a penniless, homeless single mother. Even during the sound-check she sang with a rapt intensity, rooted to the spot, eyes closed, gripping the microphone stand as if for support.

I was looking at her when I became aware of Amelia beside me.

"I really feel it when Angie sings. There's something – I don't know – *concentrated* about it," she said.

"I know what you mean. What do we do now?"

"Well, doors open at 7.30pm. They want us to sit at that table over there and sell books and cassettes. They don't charge people to get in, but they have to pay the landlord for use of the room. The idea is that we sell enough books and cassettes to pay him, and if there is any left over we give it to the Olive Grove."

She gestured to a trestle table to the left of the door into the bar. On it were several boxes, open but not unpacked. One contained copies of the book, another The Flock cassette, called *Lost Sheep Found*. There were also some leaflets about the Olive Grove. We got a few of each out and made a display, putting the boxes behind the table. Amelia wrote a price list in her neat hand:

Books £1.50
Cassettes £1
Change your life tomorrow night – no charge.

"This is how they usually do things. The band play on a Friday or Saturday night and get talking to people after the show, and invite them to church. A lot of people have joined that way…" she broke off, and smiled over my shoulder, her head dipping a little.

"Hello, you two – thanks for coming along and helping the cause."

It was Magnus. He and Simon had turned up unnoticed. By me, at least. Simon was standing on the stage talking to the musicians, who had finished setting up. He had grown his hair and it was now long enough to tie back into a silver ponytail. I felt the mix of pride and faint nervousness I always did when one of the Two spoke to me directly. I couldn't think of a response but didn't need to.

"Everyone up here. Doors open in 15 minutes and we've got work to do," Simon called.

We clambered onto the stage and at Simon's direction everyone not in the band surrounded the musicians and began to pray for them. I wondered what the barmen and scattering of customers in the bar thought of us, if they looked through the glass pane in the door. A circle of latter-day hippies standing in silence around the band, directed by two somewhat older and more conventionally-attired men. Like teachers cajoling a drama group to enact Stonehenge. We prayed for a strong performance, for a big crowd, for a good time. Angie clutched her hands tightly at her breast, eyes closed, and began to sway. With her blond hair and green dress she looked like a solitary early daffodil in a spring breeze. We stood like this for a minute or two, no one speaking. I was conscious of being the only one with my eyes open, and I made the effort to close them, to focus, to enter the moment. I was almost succeeding when Magnus and Simon broke the transported silence, calling out in unison "more life, Lord of life and power. More power," and in spite of myself I started, and opened my eyes. At that moment I saw Angie fall, folding in on herself and crumpling to the floor. Simon and Magnus knelt beside her, each with a hand on her head. After about thirty seconds she opened her eyes, appearing momentarily confused in the manner of someone who has fallen asleep on a train, and wakes not immediately certain where they are. She sat up, helped by Magnus, and the group burst into spontaneous light applause and murmured blessings. Angie smiled as she got to her feet, and Simon said: "People, I think it is going to be quite a show tonight."

With that, the prayer meeting broke up and the band retreated to their dingy quarters backstage. I helped carry guitar cases into this damp, windowless cavern, decorated with an intricate mural of obscene graffiti from the hands of hundreds of musicians who had lurked there over the years. Angie, now voluble and excited, took a marker pen from her bag and wrote *Jesus loves you* on the wall. When I came back out into the main room the doors to the bar were open and a trickle of drunks, regulars and Olive Grove members had wandered in and were standing around in disconnected groups. Someone put on a Larry Norman record to fill the space and the palpable sense of awkwardness vanished.

The Two were now nowhere to be seen. Amelia was already standing behind the table and I joined her. She'd found a tin for the money and I put two 50p pieces into it and slipped a cassette into my pocket. We stood for ten minutes or so watching the room fill up and talking to the few potential customers who came to flick through the book and run their eyes down the tracklist on the cassette. We'd sold a handful of each when a crumpled little man of uncertain age swayed toward us, dark hair long and oily. He leant on the wobbly table and stared at the display for a short while before looking up and saying:

"Young man. Young lady. I have surveyed your wares. So this is Jesus-freak hippy zealotry? Can we expect plainsong and hymnology? Do they honour our lord Gene Vincent?"

Displaying not the slightest hint of unease, Amelia held out a leaflet and said:

"Why don't you join us tomorrow?"

The man studied the leaflet for several seconds, holding it in front of his face between finger and thumb. Then he dropped it to the floor, looked up at Amelia, smiled a drunken smile, and said:

"If Ken says it's Jesus-freak hippy zealotry shite, then that, my dear, is what it is." Hands in the pockets of his rank donkey jacket, he turned and followed an unsteady course back toward the bar.

Amelia looked at me, eyebrows raised. "Well, worth a try."

"I can't help but think this isn't quite the right audience," I observed.

"You'd be surprised. I went to a Flock concert at New

Cross one Saturday a month ago and three people we met there came to church the next day."

"I didn't know you'd seen them play before."

"Oh yes. Quite a few times."

We stood behind the table for maybe another half an hour. A few people we knew from the Olive Grove came over and chatted. Amelia managed to sell a book and a cassette to a teenager who had heard the band once before. He wanted both signed so she escorted him backstage.

The room filled up. By 8.30pm there must have been 150 there, no more than a third of them from church. Amelia returned. Somebody edged up the volume of the record playing over the PA to compete with the background chatter of the audience. Everyone began to talk that little louder, leaning over and speaking into each other's ears. Then the lights, already dimmed, were switched off, the only illumination coming from the bar through the open door. The music stopped and conversation with it, as people realised how loudly they had been speaking. For a minute or so a near-silence held, and we all became aware of shadowy figures walking on stage, the click and buzz of electric guitar leads being plugged in, the twinkle of little red amplifier lights. Then someone hit a snare drum hard and loud and dim green stage lighting faded up like an accelerated dawn, revealing The Flock in position on stage. Angie stood stock still with her arms at her side. Over a swelling organ chord she began to sing a wordless ululating improvisation, the rest of the musicians joining in around her, one by one.

That first piece – you couldn't really call it a song – went on for about five minutes and split the audience. The greater number seemed absorbed, transfixed even, eyes closed and heads nodding, and I myself couldn't deny the music had a certain hypnotic power. But a small number were laughing among themselves, calling out the occasional insult and dancing in exaggerated parodies of the band's onstage movements. As the music ebbed away back to the organ chord that had introduced it a shout came from the midst of crowd:

"Weeeellll, be-bop-a-lula, she's my baby – I don't mean maybe, woah she's the girl in the green velvet dress!"

In response came jeers and catcalls and lascivious laughter. Angie appeared oblivious to this, still standing motionless but now once again gripping the microphone stand. Without even giving the appreciative element of the crowd time to applaud the band launched into a faster, rhythmic piece derived from an old gospel song. I knew it from church services. The chorus had a refrain something like "I've got life in my legs, I've got power in my arms and I've got eyes to see." Whether this was intended to appease the disruptive minority I don't know, but it had the opposite effect. Within seconds, a group of people in the middle of the crowd, just in front of the stage, began jumping around, arms flailing, barging into the people around them. I heard screams above the noise of the music, and the crowd began to sway backward and forward around the turmoil at its centre. I saw bottles and glasses fly toward the stage and a big heavy man with a shaved head jump up, hang momentarily above the melee, and hit someone on the top of their skull with his fist as if banging a table to call a meeting to order. Ken the drunk staggered from the knot of people, blood trickling from the corner of his laughing mouth. He stood for a moment looking around in dazed appreciation before turning and diving headfirst back into the throng.

The song broke down bit by bit as first the guitarist

stopped playing, then the bassist. Soon just the drummer was left, until he realised he was on his own. Angie had been hit by a bottle and was bleeding from the head, the scarlet streaks in her white-blond hair lurid and sickly in the green stage lights. Someone was helping her from the stage while below a full-tilt brawl had broken out among a group of about 20 people. Everyone else stampeded toward the door. I saw a woman fall in the midst of the rush. Amelia grabbed my arm. I was in two minds whether to make for the door like everyone else or join a couple of beleaguered young men from the Olive Grove who I could see trying to break up the fight.

Before I could decide a ringing metallic crash exploded from the speakers, sudden as a gunshot, and a voice began repeating "be still, be still, be still." I looked to the stage and saw Simon and Magnus, each standing at a microphone. It wasn't one voice but two, the Two, speaking in perfect unison. I had not seen them at all during the performance but there they were, standing on the stage while bottles flew around them and the fight raged at their feet. They continued their chant and one by one the brawlers broke away from the fracas and stood becalmed, looking at the stage. Some sat down on the floor, embracing. The big man with the shaved head ambled from the room smiling to himself, the remainder of the crowd knotted around the door parting to let him through. Soon only Ken was left, flailing at thin air and laughing. After a few seconds he too stopped, realising his bloodied fists were no longer making contact with flesh and bone. He cut an almost comic figure now, deflated and puzzled. Without noticing them stop I realised that the Two were no longer chanting. Simon had already climbed from the stage and was walking among the battered combatants, touching each lightly on the shoulder and murmuring invocations. Magnus joined him and they knelt beside two embracing men on the floor.

"That's amazing," Amelia said. "That is power. It's undeniable. How can anyone see that and not respond?"

I felt a little frightened. "How do they do it?" I asked. "What was that noise?"

"Who knows? A thunderbolt?" Amelia was standing on tip toe to see over heads to where the Two were ministering to the pair of sitting, embracing men, like stretcher-bearers in no man's land. She was leaning on me for balance and I could feel her trembling. "You can't deny that."

"But how do they do it?" I repeated.

She looked at me. I'm sure I saw disappointment in her eyes. "*They* don't do it, Martyn. God does it through them. They are channels. We can be channels too. It was God."

I smiled at her but felt uneasy, undecided whether I had seen a miracle or stagecraft. Or had some kind of collective hallucination overtaken the brawling men? Was it peace or control? The room had fallen silent once the Two had ceased their refrain, but it was now filling up again with laughter and chattering. Men who had been beating each other to a pulp minutes before slapped each other on the back in a sort of mirthful bemusement. The rest of the audience that had rushed for the door was now spilling back into the room. The band didn't return but no one seemed to mind, or even notice. Someone put music on over the PA, and members of the Olive Grove took handfuls of leaflets from the table and circulated among the crowd, inviting people to come to church. Trade in books and cassettes picked up and an hour later we had more than enough money to pay the pub for the hire of the room.

By about 10.30pm the event was drawing to a natural close. People were drifting out through the bar into the cold night, and a few men from the Olive Grove began to pack up the band's equipment. Still feeling unsettled at the events I'd witnessed and anxious for something to do I joined them, climbing onto the stage and picking up a guitar amplifier. I didn't realise it was still plugged in and as soon as I moved it I heard that same metallic crash that had heralded the Two's appearance on stage.

"That's the spring reverb," the guitarist, who'd appeared from the dressing room, explained. "Did you see Simon give the amp a kick to get everyone's attention? Makes quite a noise when it goes through the PA."

Together we carried the amplifier through the dressing room and out a back door into an alley where the minibus was now parked, back doors open. As we lifted it into the vehicle I noticed, further back down the alley, Ken the drunk. He was sitting upright on a low wall, with his hands folded in his lap. The Two were standing in front of him, their backs to me. Each had a hand stretched out onto Ken's shoulders. I went back into the pub to see if there was any other equipment to lift out. When I saw that everything had been moved already I stood for a while on the bare stage looking out over the room. Only a handful of people now remained. The lights had been turned on. The floor was littered with crumpled leaflets, broken glass and cigarette ends. Amelia was sweeping up the debris and emptying it into plastic rubbish sacks. Someone else was mopping at a bloodstain on the floor in front of the stage. There was a sense of deflation, anti-climax, and I felt a longing to go home. I went to say goodbye to Amelia. She pecked me on the cheek and embraced me with one arm while holding the broom with the other, saying "see you tomorrow."

Outside, several of the musicians were climbing into a car and one of them called me over.

"Thanks for your help, Martyn – there's room if you want a lift."

"Thanks, but I think I'll walk. I could do with some air."

The car drove off and I realised I was hungry. I knew a chip shop around the corner. I got there just before it closed, bought a bag of chips and set off back in the direction of East Dulwich. It was a cold night and after I'd been walking for ten minutes a light snow began to fall, soon rendering parked cars ghostly in the streetlight. Progress was slow, my feet slipping a little with each step. I trudged on for some time, preoccupied, until I found myself in East Dulwich Grove. It was about 11.30pm. There was no one about, and few passing cars. By now I was shivering and wet, but there was something peaceful about the white deserted streets so I stopped for a while and looked to the sky, watching the snow fall.

"We thought it was you," came a voice from the other side of the road. "It's beautiful, isn't it?"

I looked over to see Magnus and Simon standing under a large umbrella thickened by a layer of snow. I remembered that Magnus lived just around the corner. "You look cold – do you want to come in for a hot drink?"

"Thanks, but no. I need to be getting back."

"Sure. Great night, wasn't it? See you tomorrow. Blessings."

They turned and walked up the street toward Magnus's flat, fading into the heavy snow. I turned myself and set off toward Peckham Rye, getting home after midnight. The flat was cold and I was tired, but I didn't feel like sleeping. I wrapped myself in a blanket, pulled a chair to the window and sat in my dark room watching the snow fall for a long time.

CHAPTER 7

February 1973

That night after the Flock concert I didn't go to bed until gone 2am, and even then I lay awake for a long time. I must have been deeply asleep when I was woken by a banging noise. I lay in bed not understanding what it was. The alarm clock said just after 10am. The noise continued – three hits at a time, followed by a pause – and I realised it was someone knocking on my door. This had not happened before. Anyone calling for me had to use the entryphone to get into the building. A neighbour? But I barely knew any of them. The insistence of the knocking made me worry something was wrong, maybe a fire, so I put on my dressing gown, picked up my keys from the bedside table and walked to the door.

"Oh, Martyn, so sorry, man, were you still asleep? We assumed you'd be up by now."

They were standing there filling the doorway, Simon speaking, half a step in front of Magnus. Both smiling. I probably mumbled something about being late the night before, I don't really remember, but I can see them both now – just nodding and smiling and saying "sure, sure", and showing no sign of moving. Then something seemed to occur to Magnus, and he put up a hand as if asking for permission to speak.

"Idea. Why don't you let us come in and fix breakfast for you?"

They both beamed at me. What could I do? I thanked them and stepped to one side while they squeezed past me and walked down the corridor into the main room. They knew where they were going. They'd visited before.

"We were downstairs preparing for tonight's gathering and we thought we'd drop in and say hello. We don't use the office much but sometimes we find it conducive to concentration." Simon was speaking over his shoulder from the little kitchen. Magnus was standing at the window in the main room, hands behind his back, looking up and down the street.

"If you don't mind I'll just take a quick shower and get dressed before breakfast," I said.

"Yes, of course. See you later."

When I came back into the room fifteen minutes later, hair still wet but feeling a little more awake, they were both in the main room standing next to the table. It was laid with coffee, cereal, toast, marmalade. Much more than I'd have made myself. Just one plate, and one bowl and one cup.

"Want an egg, Martyn? We've already eaten. Just sit down and enjoy some bespoke waiter service for once."

It was Simon speaking, as it generally was. Magnus had moved from the table and was running an eye along my shelf of books.

To my surprise I was hungry and I ate with enthusiasm, only very mildly discomfited by the Two's hovering, smiling presence. I suggested that they sit down but Magnus said they'd prefer to stand. When I'd finished they took the dishes into the kitchen and made some fresh coffee. I sat on the sofa, Simon next to me, Magnus on one of the dining chairs that he'd pulled over, facing me. We sat in silence drinking coffee for a minute or two, then Magnus – leaning forward from his chair – spoke:

"We've really valued your commitment over the past months, Martyn. Any set-up like ours, which has so many people who have – how shall I put it? … well, people who've taken some hard knocks – we need steady, reliable types like you to steady the ship. Simon and I were wondering if you would like to get more involved."

I must have given some kind of positive response, or at least not negative, because he continued. This time his tone had changed. Not quite as easy-going and informal:

"Don't want to sound heavy-handed, but we have to insist on complete confidentiality. Not everyone gets to hear what we're about to tell you. Do you understand?"

"Yes, but hear what?" I said.

Simon took over: "Sometimes we notice people in the Olive Grove who seem to have something special, so we formed a group that meets from time to time to go a little deeper into the mysteries. We call it the Servants, because we're all about self-sacrifice and serving, aren't we? Invitation only. And we'd like to invite you. It's completely private, of course, so you must not mention it to anyone."

"I've never heard of it before. Who else belongs?"

"I'm glad you haven't heard of it. That means the Servants we've already chosen are faithful to their vow of silence. We can't say, of course, who belongs unless you join. But you'll see some familiar faces if you come along."

The conversation continued for a while. I recall asking them when and where the Servants met, what they did, what the point of it was. The answers revealed little. As the group was secret they couldn't tell me much, but I'd find out if I joined. And I wouldn't regret it if I did. Actually, 'private' was the word they used most. "We're not like Freemasons," Simon joked.

"Well. Thanks for asking me. I'm honoured. Is it OK if I think about it for a bit?" At that point I was as close as I could be to saying yes without doing so. Only a temperamental reluctance to join in, a tendency to stand to the side and observe rather than plunge in, held me back.

"Sure, man," said Simon, then he paused, as if wondering if he should continue. I saw him catch Magnus's eye. "Only fair to say at this stage that a couple of people we've asked to join who decided they didn't want to ended up leaving the Olive Grove soon after."

"You mean they were asked to leave?"

"No! No! Of course not," said Simon, all smiles and geniality, gripping my shoulder and giving it a little shake. "We'd never ask you – anyone – to leave. That's just not where we're at. Just that … sometimes when people decide to stop halfway on their journey they slip back to where they started. I guess they think if they can't reach the goal, why keep travelling? We think you've got to keep climbing the hill, else you slide back down." It was Magnus who finished the sentence, leaning over me from his chair.

If they hadn't had said that, if they'd just left it with me for a day or so I'd have said yes and joined before the week was out. As it was I was left not knowing if I was being chosen or compelled. No, that's wrong. I say that with hindsight, but I'll leave it in here so you can understand that I understand that memory plays tricks. I didn't really think that at all at the time. But somewhere, not even in the back of my mind but further away, I think I felt the faintest itch of uncertainty.

The Two stayed for a little longer and conversation turned to easy, inconsequential things. They could do that. Especially Simon.

Then Magnus stood up and said to Simon, "Come on brother, we've got a lot to do." They walked down the corridor, turned at the door and embraced me, one by one, in the narrow hallway.

"See you this evening," I said, and closed the door.

I spent the rest of that day in the flat. When the time

came to go to church I couldn't find my keys. I didn't have a regular place where I kept them. I recalled taking them from the bedside table to open the door in the morning and I thought I'd left them in the lock – though I couldn't be sure – but they were nowhere to be seen. I didn't want to waste too much time looking so I took the spare set and set off for church.

The Olive Grove evening service began at 6.30pm but people tended to drift in an hour or more early for coffee and chat. That day I was one of the first, eager to see Amelia. For me, at that time, a perfect Sunday evening was chatting to Amelia before the service, sitting with her during it, and eating out with her when it had finished. That Sunday it was perfect.

Looking back I think my feelings for Amelia reached a peak that following week. I didn't see her, but we spoke on the phone and she sent me a card with some affectionate message that hinted at future possibilities. That was the thing about the two of us. The relationship being unconsummated – not only physically but in some sort of hard-to-quantify emotional sense too – meant that much of the excitement derived from wondering what might happen. People live their whole lives like that. Imagining some unspecified future in which everything comes together, or – just as bad – looking back to an irretrievable lost age that never existed. Missing the life they're living, the things right in front of them.

We had agreed to spend the whole of the following Saturday together. When we met at Peckham Rye train station at 9am I had already been up for hours.

"Did you keep your promise?" she asked, kissing me on both cheeks.

"Yes, and I'm starving. You?"

"Of course. And yes, me too."

"Maybe we should find a café here before catching the train? Or there's that place over there?" I pointed to a booth by the station, the sort of place taxi drivers congregated around.

"Let's find somewhere on the South Bank. There's a train coming in now. We'll be there in half an hour."

I caught the same train into work during the week, and I'd come to enjoy the journey. The sense of being right in the middle of the metropolis yet simultaneously slightly removed from it too. Of looking in on the city from an elevated perspective, like a minor god, as the train rattled across bridges, the archways of which contained car workshops, or opened into builders' yards. And, if the papers were to be believed, provided refuge for criminals and their stolen goods.

"Let's look in lots of second-hand bookshops today," she said.

I agreed, and we got talking about our own book projects, me feeling duplicitous, as I'd barely opened the manuscript for months, she eager and engaged.

"What is it exactly you like about golden age crime – that's what they call it, isn't it? I'd have thought it was all a bit old hat."

"Well, the stories are clever and I like trying to work out the puzzles, who did it and why. But then everything is tied up at the end. Never mind how messy and complicated life gets, order is restored. I once read a poem that summed it up but I can't remember what it was called or who it was by, but one line stuck in my head: *thus the universe is clarified.* Everything becomes clearer. It all makes sense."

"Life isn't like that. Mine isn't, anyway."

"Life can be like that, Martyn," she said, gently taking

my hand and turning to look me in the eye. "Yours and mine."

I probably replied, or maybe I didn't. I can't recall all the detail at this distance. I do remember, though, that her words felt like an offer.

We walked a lot that day. From London Bridge station along the South Bank to Waterloo Bridge, then up to Covent Garden and across to Charing Cross Road. We must have found somewhere to stop for breakfast, but that detail escapes me. I remember, though, that we had lunch in Bunjies. "Mind your head," I said, as we walked down the stairs into the cellar, enjoying the sense of being able to introduce her to something new, something that felt like a secret. We sat under an archway, a step down from the main floor that she didn't notice, grabbing me for support after stumbling. A woman with an acoustic guitar was singing in the back room, just audible. "Bob Dylan played here," I said, and she shrugged her shoulders. For some reason I loved her indifference to contemporary popular culture.

"The protest singer. Oh yes, curly hair. I don't like his voice." We sat there for two hours, eating, reading from the books we'd bought from stalls by the river, making meandering small talk. Before or since, I've never felt as at ease with a woman as I did then.

"I could lie down and sleep – what do you say, 'doze'? – right now," she said. I knew what she meant, and how I would have loved to lie down with her then.

We'd been in that cellar for so long that stepping out into a gloomy, nondescript afternoon, the pavements milling with tourists and day-trippers, jarred. It was the sort of place and moment from which you would expect to emerge into a bright dawn, with everything new and opening up like a flower in front of you.

"How about going over to Leicester Square and seeing what's on?" I suggested.

"Good idea," she replied.

I know we did go into a cinema, because the memory of sitting in the darkness holding her hand is vivid still, but I have no recollection of the film. Maybe I fell asleep.

After the cinema and more aimless, deeply pleasurable wandering we found ourselves in a little Italian restaurant in Soho.

We drank beer and wine and our habitual mutual reserve loosened.

"What is it like to have been married and to have known someone so well, and then for them not to be around?"

We rarely spoke of my marriage, and by that stage I could go days without Lillian even crossing my mind.

"Hard to explain, really. It just feels like another life, one that has no connection with this one. I can remember all the details, but it's as if that life ended and I started another one that had no links back to married life. I feel more in touch with my life before I was married."

"We've both started new lives really, I guess."

"You mean the Olive Grove? Yes, I suppose so. Funny how the Two don't talk that much about being born again. You'd have thought that was the sort of language they'd use."

"Well, they aren't conventional. It feels like we've been born again, though, doesn't it?"

I thought for a moment before answering. I was conscious of her waiting on my response, and I wanted to get the words right.

"For me, in a way it does. I love being there. Nothing in my life up to this point suggested to me that going to a church would actually become the centre of my life. But sometimes I do think that there's something about it I don't quite *get*." I put an emphasis on the last word, hoping she'd immediately come back with, "I know exactly what you mean". But she didn't. She just looked at me, all earnest eyes.

I continued: "I went to a classical music concert once with some friends from work. They were aficionados of that sort of thing – very knowledgeable. I really enjoyed it. Parts I found moving, parts exciting and dramatic. But I had the sense of not quite appreciating it in the way that my friends did. As if they heard something that I couldn't hear. Sometimes I feel like that about the Olive Grove. I love being there and wouldn't miss it for the world, but I look around sometimes and wonder if everyone else has *got* it in a way I haven't. As if I might have missed some crucial detail. The Two visited last Sunday. They made me breakfast. And they asked me ..."

I stopped and took a drink. I wouldn't say I was disinhibited, but I was talking more than normal, and I had to check myself when I realised I couldn't tell Amelia that they'd asked me to join the Servants. "Go on," she said. "What did they ask?" Though we were talking about serious matters she was in a playful, teasing mood, and the sense of light-hearted intimacy was more intoxicating than the Italian wine and beer could ever be. I held off for a while, saying no, it was a private matter, and she was laughing and squeezing my knee under the table and saying "come on".

"Funny", she said, pursed-lipped and coy. "They came to see me late Sunday morning last week. Said they'd like to make me lunch."

She stopped there and looked at me, eyebrows raised, head to one side.

"What?" I said, laughing.

"I think you know."

"What do you mean?"

She looked down at the table for a few moments, then looked up again, and pushed her hair behind her ear.

"OK. Tell me if I am wrong. They asked you if you'd like to become a Servant."

"You're not meant to say that," I replied.

"If you know I'm not meant to say it you must know what the Servants are because otherwise how would you know they're a secret?"

"But they told me not to talk to anyone about it."

"Did they? They told me the same, except they said I could speak to you about it, because they'd just asked you too."

"So if they said you could talk to me about it, why have you waited all day – all week – to mention it?"

"I was choosing my moment. I just wanted to be sure we were both going in the same direction. After today I'm sure we are."

"So you're going to join?"

"Of course. You?"

"I guess so, yes."

Would I have joined without Amelia's encouragement? I'd like to say no, but I think I would have. I was excited. Joining meant going further into whatever it was that Amelia and I had together.

I was late back that night, after walking Amelia to her door. As I drifted down the street toward my flat I noticed a light on in the Olive Grove office. I thought about telling the Two – it was bound to be them in there – that I, we, were going to join the Servants. But I was tired and elated and I wanted to luxuriate in my recollection of the day so

I decided to leave it. I'd had a new key cut and it was stiff in the lock. The old one hadn't turned up. But that night as I went into the lounge and turned on the light I took a book from the shelf as I felt like reading some poetry, and there were the old keys, behind the book.

CHAPTER 8

February 1973

The next day, after the service, Amelia and I approached Magnus and said that we wanted to join the Servants. "Great," he said, smiling and nodding once. "Come and see us this Wednesday evening and we'll start the induction."

That Tuesday our small group met in my flat as usual. Several times through the evening I caught Amelia's eye. The sense of being in on something with her was better than the anticipation of what might happen the following evening.

We arrived at the bingo hall at 8pm, as instructed. Magnus and Simon were both waiting in the foyer, and they led us through the main room back into one of the smaller rooms used for prayer and counselling. There was no one else there.

"We like to see new Servants on their own for a few sessions before introducing them to everyone else. Just to explain what it's all about. But as you two are an item we thought it only right to see you together."

An item. An electric thrill went through my body. I glanced at Amelia but she was looking at Simon, nodding in agreement as he kept speaking.

We were there for about an hour and I left with a mixed sense of relief and anti-climax. I'd been expecting intensity and maybe ritual, and had been a little nervous, but it was just the Two talking. About layers of spiritual experience, and techniques for moving from one layer into a deeper one, like miners digging ever further in for a glimpse of the precious seam. And how sometimes some people weren't ready to go from one layer to a deeper, more profound layer, but we were. They were sure of that. Then they asked us to come again next week, same time, to continue with the induction.

"How did you find it?" said Amelia as we walked, holding hands, down the high street from the bingo hall.

"Fine. Not quite what I expected, but fine."

"What did you expect?"

"Don't know, really. Something a little more intense. Signs and wonders. I still feel I don't know much about this. It's a small group for people going deeper into things, but what does it actually do?"

"From what I've heard we will get our signs and wonders."

"What have you heard?"

"Oh, just something Simon said to me. I bumped into him earlier today. Shall we go to the Clockhouse? It's only just after 9pm."

After that evening I didn't see Amelia again until the following Sunday, and then again on the Tuesday. She said she wanted to put a lot of time into her book because it was getting stuck. At the Tuesday meeting at my flat she seemed distracted and I was disappointed when she said she needed to leave early to do some more work. But in the corridor, as I walked her to the door she held both my hands, kissed me, and said "tomorrow", and that was enough.

We'd agreed to meet at the bingo hall, and when I arrived promptly at 8pm Amelia was already there, talking with the Two in the foyer. "Here we all are," said Simon, leading us to the same small room. Whereas the previous week it was just as we found it, this week it looked to have been prepared. A table and some chairs had been removed, leaving just four hard, upright chairs, arranged in a square

– two facing pairs. Simon gestured toward two of the chairs and Amelia and I sat next to each other, me facing Magnus, she Simon.

"This week," Simon started, "we want to tell you about how the Servants work. When we meet, and what we actually do. The practicalities. OK?"

We nodded, me feeling that finally I was going to understand what this was all about.

"We meet on Thursdays about this time. We keep Wednesdays for more personal work like this. Various venues. We'll call you early evening and tell you where to go. Apart from the four of us here you can expect maybe another half dozen people. Membership is fluid because people move on through the stage of the inner journey that the Servants are concerned with. So you might see someone there the first week, then not see them again after that."

Magnus took over. "I expect you'll recognise a lot of the people there, but you may not know them. This isn't a group for people in prominent positions in the Olive Grove. It's not a council of elders. There's no one from The Flock there, for example. So it is very important that you don't mention this to any leaders. Anyone at all. It's not to do with position or influence. Understood?"

We nodded. Magnus could assume a peremptory manner that jarred with the informality of the Olive Grove. In this context it brought a sense of gravitas. We were talking about something serious. Simon picked up the thread, reverting to the usual casual style: "There is a bit of ... what would you call it? ... ritual. I must tell you, friends, you will see some pretty amazing things. Undeniable things."

They continued speaking. We were not to bring anything with us. 'No baggage' was the term they used, meaning Bibles, wallets, bags. Nothing apart from our keys and the clothes we wore. The rooms where we'd meet would be only faintly lit. There would be no singing. Just the words – which we would repeat after the Two – and a lot of silence. We must come and go alone. No groups, no pairs. "Sorry, not even you two," beamed Simon. And then they stopped. Just before 9pm. Shorter than the first week. No prayers, just a practical, business-like tone.

"Same time next week for the final session of your induction? It's the demonstration." Simon winked at Amelia as he said this, then turned to me and said "she'll explain, man. We had a little chat before you got here."

"Clockhouse again?" I said as we walked away. She agreed and we turned left in the direction of the Rye. I asked her what the demonstration was but she said "wait until we're in the pub". It was quiet on a cold February Wednesday night and we found a table in the corner out of earshot of the few other drinkers. "So, tell me," I said.

"Don't build it up so much, Martyn. You know when Simon said we would see some amazing things? He said before you came that some people get a bit frightened at first, so he and Magnus do a demonstration in private for new Servants like us, so we know what to expect."

"So it'll be a miracle of some sort?"

"I suppose it will. Exciting, isn't it?"

I probably answered yes, but I felt resistance, like walking with weights on my feet. We talked some more about becoming Servants, and what it might mean, and I could tell she was absorbed in the notion in a way I wasn't. I wanted to change the subject so asked her about her book.

"Oh, I don't know," she sighed. "It was going so well but over the past few weeks it has all seized up. I think I need to take a break from it. What with all this …" she gestured with both hands, blew out her cheeks and looked around the room, but I knew she was talking about the Olive Grove and the Servants.

That weekend I went to an old friend's wedding, and Amelia didn't come to the Tuesday meeting at my flat. She called just before saying she was tired and wanted to be at her best for the demonstration.

The wedding was in Cheshire. There wouldn't have been time to go up on Saturday morning so I took Friday afternoon off work and stayed that night and the Saturday night in a village pub with some other guests, a few of whom I had met once or twice. I was there out of a sense of duty more than friendship. I hadn't seen my friend, Pete, for years and never saw him again after his wedding. Though I suppose I might have if things had turned out differently. He came to the pub on Friday and, thinking that going to a wedding might bring back painful memories, took me aside and said how sorry he was to hear about Lillian. He was kind and sensitive but by that time I rarely thought of her and didn't really care at all what had happened. But I couldn't say that to him on the evening before his marriage so I endured what he thought was a deep conversation. I tried to call Amelia from the pub payphone that evening, then again after breakfast, but she didn't answer.

The wedding itself took place at midday in the village church just over the green from the pub. In spite of myself I felt tears pricking my eyes during the vows, and after the ceremony, when the photographer was ushering guests into formation on the green I hid away in the graveyard and cried like I hadn't cried since I was a child. It was more than wedding sentiment, and the tears weren't for Lillian. At the time I might have said I was crying for Amelia, for my longing for her, for wishing it was me standing at the front of the church with her. Looking back, though, I think they were tears for something I feared I was losing. But a loss I couldn't articulate – an indeterminate sense of being cut adrift from ordinary, humdrum, good things and never getting back. But that's hindsight speaking again, and like I said, memory plays tricks. In the years that followed I sometimes wondered if Pete and his wife (what was her name?) ever looked at the wedding photos and wondered why I wasn't in any of them.

I didn't see Amelia again until I turned up at the foyer the following Wednesday. I was early this time, and just Magnus was there, waiting for me. "Simon and Amelia have already gone in," he said, leading me through the bingo hall toward the same room. They were standing at the door, which was closed, waiting for us. Simon opened the door and went in first, then beckoned us in. Magnus closed the door. The room looked different again, this time empty of all furniture. The central overhead strip light was not on. Instead a dimmer light, the source of which I could not see, cast a yellow glow over the walls, while the centre of the room remained almost dark. Simon asked us to stand in that near darkness, and we took positions in a diamond, facing inward. Then he spoke: "I will speak, and we will wait in silence, our eyes closed. When I say 'open', we will open our eyes, and see what gifts we have been given."

If not exactly that, then something pretty close. It's stuck in my mind all these years because of the more formal language, and the incantatory, ceremonial delivery, so out of character for Simon. It's only now, writing them down that I notice the words he did not say.

I find it impossible to say how long we stood. In a silent room with your eyes closed you have only the beating of your heart to measure time. I knew even then that I was not entering into the moment. I was keeping part of myself back, and after what was probably just a few minutes I risked a slit-eyed glance around the room. Simon and Magnus were both stood stock still, legs slightly apart, arms raised. Amelia held her hands in front of her, palms faced upward. She was swaying. I closed my eyes again and waited, waited, waited for whatever it was that was about to happen. After another indeterminate pause I heard a noise, faint at first then growing in power, like air being released into the room. I chanced another glance, to see the other three exactly as they were. The noise continued, rising in pitch and intensity if not in volume. It seemed to be sound only. I felt no sense of wind on my skin. Then the Two, together, cried "open!", loud enough to make me jump, and the noise stopped.

In our midst, in the centre of the diamond, a blueish flame about the size of a finger was glowing. It seemed to be hovering in mid-air, about three feet from the ground. As we watched, it thickened out into a rounder shape like a fist, then grew in size and rose until it was as big as a football, hovering at head height. I could see Amelia staring, utterly transfixed.

We watched the ball of blue flame for some time. It could only have been four feet from me, but I felt no heat. Then, without warning, it vanished. No gradual flickering decline, it just wasn't there any more. Magnus reached over to the light switch and the bare room became, immediately, just like any other tatty, dusty bare room at the back of an old bingo hall. A room that at one time may have been used for storage, or as an office, or a place for the caller to rest and have a cup of tea before eyes down.

"There we are. We were given fire, as a sign of the fire that purges," Simon said. Amelia was shaken and emotional, tears in her eyes. Simon put an arm round her then stood back and indicated that I should take his place. Magnus and Simon ushered us out of the room, talking easily and informally. Amelia leant on me as we walked and I could feel her trembling.

Outside the room, in the main hall, Magnus said that we should make sure we were at home and by our telephones at 7pm on Thursday evenings. We'd get a call, though maybe not straight away, telling us where to go for our first full Servants meeting. We might not both get a call on the same Thursday. They knew it was hard but we really shouldn't be talking about this to each other.

There was nothing in his manner or tone of voice to imply that he was discussing anything important or dramatic. Nothing. But he had a sort of command that it was hard to resist. "Cheers then," he said, as we stepped out into the dark.

"Cheers," said Simon. "See you on Sunday."

"Clockhouse?" I said to Amelia, as we walked from the bingo hall.

"Not this time, no. Can you walk me home? I feel drained."

She didn't say much after that. I tried to engage her in conversation about what had happened, what it might mean, why there was a sound of rushing wind but no feeling of it on our skin, why the fire gave no heat, but she just kept saying "it's a sign."

It was a sign.

CHAPTER 9

March to April 1973

Things change. Sometimes you look back and think you can pinpoint the moment they changed. Other times you can't work out when or how it happened. For a long time I thought the demonstration was the turning point. Now, writing it up and reflecting back all these years later I wonder if the signs were there before, but I was too blind to see them. Her look of disappointment at the Flock concert. The time I told her there was something about the Olive Grove I didn't quite get.

Possibly, I really don't know. I couldn't put my finger on anything in particular, but in the few weeks after the demonstration Amelia seemed less clearly defined, more circumspect. The purposeful leaning into our conversations less apparent. Reserve became distance. Often when I called the phone went unanswered, and when I did manage to speak to her she didn't seem to be concentrating. "Sorry, I missed that. I've got a lot to think about at the moment."

Around the same time I found myself beginning to think differently about the Olive Grove. There was no definitive change, but I became less a participant, more a spectator. Increasingly I found myself standing, eyes open, looking around the room, while everyone else seemed to be in rapt mystic conversation with what they believed was God. One Sunday Simon walked past me and said under his breath, "we'll call soon, brother," and winked.

But I never got the call at 7pm on a Thursday. Did Amelia? Subsequent events made me think she did, but I can never know, really. I had tried to talk to her about it after the first Thursday, the day after the demonstration.

Asking "did the phone ring?" with what I hoped was twinkly, good-humoured intimacy.

She said "no, but they said it would be a few weeks anyway. And besides, I don't think you and I should talk about it. They asked us not to."

The last time I saw Amelia face to face was early one evening, the last Wednesday in March. The group that met in my home was taking a break that week, and I managed to persuade her – it felt like persuading – to go out to dinner. We arranged to meet at 7pm in a vegetarian restaurant in Peckham.

Despite what I took to be her reluctance to meet, when she walked up to the restaurant she seemed at ease, if a little distracted. She kissed me and took my arm. I felt hopeful. I had decided before we met to speak directly, to ask her what was wrong and why she appeared to be avoiding me. Even though I knew the risks. The worst thing a man can do is crowd a woman with anxious questions.

"What's wrong. I can tell you haven't been yourself for a while. Is it me?"

"Nothing's wrong. No Martyn, it's not you," she said, squeezing my arm again. It was the last time she touched me.

I don't recall much detail from our conversation after that. In contrast to that first meeting in the Clockhouse, which I remember even now with a sort of super-perception, my memory is dull and indistinct. One detail I do recall is an attempt to catch her attention when she drifted into one of many absences. "Looking for angels?" I asked, hoping that the reference back to that first Clockhouse date would elicit a fond response. She just looked at me with a frown and a question in her eyes.

What I did get from her, after much coaxing and cajoling,

was that she wanted to go further in her spiritual journey. After the demonstration she had met the Two on several occasions for private counselling. They had singled her out as someone with potential, a special destiny, and that this meant that she couldn't see me anymore. It wasn't that there was anything wrong with me. In fact she liked me a lot. It was just that she needed to remove herself from all distractions. It was her decision, not theirs. She speculated that she was hearing clearly now the call she had heard indistinctly when she'd considered going into a convent. She said this quite gently, but with little emotion. Or at least, compared to the turmoil I was in.

I didn't know what to say. Casting around for a change of subject that might engage her I asked about her Sayers book. She shrugged, saying she hadn't done much on it for a while. She wasn't sure where that fitted in. She'd have to see how things worked out.

At about 7.45pm Amelia started to put on the jacket she'd hung on the back of her chair, saying she had a meeting at church at 8pm. She hadn't finished her food. I remember I asked if I could walk her there, as it was about ten minutes through some rough streets, but she said she'd be OK. She offered to pay for the meal, but I refused. Then she stood and, ducking her head, said goodbye. The last I saw of her she was walking through the open glass doors of the restaurant into the night, as a group of students came in. She didn't look back. I had an impulse to run after her but by the time I had paid the bill and got out of the restaurant she was nowhere to be seen.

I did try to call her at home after that, several times, but there was never an answer. I phoned her workplace once, but was told she had left. She was only a temp so this in itself was plausible, but I felt a pang of humiliation as I imagined her sitting in that office, her colleagues primed to throw me off the scent if I called, their hands over the receiver mouthing "it's him" while she waved her hands in dismissal. I admit I even hovered outside her flat, standing in the shadows like a private detective. But I never saw anyone coming or going, or even any lights on in the place. This went on for two weeks, during which time she didn't come to church. I asked a couple of people in what I hoped was a casual manner if they'd seen her, but no one had. I had a sense of people skirting around me, not avoiding me exactly but keeping a distance. One of the elders, an older man called Peter, said he'd heard she'd gone away for a while. He spoke in a deliberately gentle tone. I began to wonder if she was at Undercliff.

I started to think about going down there unannounced. I mentioned to my manager at work that I'd like to take some time off. We were in a small open plan office so everyone I worked with heard my request. Someone asked where I was going. Just vague office chat. I didn't want to speak about Amelia so I said something about spending some time walking in Devon, coming back after Easter. "I feel like I need a break."

"Are you driving down?" asked someone else. I hadn't thought that far ahead, so I replied that I'd probably catch the train to Exeter and pick up a bus to the coast. Then Oliver, who sat opposite me, offered me his car while he was out of the country. From time to time the permanent staff got sent out on research trips, and it was Oliver's turn next. He was going to Peru. I put up token polite resistance – very kind but I couldn't possibly – but he said as the car was quite old he found it wouldn't start when it had been left idle on the street for a while. I'd be helping him out. So I accepted. That was on a Tuesday and I picked up the car, a Herald, that evening. I booked Tuesday, Wednesday, Thursday and Friday of the following week off, then all of the week after that up to and including the Easter long weekend. I planned to drive down to Devon later in the first week after a few quiet days in London. When I got home I couldn't find a parking space outside my flat or anywhere nearby on my road, so I left the Herald around the corner near a service lane that ran to the back of my building. Whenever I took it out over the next few days I'd find that was the only space to park on my return.

I decided to speak to the Two directly. I wasn't really expecting to change anything by doing this, I just wanted to know if they knew where Amelia had gone. Although she'd told me quite clearly that our relationship was over I didn't have any sense of what people now call closure. I suppose at that point I still hoped to change her mind. It was on the day after I'd picked up the car, a Wednesday evening, when I went to see them. As I walked toward the old bingo hall just before 8pm I realised it was exactly two weeks since I'd last seen her. I didn't tell them I was coming, as I didn't want a prepared response. But I was pretty confident they'd be there.

The swing doors into the main lobby were unlocked, as they generally were. The church had an open-door policy, though in the evenings this meant that anyone who walked through those first open doors would find themselves in a lobby from which four other doors led. Chances were these would be locked, and indeed they were when I arrived. If I had been passing trade the Church's welcome would have consisted of some free literature on a table and a form to fill in, which I could have posted through a letterbox in one of the locked internal doors. This would trigger a friendly follow-up call within a few days.

That night I looked on it all with growing disdain.

The place had been a cinema before it was a bingo hall. Directly in front were double doors that led into the main room. These were old, battered, a little warped, probably survivors from the building's former life. On that night they were locked. There was no bell to ring, so I tried the handles to the other three doors, and pushed at the double doors. But something kept me from calling out. Instead I put my eye to the gap between the double doors, to see if I could get a glimpse of the main room. I knew that heavy curtains were drawn across the entrance immediately behind the doors, but their runners were old and sticky and they didn't close properly. I knew this because sometimes I helped to lock up on Sunday nights.

As I looked through the crack I could see that there was indeed a gap in the curtains. Dim lighting glowed near the stage. I could see an area around the stage, though I had no sight of the rest of the cavernous room. And I could see the locked door, the one marked STRICTLY NO ADMITTANCE. The one I had once tried to open, by mistake.

I could also see the Two standing about six feet apart in front of the stage, facing me. They both had their eyes closed, their hands held out in front of them in a posture of anticipatory acceptance. This was a familiar prayerful stance in the Olive Grove, and we all did it. I could just see on the right-hand side one other person, who appeared to be standing at an angle facing the Two, but I couldn't see who it was. Black trousers, white shirt. Then three people walked in from the left-hand side. Two men who I recognised from the congregation but didn't know. Again, black trousers, white shirts. They were supporting a limp, stumbling woman. Her feet were dragging and her head lolled. Her hair partly covered her face. I was not able to identify her, but she looked young. Slim, and her hair was thick, shiny and dark. She might have been Spanish or South American.

The two men lowered her into a kneeling position facing the Two. I remember being surprised that she was able to remain like that when they let go of her, because she looked so floppy. Then they assumed position in a three-point formation with the third man I'd seen, their backs to me, so that they and the Two surrounded the woman. She knelt there, her head bowed. From the position of her elbows I think she was holding her hands cupped together at her breast, like a Catholic at Mass. The Two then lifted their hands above their heads, perfectly synchronised, and held this position for some time. I could see their mouths moving and could hear very faint voices, but I couldn't make out what they were saying.

After a minute or so the Two stepped forward together, and each laid a hand on the kneeling woman's head. Simon, who was standing on her right, reached out his right hand, while Magnus reached out his left. At the moment their hands joined on the woman's head the sound of voices stopped, and I realised at that point that the other people in the room had been contributing to the murmur. There followed a short period of absolute stillness and quiet. How long? Twenty seconds, maybe, before the woman fell forward onto her face, her arms beneath her body, her hair spilling onto the carpet. As she fell the Two withdrew their hands and held them again in the cupped, anticipatory position. They stood like this for a couple of minutes, eyes closed, while the woman lay motionless. Then, as if in response to some signal that I couldn't see, the men who had supported her walked over to the woman and lifted her sagging form into a parody of standing. The other man, who

I had glimpsed to my right, then moved fully into the scene. It was Harry, the caricature plumber. He knelt and picked up the woman by the legs, and the three of them carried her toward the door marked STRICTLY NO ADMITTANCE. Simon opened it and they all passed through.

It might seem odd to you, but at the time none of this troubled me or even made much of an impression. Strange things soon seem normal when you experience them as a matter of routine. I was quite used to seeing people crumpling to the floor during prayer sessions. 'Being slain', we called it. I'd experienced it myself, a sort of pleasant weakness in the legs and a longing to give in, to lie down, to surrender. I'd prayed for people, laid hands on them and seen them keel over. I remember seeing a television documentary exposing corrupt American televangelists that included slowed down footage that clearly demonstrated that the preachers had given the supplicants standing in front of them, eyes closed, a shove. At the time I'd have sworn that we didn't push people or allow ourselves to be pushed, but I'm not so sure now. Try standing still with your eyes closed, hands cupped in front of you for a few minutes. You'll start to sway and it would only take a touch to unbalance you. But that's going off the point. At the time, praying like that and falling over had become normal in my life. The only thing that was a little odd was that the woman had seemed barely conscious before the praying started.

I left the bingo hall and walked back up the high street. A Vauxhall estate, like Harry's but a brighter shade of blue, slowed for a moment as it passed me, and a man I didn't recognise in the passenger seat caught my eye. He held my gaze for a second then turned to the driver, and the car moved off. I turned into my road and walked on, absorbed.

Not far from my flat I heard a voice behind me, and as

I turned to look over one shoulder a hand came down on the other. It was Simon who had spoken, and Magnus who held my shoulder. He slackened his grip and it became a friendly pat. They were both smiling.

"You were in a world of your own, Martyn. We called a couple of times and you didn't hear. Lovely evening, isn't it? Been anywhere special, or just out for a stroll?"

We had stopped by this time, about 30 yards from my flat. I might have been imagining it, but I thought Simon put a stress on the word 'special', very subtle, as if he were humouring me. Before I could answer he said they were going to the office to pick something up. He was standing a little too close to me, as he sometimes did. Only a few inches, but still.

"Actually, I've just been over to the building," I said. We sometimes called the one-time bingo hall and cinema 'the building', rarely 'the church'.

"This isn't the church," the Two used to say. "It is just a temporary shelter. We are all the church, so the church goes wherever we all go."

"I wanted to ask you something but I couldn't see anyone around," I added.

It was equal parts lie and truth, but spoken out of embarrassment more than anything. It seemed wrong to interrupt a private prayer meeting. I felt awkward, as if I'd seen by accident some intimate act.

There was a break in the conversation. They looked at me, expressions placid and amiable. Then they spoke together, in perfect unison:

"We were there, Martyn. You would have been welcome to join us."

It was the first time they spoke to me in unison. Personally, I mean. I'd heard them do it from the front many times. I was about to speak when they started again:

"What did you want?"

Spoken with a smile, with something like warmth. Or was it heat?

I managed to piece together a few sentences about being upset about Amelia's absence, and wondering if they knew where she was, and if I could, or should try to contact her. Simon said they didn't know, they'd look into it, and suggested I meet them at the bingo hall the following Tuesday morning. "As it's the first day of your break from work," he said.

Later I couldn't recall if I'd told him about that or not. I agreed and we walked on toward my flat and the office. In the little foyer Magnus again held my shoulder and they said, together, "see you Tuesday."

I walked up the stairs resolved to wait patiently, prayerfully for Amelia's return. Or to accept that she might not return and that was that.

Next Tuesday I arrived at just before 10am.

When I look back on the subsequent interview now I am astonished. All I can say is that when they, dressed in their everyman casuals, talked about eternal life and how to find it, they sounded oh so reasonable. And I can see now why that is. The two of them had developed a system that was a model of clarity and completely logical, as long as it was expressed matter-of-factly in an environment they controlled.

I know – I realise that's virtually a definition of a cult. But most of what they said seemed standard-issue orthodoxy to me. You could have heard something virtually identical from church leaders the length and breadth of the country. Virtually identical, but not quite. And when you were with them, in that environment, and you are being praised and affirmed, and it seems like everyone's attention is directed at you, and you were lonely before you came. Well, all I can say is that when you are there you can't see that they've made you their puppet, and you dangle on their strings.

They sat in high-backed wicker armchairs, beckoning me to sit in a single, vacant armchair in front of them, a little lower than theirs. They gave me a cup of coffee and proceeded to affirm me. I heard about all the qualities they discerned in me, how valued a member of the Olive Grove I was, and how I had grown in faith. After a few minutes of this I felt myself being lulled into a comfortable state an increment below full consciousness. It was with some effort that I reminded myself I had things I wanted to raise. I said I was worried and upset about Amelia. Did they know where she was, and could they tell me what was happening.

They didn't answer directly.

"The pair of you have given so much to the Olive Grove, Martyn," said Simon, stroking the end of his ponytail that fell forward off his shoulder onto his chest.

"You've grown so much in what? – it is only a few months, isn't it?" continued Magnus, taking the conversational baton and staring at me, unblinking. "You've both got something special to offer."

I believe now that all of this was careful manoeuvring. Setting me up on an intricate little scaffold of compliments. At the time I half recognised this, but I was intrigued and flattered too. I think I must have asked questions, and I remember a few snatches of what followed:

"Remember what we are told? That the greatest thing is to lay down your life for others, yes?"

"...It isn't just about diving into the sea to rescue a drowning child, and drowning yourself. It isn't just about giving up your time to serve people. Those are the lower expressions of a profound principle. The highest expression is something so much more wonderful…"

"The olive must be plucked and pressed to release its life-giving oil."

"…humble submission. Submit to us, your leaders, just as we submit to a higher force, and we will guide you …"

And then things become fragmented. My memory of the conversation becomes increasingly patchy, like a newspaper from which somebody has cut certain crucial passages, and each time you turn a page there is more missing. They did some of their unison speech. I recall they asked me if I really believed in an afterlife, but what my answers were I couldn't say. There was something about the principle of death giving life to us, and how we were meant to live it out. "You've got to give to live." That phrase sticks in my mind. Give to live.

I don't know how the meeting ended, nor can I remember what happened over the next twelve hours. All I know is that I walked into the bingo hall at about 10am, and that by about 11pm I was sitting at home alone.

This was when doubt began. No, that was when doubt took on a vague yet tangible form, like a mist that blew in sometimes. Did I make my own way home or did somebody bring me back? Was it hypnosis, or drugs in my coffee that accounted for a memory smudged to illegibility? Or was it the power of God? What had happened? As my head cleared I was left with one abiding impression, stark in its clarity amidst the confusion. I was to return to the cinema the following evening, Wednesday, at 8pm, to pray with the Two and a few elders. This fragment of clarity unsettled me and I couldn't work out why for a while. Then I recalled that Amelia, too, had been called to pray with the Two at 8pm on a Wednesday. I had seen her leave the restaurant to make that rendezvous and hadn't seen her since. And then there was that memory of the other woman, unknown to me, falling face down. Also on a Wednesday night.

Then the phone rang. It was Simon. Easy-going. Cheerful.

"Martyn, I left it a while before calling. We had such a powerful time I thought you'd be out for a while. We brought you home and let ourselves in with the keys in your pocket. Are you OK, brother? It was a fantastic time. There was great power there today, it really fell on you."

I mumbled some response and he continued as if he hadn't heard me.

"Take it easy. Just relax. My advice is don't try to put too much effort into praying right now because we're weak mortals and there's only so much we can take in one go. Just relax. Trust me."

I asked him what had happened.

"We know you're upset about Amelia. It often happens that when we get upset about something and we're at a low ebb doubt crowds in and drives us half crazy. Just relax and all that will fade away. Come and see us again tomorrow night, and we'll work through to victory. There's a breakthrough in sight."

I said I'd do that, and as I put the phone down I felt a release of tension from my body, as if I'd taken an opiate. I had let my mind get overcome with absurd, paranoid thoughts. Amelia leaving upset me, but I would be OK because God was with me. I went to bed exhausted, not happy exactly, but humming a hymn to myself.

CHAPTER 10

Wednesday April 11th, 1973

I sat up at 6am, as if a loud noise had woken me. If it had I didn't hear it again. I listened for a minute but all was quiet apart from scattered birdsong and distant traffic. I had slept heavily and yet felt sluggish and weak, not refreshed at all. I had a dull headache behind my eyes. The details of a dream came back to me. I was trying to persuade my parents and Lillian of something I had discovered that seemed transparently obvious to me, and on which our safety depended. Yet despite being absolutely clear in my mind of what I wanted to say I could not find the words, and every time I started to try to speak my parents and Lillian would change the subject or appear not to be listening. My frustration rose to a pitch as I felt increasingly impotent, alone in my knowledge of impending doom and trapped in my inability to warn everyone of it. I awoke as my parents and Lillian walked away from me down a footpath lined on each side with tall hedges, me walking just behind, trying to force words from my mute mouth.

I lay in bed for a long time, alternately dozing and reflecting on my late night conversation with Simon. I had planned to go into central London to get a few things for my trip but there was no hurry. Last night's acceptance of what he said was now tempered with – not doubt, exactly, but something like it. When I was at the Olive Grove and speaking to the Two it was OK for that moment. Belief was viable in the company of believers. But left to my own thoughts, lying in bed with a headache, I had a feeling of claustrophobia. The Olive Grove seemed not a fertile fruit-bearing place but a creeping, constricting thicket. I just wanted to get some space, get away from the Olive Grove for a bit. I wanted a change of scene, to see some different faces. I had a sense of people crowding around me, which is something I've never liked.

I got up at about 9am. I decided to do my shopping that morning, be back in time for lunch, and spend the rest of the day packing and getting ready. I didn't want to go and pray with the Two tonight. I'd phone them later and cancel.

As I walked down the stairs to the front door the post spilled from the letterbox. I gathered the scattered letters into a pile and flicked through them, noticing one item for me, a postcard with a picture of St David's cathedral on the front. I put the rest of the letters on the shelf and walked out of the door looking at the cramped, scratchy handwriting, recognising it immediately, though I hadn't seen it for a while:

Martyn

I'm at a conference here at this most humble of cathedrals and I thought of you as I remember you once said you used to come here every year for family holidays. I hope you are well. We should catch up soon. It's been too long.

George.

George Parsons. Now the Revd. George Parsons. A most appropriate name, as George himself was fond of saying. A friend from the *South London Press*. He'd left to train for ordination shortly before I'd moved to Leicester with Lillian. Older than me by about five years. I hadn't seen him since leaving London, but had sent a change of address card when I returned, telling him Lillian and I had split up.

It was a second-class stamp on the postcard. I decided to call him immediately and turned and walked back up the stairs to my flat. Avuncular, salt of the earth George was an appealing prospect right now.

He was in when I phoned.

"Martyn, lovely to hear from you. Have to be quick as I've got a funeral."

We spoke for a few minutes. He asked what I was doing. I told him about my job, and going to the Olive Grove. He said he'd heard of it. I said we should meet up. "Yes! Why not this evening? There's a place I go to by the river in Hammersmith, just outside the parish. Don't want to be bumping into parishioners. Even a vicar needs a night off."

There was, as ever, something staged about George's bonhomie, and yet at the same time it was authentic. It was as if he, an extrovert, good-natured man, was somehow unable to act intuitively in accordance with his character, and had instead learned from books how to behave. In the past this had rankled a little, but today I was filled with a sense of relief at returning to somewhere I oughtn't have left. I decided I'd call the Olive Grove when I got back from shopping to tell the Two I wouldn't be coming tonight, but as I left the front door of my block I saw Magnus strolling toward me. "Just going to the office," he said. This was unusual. The place was rarely used as there was another office in the bingo hall, and I'd often wondered why the Olive Grove kept on the room in my block. I told him I needed to see an old friend tonight who'd just got back in touch and that I couldn't come at 8pm as arranged. "That's fine, brother," he said, smiling. "There's always another time."

Glad to be free of that commitment I went up to the West End on a bus and bought a sleeping bag. It was a sunny morning and on the journey home, looking out from the front seat on the top deck as we drove across Waterloo Bridge, I felt a renewed surge of optimism. Olive Grove or no Olive Grove, I'd find Amelia and work it out with her. But even if I didn't, things would be alright in the end.

I got off the bus a few stops early as I felt like walking, but immediately regretted it. Harry the plumber called from over the road. I could hardly avoid him as I had to cross over to get home. I'd never liked him at the best of times. "Look forward to seeing you tonight," he said, slapping me on the back. I must have looked puzzled because he immediately followed this up: "The telling? Tonight at 8pm? A few of us will be there. I thought you were coming along?"

"Oh no, I can't come after all. Sorry. I've got to see an old friend."

"Oh well, shame. There's always another time."

As I walked on I felt doubly relieved that I was not going. I had thought I'd just be seeing the Two. I'd experienced a few tellings before. Not unpleasant experiences in themselves, but on that day the thought of the Two and Harry and God knows who else surrounding me, laying hands on me and speaking platitudes at me made me recoil.

I spent the afternoon packing my old rucksack, which I hadn't used for years, then at about 6.30pm I set off to Hammersmith in the Herald. It had a cassette player in it and I slotted in a copy of the Flock album *Lost Sheep Found*. I hadn't got around to listening to it properly since buying it at the pub in Herne Hill. It was the same ebbing and flowing, polytonal, free-form music that I remembered from the severely abbreviated concert, but the recording quality was poor, the sound thin and drained of any power it may have had. I found it a distraction while driving and ejected it, leaving it on the front passenger seat.

In those days it was a lot easier getting around London by car. Fewer parking restrictions, less traffic. Even so, it was getting on for 7.30pm by the time I reached Hammersmith. As I got out of the car the cassette caught my eye and I decided I'd take it in for George. He'd probably hate it.

George was sitting at the bar reading a paper. He wasn't wearing his dog collar, which pleased me for some reason. His sandy hair had thinned since I last saw him, now looking like a patchy lawn seeded by an incompetent gardener. As I got closer I noticed the cheeks of his big face were criss-crossed with tiny thread veins, the nose a little red. He'd always liked a drink, I remembered. He was a big man but he'd lost weight if anything, and he was getting jowly. In fact he looked much older – probably I did too – but he was as hearty and cheerful as ever. I was relieved to greet someone with a firm handshake rather than the warm embrace customary at the Olive Grove. I'd never felt comfortable with that. He said he was sorry about Lillian and I realised I'd barely thought of her for months. I didn't want to talk about that so I asked him about life as a vicar.

"Oh, usual parish stuff most of the time. Bit of tension on the PCC about whether a local yoga teacher should be allowed to use the hall. It's hard work at times, but that's what I signed up for. Can't complain."

"I was always surprised you chose that life. I imagined you taking on a regional daily somewhere in the shires."

"It chose me, would be more accurate, I think. But yes, that was what I imagined too – the shires, I mean – but when you hear the call you have to answer. At least I did."

"How did you hear the call?" I asked. I'd never heard the story.

"Oh, a few things happened. There was a fellow called Cleave, a detective. Remember him? No? It was probably

just after you started at the *South London Press*, actually…"
he tailed off and took a drink. I got the impression he would
prefer another subject.

"How's your sister?"

"I forgot you'd met Annabel. Yes, she is doing well. Two
sets of twins now. They're in Berkshire. David travels a lot.
Big house, Labrador. You get the picture."

"Still single yourself, George?"

"Yes, I'm afraid so. Who'd have me? Still time though.
Only 41."

The conversation meandered pleasantly for half an
hour, but I noticed that George was looking increasingly
drawn. I asked if he was OK.

"Yes, fine, I just get tired easily, and what with a couple
of these," tapping his beer glass, "I'm feeling a bit drained. I
didn't tell you about my illness, did I? I had cancer, actually,
about three years ago now. I won't tell you what of as it's an
eye-watering prospect, but it seems they got it out alright.
Slash and burn – that's the way to do it. I'm fine now. Takes
a lot out of you, though. But enough about that. As a man
of the cloth I'm obliged to ask you, what is the state of your
soul?"

"Well, I mentioned the Olive Grove on the phone earlier.
In Nunhead? I've been going there for a few months."

"Yes. I've read about it somewhere. Some kind of free
church, isn't it? Two men leading it?"

"The Two – Magnus and Simon."

"There was something in your tone when you said
that, Martyn, that makes me think you are harbouring
reservations. Correct?"

"Well, yes, I suppose so. You'll remember from our
conversations at the paper, or should I say arguments, that
my faith has always been a rather variable prospect. But

when I first went to the Olive Grove I thought I'd finally found my niche. It felt real for the first time, whereas before it had always felt a bit like borrowing someone else's suit for a wedding. But now... I don't know... I'm starting to feel a little bit claustrophobic..."

"And?"

"Well, I met a woman there but she..."

George hit the table hard enough to cause the barman to cast an eye in our direction. "I can always tell a heartsick man. Must be on account of my extensive personal experience. Keep going."

And with that we talked for an hour about the Olive Grove, and Amelia, and the state of my soul. I showed him the Flock cassette, trying to illustrate a point I was making about the hippy, counter-cultural trappings that I now didn't find quite so appealing.

"The thing is, Martyn," said George returning from at least his fifth visit to the toilet. "churches are like families, but they're also like organisations or even armies, and I'm a little wary of these independent set-ups. No chain of command. Who are those two accountable to? They'll say God of course, and fair enough, but there's nothing like a pedantic PCC and a fussy Archdeacon for keeping your feet on the ground. There's power in leading a group of several hundred people, and power can corrupt anyone – it can even corrupt church leaders. Ah, Adam! Sorry Martyn, forgot to say Adam was joining us."

I turned to see a man much younger than George and a fair bit younger than me. Short and slight, with dark curly hair, dark brown eyes and the hint of a hunch in his shoulders.

"Martyn Hope - Adam Ncucquet," said George, standing and gesturing to us both. I stood to shake Adam's hand just as he sat down, nodding in my direction without quite making eye contact.

"Adam's a friend and," George explained, "parishioner, too, I suppose. Catholic, though, so don't see him on Sundays. So he's spared my sermons. Thought you two might have something in common. Olive Grove and all that."

Introductions over, and another round of drinks bought, the conversation went off on a different tack, though I would have liked to talk more with George about the Olive Grove. Adam asked me what I did, a question I always disliked because what I really wanted to say was "I'm a writer" but I couldn't, and was beginning to think I never would. So I gave as brief an account of myself as possible before asking him what he did. At this point George broke in:

"Tell him, Adam. I bet you've got a copy in that bag, haven't you?"

Adam, without a trace of the reserve I'd have felt, produced a book from his satchel and said "well, I'm a lecturer at King's, modern history, but this has just been published."

I took it and asked what it was about and he, clearly glad of an audience, explained in some depth that it was a study of an Edwardian utopian sect that flourished briefly in a manor house in Hertfordshire. New Dawn, or Dawnists as they came to call themselves. In 1910 there had been several hundred of them living communally but the war decimated their menfolk and destroyed their idealism.

"You can have that copy if you want," Adam said.

"Oh thanks, that's very kind."

"He's got boxes of them under his bed, I expect. He spends his time wandering around Hammersmith giving out freebies to unsuspecting passers-by, calling them review copies," said George, which Adam ignored.

I've still got that book. It's here before me on the desk as I type this. *New Dawn: Utopian Dreams and the Great War* by Adam Noucquet.

Adam picked up the Flock cassette I'd left on the table. "So you go to the Olive Grove, George tells me. I'm interested in that sort of thing. From a cultural perspective, that is. I've heard about this band. I read a review of it in *New Life!*"

"Surprised to hear a Roman would read radical evangelical propaganda, Adam," butted in George.

"Well, it pays to be broad-minded in these matters, I think," said Adam, entering into the banter like a man dragged from his deckchair to build sandcastles with his children. "I like to keep in touch with what's going on. The review said it sounded a bit like the Trees Community. I don't expect a man of your vintage, George, to have heard of them, but it's the sort of thing that interests me. They're a community at the Cathedral of Saint John the Divine in New York City. They perform a sort of free worship music, sounds a bit like The Incredible String Band? No, thought not. Anyway, I was over there for three months on a research trip last year and I used to go and see them play – the Trees Community, that is. I've been looking out for this," said Adam, holding up the cassette.

"Well take it, please," I said. "A swap for the book. The music isn't really my cup of tea to be honest, but I'm told by people who seem to know that it's very good, so you might like it."

Adam thanked me and slipped the cassette into his satchel. He only stayed for one drink.

"A bit sharp, but a nice fellow when you get to know

him," said George. By now he was looking very tired and before long he too stood to leave. We shook hands, agreeing that we ought to meet more often.

"Lovely evening. It's been too long," he said, and with that he was off. For a cumbersome, doughy-looking man he was a brisk, keen walker. He thought nothing of trekking the two miles home through London's darkness to his flat. Even so, there was weariness in the slope of his back as he worked his way through the now crowded pub.

With no work the next day and nothing much else to do, I decided to stay until closing time. I bought myself another drink and a packet of crisps and settled on a stool at the end of the bar. On the wall next to me was a framed document claiming that *Rule Britannia* had been written in the pub. I opened Adam's book and flicked through it. A bit sharp, George had said. He was right. I'd noticed something waspish in Adam's conversation that was mirrored in the tone of the book. The unpicking of the hypocrisy bound up in gender relations in the community, the confused mix of Theosophy, proto-Marxism and a dash of Tolstoy. I decided then I'd read it properly on my break in Devon and I did, and have again, many times since. I always like this bit:

Whether rank-and-file members experienced New Dawn as a patriarchy or a matriarchy is hard to say. On the one hand, interpretation of Dawnist doctrine was strictly in the hands of a small group of men. That same doctrine, however, held that women were more alert to the mysterious voice of the Divine. They were the lightning rods that drew the bolt of revelation. In practice, this meant that women spent much of their time in repose, waiting for insight, which they then passed on to male elders. On the other hand, men – or at least most of them apart from that core group of elders – worked

12 hours a day, six days a week, scratching the community's living from the recalcitrant Hertfordshire soil.

There's a plate section in the middle with a dozen or so photos of the commune, bearded men in heavy tweed trousers, boots and collarless work shirts, women in white linen gowns, all gathered around the thatched cob shelters and shepherds' huts where they lived. There was something about one of these photos that caught my eye, but I couldn't quite work out what it was. I looked at it for a while and then closed the book. The barman rang for time. I finished my beer and got up to leave, realising as I did that I was a little unsteady on my feet. I'd had a bit to drink and nothing to eat. It was a warm, clear evening and I decided to stroll along by the river to clear my head before driving home.

The pub had a terrace that looked out over the still, grey water. I stood there for a while, breathing in the air. With the beer and George's company I was feeling happier than I had for a while. I walked down steps from the terrace to the path that runs along by the river and set off westward. The path was well lit and there were still quite a few people around – couples, dog walkers, a group of teenagers. I had only been walking a few minutes when I saw, 50 yards ahead of me, a man with his back to me, leaning against a lamppost as if in some discomfort. It was a rather grand Victorian gas lamp, converted to electricity. As I approached the man his outline clear in the lamp's pool of light, he turned half toward me so that I could see him in profile. The shape of his head looked familiar, but I didn't recognise him immediately. I found myself thinking that I ought to ask him if he was OK, while at the same time resisting the impulse to help, uncertain about approaching a stranger in the dark. I was about 30 feet away when I recognised him. I called out "can I help?" or something like that, and he looked in my direction. As I walked into the lamplight he seemed to recognise me, though I couldn't be sure.

"Life, my friend, is full of surprises. Surprise is the spice of variety. My advice to you, if you are a taker of advice, is to give the widest of berths around religious zealots."

"Are you OK?" I replied, standing ten feet from him.

Ken the drunk made a swinging gesture through the air, as if pushing people out of his way.

"Young man, suffering is my constant companion. I have learned to accommodate him, even if I relish not his company. So piss off. Enough."

With that, he turned his back to me, leaning his forehead onto the cold iron of the lamppost, and retched. He swung his arm behind his back in my direction and said something else I couldn't hear. I turned around and walked back to my car, wondering if he had recognised me, and how he came to be in Hammersmith, and if his words meant anything or were just the sad arbitrary poetry of a mind scrambled by alcohol.

As I walked along the row of parked cars, I noticed little oblongs of paper tucked under windscreen wipers, mine included. I unlocked the driver's door and took the paper, glancing at it as I sat in the car. It was a leaflet from what I assume was the local parish church, listing forthcoming Holy Week services. It awoke an obscure longing in me, like a memory of something that had never happened. I wondered if George had put it there, then remembered he'd said the pub was just outside his parish. I sat in the car for a few minutes and thought of those services in that church. What sort of people would attend? What sort of God would listen to their prayers?

Then I turned the key and put my hand on the gearstick.

***

Adam leant back in his chair, thousands of miles and many years away from that meeting in that Hammersmith pub. He was still slight, but the hunch was more pronounced and the hair was gone. He had realised a few pages into the manuscript that it was written, purportedly, by Martyn Hope. He had remembered him, but more from reports of subsequent events. The details of their meeting – that one brief meeting – had remained just out of memory's reach until now. He smiled at the description of his younger self. Waspish. Not unfair.

CHAPTER 11

Thursday April 12th, 1973

I got back just after midnight, parking around the corner as usual. I had drunk quite a bit so shouldn't have been driving at all, but everyone was slack about that sort of thing in those days. Though I was tired when I got home I still felt the benefits of the evening's company and the beer, and I felt relaxed as I strolled toward my flat. I'd forgotten about Ken by now, putting our encounter down to coincidence.

It was with faint relief that I noticed that the Olive Grove's office was dark, the blinds drawn. Not that I thought anyone would be in there at that time. When I went into my flat I half expected to see a note from the Two pushed under the door inviting me to make another date to see them, but there was nothing on the floor. From force of habit I walked over to the answer machine on a table at the end of the short hallway. For the past couple of weeks I had lived in hope of a message from Amelia, though so far there had been nothing. In fact I rarely got any calls at all. But this time I could see the red light winking at me:

"Hi Martyn, Simon here. Just to say I'm camping out in the office downstairs from you as I'm having some work done in my kitchen at home. I thought we might have breakfast tomorrow? Knock on the door when you get up if you want to. Cheers."

I played it again, as if the second time it would say something different. But no, the same cheerful, casual, friendly voice. I didn't like the idea that he was down there, two floors below. I want you to understand that up until this point I hadn't really suspected anything more than that *perhaps* the Olive Grove was a mildly cranky cult, and the

Two a little more controlling than they'd have you believe. Amelia's departure had changed my view of it, though.

Or maybe it was changing anyway and her absence just accelerated the process. I recognised that I had shifted position. No longer was I a member of the group. Rather I was outside, observing it (and, I thought, seeing it for what it was). And like a lot of things, it looked different depending on where you stood. I had a sense of what, just a few weeks before, had seemed like a welcoming, friendly set of like-minded people now surrounding me, hemming me in. And then I thought about George and what he represented. For all his idiosyncrasies, his weaknesses, his faults, how much more substantial he seemed. More durable, more rooted.

What I most wanted at that moment was to speak to Amelia. Maybe she'd gone home to Belgium? But she'd told me often enough there wasn't anything there for her anymore. My best guess was that she was at Undercliff. If I spoke to her ... maybe? Maybe?

I was restless. I paced around the small living room, sitting down from time to time but unable to settle. I tried deep breathing exercises, I poured myself a whisky, I put a record on and took it off, I even tried praying, but nothing could settle me. It dawned on me how hungry I was. I hadn't eaten since lunch, apart from crisps at the pub. There were two bananas in a fruit bowl, and I ate them in quick succession. As I was peeling the second I decided to draw back the curtain and look out of the window. I'd noticed a strong crescent moon in the clear sky when I was driving home and I thought I'd look at it for a while as I tried to unwind. In the silent road bathed in the frail silvers and yellows of moonlight and sodium, I caught a momentary glimpse of a figure on the far side step behind a van and out of sight. I drew the curtain closed and sat on the sofa.

Was someone watching me? Was someone from the Olive Grove watching me? I don't know why that idea came to mind but it did, and once it was there I couldn't shift it.

My thoughts accelerated through a succession of possibilities. It occurred to me that the ground floor office was a handy guard post, and in it sat Simon. He would have heard me come in, and would be perfectly placed to apprehend me if I tried to leave by the front door. The hallway passed by the internal office door, which was immediately to the right of the front door as you were leaving. "Hello Martyn, how are you?" I could hear it.

But what was I thinking? Was there really anyone standing guard on the other side of the road, watching my windows? Why on earth was I imagining that? Well, that's what it did to you. You get involved, you give of yourself, then when you step back, you find your feet are stuck in quicksand and it's hard to get away, and you panic.

I crawled across the room below the level of the windowsill, so my shadow would not be seen. A part of me was feeling ridiculous, another part afraid. I suppose I was enjoying it a little too. When I reached the window I pulled back a corner of the curtain a fraction and looked out. There was somebody there. No question. An impassive face partially hidden by the cab of the van, staring up at my flat.

I slunk back to my seat and attempted to compose myself again. I *was* being watched. So who was watching me? As I tried my best to consider this question with a clear head I noticed on the coffee table a sheet of notepaper that I hadn't seen before. I picked it up. Written in pencil in a hand I didn't recognise, on the Olive Grove's headed notepaper, were these words:

But the eyes of the LORD are on those who fear him.

That was all. *LORD* written in capitals. No signature, no message. Had the Two left it when they'd brought me home yesterday? I'm sure it hadn't been there in the morning. I'd have noticed it. Or maybe someone had been into the flat while I was out during the evening. There was something about those words that clarified my mind. Or rather it wasn't the words as such, but the context of them, appearing unexplained on my coffee table while someone stood outside staring up at my windows and Simon sat in the office below. I thought of calling the police but almost immediately discounted the idea. Simon was, after all, perfectly entitled to be in his office. The note could be read as reassuring, and the person over the road – whoever he was and whatever he was doing – would just melt into the night if he saw a police car come round the corner. There was nothing to report, yet much to feel uneasy about.

I tried to be logical. I wanted to get away from the Two even more than I had 30 minutes before, and I wanted to find Amelia. The obvious place to start looking for her was Undercliff. But I knew the Two often went there as well. So by going and looking for her, I ran the risk of running into them. I sat for a while, thinking. If she was at Undercliff she'd go out for walks – she always did – so all I needed to do was watch from a safe distance until I saw her, and then intercept her. I'd been planning to go the next day anyway, but I decided to go that very night.

Then the familiar double rings began. I walked into the hall and stood by the phone as it compelled me to pick up the receiver. I was about to give in when the answer machine clicked on. I heard my own voice, stilted and unfamiliar, invite the caller to leave a message. There was a second of silence.

The caller rang off. The answer machine clicked to a

stop and rewound its tape into position to welcome the next caller. I stood there for many minutes, but the next call never came. I couldn't decide if I'd missed an opportunity or escaped a threat.

I walked into my bedroom and turned on the light, knowing any observer would think I was getting ready for bed, then quickly pushed into my rucksack a change of clothes, wallet, sleeping bag, a smaller shoulder bag, a money belt and a torch. I put my keys in my pocket. I stood there for a minute wondering what else I might need. A few other things, but I could buy them when I was down in Devon. I opened the drawer of my bedside table and saw my passport, and thought I might as well take it. Thinking I'd have a lot of time to myself I threw Adam Noucquet's book in as well. I then made a show of walking back into the lounge and turning off the light, then turning on the bathroom light for five minutes. I picked up some toiletries. Then I turned off first the bathroom, then the bedroom lights so the flat was in darkness. I shuffled along the floor below window level into the lounge for another peek at my watcher. This time I got a better look as he lit a cigarette, and recognised him as a South American student from the Olive Grove, whose name I never knew. That sealed it. I crept back into my room and dragged my rucksack to the front door of the flat. It must have been about 1am by then. I lay on the floor and tried to rest, knowing that I had a sleepless night ahead of me. By dint of supreme effort I managed to keep reasonably still for about 30 minutes, before getting up, slipping on a pair of plimsolls and lifting the rucksack onto my back.

When I opened the door from my flat the latch clicked, so I waited on the threshold for a full two minutes. Nothing. I closed and locked the door and stood outside my flat on the landing, waiting again. Nothing. I padded along the landing up to the side of a curtainless window, and looked out. Below was a walled courtyard, an old lean-to extending into it in which residents kept bicycles. A door from the courtyard led to the service lane. That door would be locked, but I was given a key to it when I moved in. There was also a door into this courtyard from the downstairs hall. I had a key to that as well.

I couldn't see anyone about in the courtyard or the service lane. I stood still again for a minute, listening hard, but all was quiet. The stairs in the block were concrete so I could walk soundlessly down to the ground floor. I stepped from the last stair into the hall, no more than six feet from the door into the Olive Grove office. I turned back toward the door into the courtyard, all the while dreading behind me the sound of an opening door and Simon's bland, friendly voice. "Hi, Martyn."

I unlocked the door, stepped into the unlit courtyard, and locked it behind me.

A hand grabbed my left arm, like a clamp. Without thinking I twisted my body and lashed out with my right hand, an intuitive muscular memory of the self-defence techniques I'd been taught in the Army. As I turned I saw, standing in the shadow of the lean to, whoever it was that held me. I think the act of turning while I threw my punch unbalanced him, and although I didn't hit him with force he fell to one side and thudded against the wall. As he slumped at my feet, motionless, I recognised Harry the plumber.

I hesitated for what was probably no more than a second. Had I broken his neck? I couldn't see any blood, but he was bent awkwardly and he wasn't moving at all. Should I see if he was OK? That question was answered when he grunted and stirred, and I heard the sound of a door opening back down the hallway.

There was just time to cover the few paces across the courtyard to the door in the wall and unlock it. I slipped through as noiselessly as I could manage and turned the key in the lock just as the back door into the yard was opening. I think I heard an urgent whisper, but I'm not sure. I ran down the service lane, rucksack bouncing on my back, to a road that intersected mine about 30 yards from my block. I knew exactly where my car was, and said a silent word of thanks that I hadn't been able to find a parking place outside the flat. I unlocked the car, threw the rucksack onto the passenger seat, and slid in behind the wheel in one movement. Closing the door as quietly as I could I glanced in the mirror. Nothing. I was out of sight of the watcher in front of the flat, but not out of hearing. He might run if he heard an engine start. Even so, I reckoned I could be on my way before he got to me. It was about 50 yards down to Nunhead High Street. With a bit of luck I could get there before he could see what direction I'd gone in.

I started the car and pulled away without turning on the lights. The Herald whined in first gear.

Watching my mirror all the way I reached the main road and turned left. I didn't see anyone rush around the corner behind me, but it was dark. Once on the main road I turned on my lights and forced myself to drive like any normal, law-abiding citizen, maybe a restaurant owner coming home after locking up for the night. The last thing I wanted was to be pulled over by a bored policeman. I thought that if I could make the few hundred metres to the crossroads with Peckham Rye and through the lights I would be hard to track. There was no obvious way to turn, no way that provided a more direct route of escape than the other options, so how would anyone guess where I'd go? I turned left up Peckham Rye, then right onto Barry Road, heading for the South Circular. By the time I was crossing Clapham Common, thin prostitutes like ghosts haunting the trees by the road, I was starting to feel confident that I was clear.

The person I'd heard opening the door into the back courtyard – Simon no doubt – would have found Harry and bent to see if he was OK. I had a feeling that regardless, he wouldn't call an ambulance. Probably he would open the front door and quietly call to the South American student. They would check my flat. They were already inside the building and even if they didn't have keys to the flat, which they probably did, they'd find a way to get in. They would go inside and see that I'd gone. The best I could hope for was that they wouldn't have a clue where I was heading, even if they'd heard an engine start and noticed my car was missing. Though they might guess. But what could I do about that?

I'd have a good few hours to get to my destination. Or as close to it as I wanted to get. I looked at my watch. It was 2am – about four hours until dawn. I tingled with a charge of fearful excitement, not entirely unpleasant.

As I drove through London I decided to take the A303 toward the South West, not the M4 route via Bristol. I had it in mind to turn into Dorset and approach Undercliff along the south coast road that runs through Lyme Regis. Traffic was sparse once I'd left the capital. A few lorries and even fewer cars. What were the drivers of those cars doing and where were they going? – I found myself thinking.

The seats in the Herald weren't so comfortable and by about 3.30 in the morning I was feeling stiff and hungry. I looked out for an all-night garage and after driving on for some time found one on the eastern approach to Salisbury

Plain. I filled up with petrol and bought a can of coke and a chocolate bar. I parked the car in an area just off the forecourt and strolled up and down, eating my chocolate. There was a call box next to the parking area. I felt, as I often had in the previous few weeks, a sudden impulse to telephone Amelia. I resisted if for a few minutes, persuading myself that of course she wouldn't be at home, and even if she were she'd be angry if I woke her in the middle of the night. But supposing, just supposing it had been her calling me earlier. Then I opened the door of the phone box, took a two pence piece from my pocket, picked up the receiver and dialled her number. I can still remember it, even now.

After four rings someone answered the phone and I pushed my coin into the slot. But before I could say hello the line went dead. I fumbled in my pocket for more change but couldn't find any. I went back into the garage and asked the clearly irritated attendant for change for the phone. I gave him a £1 note and got a mixed handful of coppers and silver in exchange. I didn't even check if it was the right amount. I walked back to the phone box and dialled again, then took a coin from my pocket and held it in readiness by the slot. Engaged. I put down the receiver, picked it up and tried again. Engaged. I did this half a dozen times before opening the door of the phone box and stepping out. I had to quell an urge to cry out. I went into the phone box and tried again, and again. But always that insistent, relentless engaged tone. After about ten minutes I gave up and walked to my car.

Leaning against the bonnet and staring into the night in the blackest of moods I became aware of the attendant watching me from his booth. I considered driving straight back to London, straight to Amelia's flat. I calculated how long it would take and wondered if I'd get there before she went out to do whatever it was she did now. If indeed she had answered the phone. I wondered if there was simply a fault on the line, and that really nobody had answered. Or if I'd dialled a wrong number.

I tried to persuade myself that most likely someone else now lived in the flat, that Amelia had handed in her notice weeks ago, and that whoever that person was they understandably didn't want to be pestered by pre-dawn nuisance calls and had taken the phone off the hook. Then I remembered the man standing in the shadows outside my flat, Simon in the office, Harry in the yard, the answer machine message and the second call, and the note on my coffee table.

I got in the car and continued my journey across the deserted plain past Stonehenge. They used to illuminate it in those days.

I reached a junction and stopped to look at my map. There was no other traffic about so I waited in the road, engine running, deciding after brief deliberation to drive south through Chard. By 5am I was close to Axminster, and feeling hungry. I drove on for 20 minutes or so, looking for somewhere to eat. The sun was rising behind me when I saw a static caravan fitted up as a transport café, half a dozen lorries drawn up beside it. I pulled in. It was a cold morning but the café was warm, full of cigarette smoke, steam from the coffee machine and the smell of bacon. A few of the lorry drivers, sitting in silence around a large table, glanced up, recognising that I was not one of them. But they soon lost interest and returned to their food and newspapers and cigarettes. I ordered the biggest breakfast on the menu and made for a small table in a corner opposite the door. I was sipping my coffee when it opened and a policeman walked in. He nodded to the proprietor, raised a hand in acknowledgement of the lorry drivers, and walked straight toward me.

"Excuse me, sir. Would you mind telling me if you are the owner of the Triumph Herald parked outside?"

I explained I was driving it, but it wasn't mine, it belonged to a friend. I was borrowing it while he was away.

"And does this friend know you are borrowing his car while he is away?' he said, taking a notebook from his pocket.

"Oh yes. Yes, he does," I replied.

The policeman asked me my name and my address, and the name and address of the car's owner. He asked me where I was going and what I was doing. I didn't know the address of the car's owner, so I told the policeman where Oliver and I worked. He wrote down the information and then said he expected I knew why he wanted to speak to me. I said I didn't.

"Well, I saw you drive past about five miles back, sir, and I followed you here. I noticed that one of your rear lights isn't working, and one of your brake lights. And I've just looked at the car and I noticed the two front tyres are almost certainly below the legal limit. Does your friend's car have an MOT, Mr Hope?" He put an emphasis on the word 'friend's' that made it sound like a question itself.

"Yes, I'm certain that it has," I began to say, realising I had never given it a moment's thought, and just at that point my breakfast arrived, delivered by a large, middle-aged woman who I hadn't noticed before.

"Here you are, my lover. Look at him, Geoff, that's an honest face, leave him alone," she said, winking at me as she set my plate on the table. Geoff the policeman seemed relieved to abandon his professional persona, bantering with the woman for a minute. Recovering himself, he turned to me and advised me to take the car back to a particular garage in Axminster, just up the road, where his brother-in-law would check the tyres and replace the bulbs. Then, with a Styrofoam cup of tea in his hand, he was gone.

I ordered another cup of coffee and sat for half an hour watching the road outside as it got busier. Then I got in the car and drove on, not bothering to look for the policeman's brother-in-law's garage, instead turning toward Lyme Regis. Here I parked on a side road off a steep hill down to the seafront. Locking my rucksack in the boot, I walked into the town. It must have been around 8am, and shops were opening up. I had it in mind to buy a few things and then drive on, but I glanced at a timetable in a bus shelter and saw that a 10am bus would get me to Branscombe, via Seaton, in an hour. I decided to leave the car where it was, aiming to come back and get the tyres and lights sorted out when I'd found somewhere to stay. I didn't want to be bothered with that right now, and I didn't want any policeman pulling me up again. It crossed my mind, too, that anyone from the Olive Grove who might be looking for me probably knew the car, so better to put some distance between it and me.

I wandered around the town, buying a pair of walking boots and a few other things. I went to the bank and withdrew as much money as I could. Then I returned to the car, changed into my new boots, repacked my rucksack and walked back to the bus stop.

CHAPTER 12

Thursday April 12th to Friday April 13th, 1973

The bus pulled in at a crossroads just after 11am, and the driver called out for Branscombe. For my benefit, I think, as I was the only one among the handful of passengers who got off. I'd been to Branscombe once during a previous visit to Undercliff, walking to it across the cliffs. As I stepped off the bus I was disorientated. The place I was expecting was a scattering of beach huts and a café by a pebbly, shingly beach, but this was a nest of thatched cottages in a valley, at its heart a pub called the Mason's Arms. I wandered around for an hour trying to get my bearings, discovering that the village was unusually elongated, stretching for some miles along a road on the east side of a valley with a stream that ran down to the beach. The Mason's Arms was roughly halfway along this road. Inland there was another pub, the church, a post office and a school. I walked in this direction, catching glimpses of the valley mouth and beach that I had visited previously, before turning back and arriving at the Mason's Arms at midday, just as it opened.

Deciding it wasn't quite warm enough to sit outside I took my drink to a small table by the bar, propping up my rucksack next to me. I was the only customer and my food arrived in minutes. The barman was wearing shorts and looked illegally young. He was, he told me, the son of the landlord, back from university for the Easter holidays. He asked me what I was doing in Branscombe and as I ate I repeated a version of the story I had given the policeman earlier that day. I was down for a few days of walking;

could he recommend anywhere to stay? He said there were
a couple of places that offered bed and breakfast back up
that way, gesturing behind him roughly in the direction of
the post office and the church, but all of the rooms in the
pub were booked up for a wedding.

"You could try walking down toward the sea. About
half a mile from the beach there's a track that bears off left.
Follow that and you get into a holiday park, with chalets
and caravans on the cliff and slope down to the beach.
Quite nice, some of them. Pretty quiet. Not an amusement
arcade and social club kind of place. I'd have thought at this
time of year one or two might be free. Actually, try phoning
Maureen. She runs it. She'll know."

He gave me a card from a dispenser on the bar. *Haven
Holidays, Branscombe*. A line drawing of a chalet and
a number. I went out to a telephone box over the road.
Maureen confirmed that indeed there was a caravan
vacant. The price was reasonable, even more reasonable
if I paid cash up front. I provisionally booked it to Easter
Monday, pending inspection, and agreed to meet her at the
gate to Haven Holidays in an hour.

I went back to my seat and, taking up my drink, told the
barman of the arrangement. "Best view in Devon," he said.
Just then I heard loud voices in the street outside, before the
door into the bar opened and three shiny-faced young men
dressed in morning coats and carrying top hats walked in.

"Paul!" they shouted in unison to the barman, launching
into an exchange of hand-shaking and cheerful insults.

"On the house," Paul the barman said, lining up pint
glasses.

The ribaldry continued as Paul handed out the drinks.
For the most part they ignored me, though at one point when
the jokes became particularly obscene Paul gestured toward

me, and made a request for restraint that was ignored with a raising of glasses in my direction, which I reciprocated. Other locals wandered in, dressed in Sunday best. As I listened in to the banter I picked up that the three men – a groom, his best man and an usher – were Branscombe boys, old school friends of Paul's. They still lived locally, while Paul had achieved some fame by going away to university. The reception would be held in a function room at the back of the pub, where at that very moment the landlord and his wife, Paul's parents, were putting the finishing touches to the arrangements. I left them to it and, cheered by their good spirits and the beer, walked toward the sea.

The road narrowed the closer it got to the beach, and the houses became scattered. Just past a farmhouse, the track Paul had mentioned bore off uphill across a sloping field of cows. Some effort had been made to make it passable to cars. A rough layer of rubble and broken bricks had been compressed into the earth, but it would have been a bumpy ride. A sign limited drivers to 5 mph. I've always been a little wary of cows but they stepped out of my way as I walked among them, regarding me with indifference. As I got toward the end of the track I could see a woman waiting by a gate in the hedge that bordered the field, a spaniel sitting at her feet.

"Welcome to Haven Holidays. The best views in Devon," Maureen said, taking a step toward me with her arm outstretched. A stout, red-haired woman in late middle age, she led me through the gate and down a few steps to a bench that looked out at an angle across the beach below. I had to agree the view was impressive, but as I had seen a similar sight from Undercliff many times before its impact was reduced. The difference was that at over a mile of tiered pebbles, Branscombe Beach was much longer than Undercliff's stretch of coastline. Looking down to the mouth of the valley where the stream disappeared into the stones before rising again near the sea, I recognised the beach café and beach huts that I'd seen on my earlier visit, and the cliff path that I'd walked stretching back up a slope toward Kingcombe Vale. The beach extended to the east as well, but here it backed onto an area similar in appearance to Devil's Field, though far bigger. The caravans and chalets of Haven Holidays stood on clearings scattered around a sloping area of this undercliff Further on, a pinnacle of white rock topped with scraggy trees rose separate from the main body of the cliff. Between it and the cliff the undercliff extended, the gorse, fern and hawthorn giving way to a closely-packed copse of stubby trees. There were no signs of habitation in this area, though I could see a grey ribbon of path winding up through the greenery.

Maureen led me back up to the track, which descended toward the sea. Most of the chalets and caravans were a short walk from this track on paths cut through the undergrowth. My caravan was one of the first, set off to the left of the track up about 40 very steep steps. It must have been harder to let than many of the others on account of those steps, but it suited me. As we got to the top of the climb we came to a gate into a clearing, in which stood the caravan, itself elevated a few feet higher on a concrete footing. It was standing on four wheels and fold-down legs in each corner. The apparatus to hitch it to a towing vehicle was weighed down with a metal ball on a chain, some kind of ship's anchor, I imagine. From this elevated position the views reached even further. I wondered how they'd got the thing up there in the first place.

Nominally a four berth, the caravan had one large room containing a built-in sofa that converted into a bed, a table that folded flat into the floor, and a kitchen area with a Baby Belling and a fridge the size of a suitcase. This room had a main window that extended across one end of the caravan, from which you could look down over a vista of beach, sea, undercliff and valley. It had mains electricity and running water. There was no television, no telephone. At the back there was a small bedroom with bunks little more than hammocks, and a sentry-box bathroom connected to a septic tank. The windows were open and cleaning materials stood on the worktop in the kitchen area. A pile of bedding lay neatly folded on the sofa. I had the impression the caravan hadn't been occupied for a while. It was apparent Maureen had been trying to make the place look presentable in the interval between my call and our meeting. Actually, it smelt musty, but I didn't mind. A composite background odour: damp upholstery, Camping Gaz, plastic. Later, as an itinerant worker on the Continent I came across that smell again, many times, and when I did I always thought back to that moment.

I said I'd take it and got my wallet out. She in turn produced some paperwork on which I had to fill in my name and address. She asked if I had any ID and I thought for a moment before remembering my passport. "Thinking of going abroad after, are you?" she said, barely looking at it. Then she showed me how the few facilities worked, gave me the keys, and said to call in at the farm if I needed anything. She'd told me as we'd walked that the cows were her husband's job, the chalets and caravans hers.

"Actually, I need to get some food in. I saw the post office up in the village. Are there any other shops?"

"Not in Branscombe, no. Best bet is to walk along the cliff to Beer. Only a mile or so, and nice on a clear day."

I thanked her and she left me. I sat down on the sofa and

looked out of the window. I'd been up all night running on adrenaline. Now, after walking around the village and the drinks in the pub and the sense of having found a refuge, a delicious, relaxed weariness seeped through my body. I longed to stretch out on the sofa for a sleep, but steeled myself instead to walk to Beer straight away. It was past 2.30pm already and I didn't want to risk getting there and finding the shops closed. So I emptied my rucksack onto the sofa and put my wallet and passport in my pocket. Putting the empty rucksack on my back, I locked up the caravan and walked back down the 40 steep steps to find the coast path to Beer.

It was a few hundred steep yards before the path levelled out. At the top I stopped to catch my breath. I judged I must be more or less above my caravan. When my heartbeat settled I set off. The path was level for a mile or so. I passed an old coastguard lookout tower that showed signs of having been converted into some sort of dwelling. Books lined the windowsills of the room at the top of the tower. Gradually the path began a gentle descent. I saw a sign for another path down to the beach and judged it was the one I'd seen earlier when Maureen was showing me the view. In front of me stretched Lyme Bay, the sea flat, glassy and silvery blue in the sunlight. I saw Seaton, which the bus had passed through earlier. Lyme Regis was tucked away further along, out of sight. I thought of the Herald parked in the side street. Once I'd had a few days' rest and settling into the caravan I'd catch the bus back and get the tyres and lights sorted out.

The path got steeper and I sensed I must be approaching Beer, but I couldn't see the beach or the village itself until I came out onto a road. This ran down to the beach. On one side a terrace of stone cottages looked out to sea. On the other well-tended allotments extended to the very edge of the cliff.

It was a sheltered pebble cove surrounded by white cliffs under which green and cream beach huts sheltered. A slipway ran down to the pebbles, at the top of which a collection of shacks provided storage for nets and other trappings of the fishing that still continued. In front of the slipway on the pebbles themselves stood a number of small fishing boats, painted blue and white and red. Black, oily winch cables that dragged them from the sea lay across the stones like tentacles. A row of striped deckchairs stretched along the beach facing the sea. Though it was sunny it wasn't really warm enough for sunbathing or swimming and most were unoccupied. If I had really been a walker on a solitary break I would have sat there and relished the scene for a while. But that was a part I was playing.

I started out the walk that afternoon in good spirits, but by the time I approached Beer my mood had dipped and I was troubled by questions. Questions about that man from the Olive Grove standing outside my flat last night, and about Harry in the yard. And who had answered when I phoned Amelia's flat? Regardless of how much I told myself this surge of unease was attributable to the ebb of exhaustion after the flow of excitement, I couldn't help but look with suspicion at people around me. I decided to get what I needed as quickly as possible and go back to the caravan.

I came to one of those establishments common to English seaside villages. You couldn't have called it a supermarket because it was too small, but it sold everything. Albeit at inflated prices. I bought supplies sufficient for a couple of days. Over the road from this shop was a place called Hidden Treasure. In the packed window display I noticed a pair of binoculars. The shop was closed, so I made a mental note to come back the next day to get them.

The walk back to Branscombe was hard going, on account of my tiredness and the newly-loaded rucksack. I made slow progress, stopping several times to rest. I got back to the caravan after 6pm and unpacked my shopping. Opening the many cupboards secreted around the caravan I found assorted holiday ephemera: a picnic rug, sun loungers, paperback thrillers, an electric heater. By the door a key hung on a hook. This, I worked out, opened a padlock securing a plastic chest tucked away behind the caravan, next to a dustbin. In it were a few gardening tools, intended, presumably, for keeping the surrounding undergrowth at bay.

I made myself some food and sat on the sofa eating, while looking out at the beach. Grey clouds had come in from the sea since I had returned to the caravan, and it was breezy. I opened Adam Noucquet's book and read a few pages. There wasn't much else to do. It was more interesting than I was expecting. The combination of sleeping bag, sofa bed and book seemed like a good idea.

I was about to pull the curtains to undress when I saw, on a patch of grass next to the teashop just behind the beach, a crowd of people in a circle. In their midst was a man in dark clothes holding something white that was flapping in the wind. In the fading light it looked like he had caught a giant butterfly, or had just jumped from a plane and was gathering his parachute. It was the wedding party I had encountered earlier in the Mason's Arms, the flapping white object the bride with her dress catching the wind. I became conscious of the sound of a helicopter though I couldn't see it at first. Then it flew over the caravan from inland and down toward the waiting circle of people. The groom led the bride to one side as the helicopter hovered for a moment and then landed. The couple dashed under the rotor blades, ducking into the Perspex cabin. I saw the pilot turn to help them with seat harnesses and then turn back to his controls. The helicopter lifted off, tilting to one side to allow the bride and groom a wave to the cheering circle below. Then it soared up out to sea and back toward the coast in a wide arc. How old was that bridegroom? Twenty two, maybe? His new bride even younger. I envied them. I envied their youth, their dreams of the future. Looking back I can see I was on a cusp, still young enough to dream, but old enough to know that most dreams didn't come true. And even if they did, they didn't satisfy like you hoped they would.

I pulled the curtains and got into my sleeping bag. It was only 8pm. I was tired but the book was good. It seemed well-researched, more investigative journalism than academic monograph. As I sat turning the pages in the caravan on that April evening I hadn't yet made the compelling connection that has stayed with me ever since. Even so, Adam Noucquet held my attention and I read the whole book straight through. It wasn't much more than a hundred pages. Noucquet ended with an unsolved mystery and I wondered if he planned a sequel. By 1919 New Dawn was in steep decline. It was not a pacifist group and of course many of the Dawnists who had gone to fight had not returned. The much-diminished sect tried to regroup but broke up in disarray when two male members were arrested after the unexplained death of an older woman, one of the founders. The pair escaped from the police cell where they were being held on the night after their arrest, and were never seen again. The doors to their cell were unlocked, and the two policemen on duty were found in a confused state, unable to give a coherent account of what had happened.

I woke the next morning to a sound like a crowd of clamouring small children banging on the doors, roof, and windows. The caravan was rocking. I could see a greyish light through the curtains. Through emerging consciousness I realised it was raining hard, the banging noise raindrops beating on the caravan against a backdrop of rushing wind and a distant rumble and scrape of waves breaking on the pebbles of the beach. I got up and pulled back the curtains to see a deep-grey sky and rain coming off the sea at a 45-degree angle. I was grateful for the ball and chain on the caravan's tow bar. I looked at my watch. Just after 7am. Leaving the curtains open I got back in my sleeping bag and lay for a while flicking through the book.

By 8am the wind had subsided but it was still raining hard. I got up and as I sat eating breakfast it began to ease. I had a shower, banging my elbows in the cubicle under a feeble jet of water that wasn't hot enough. Even when I was dry and dressed I was feeling cold, so I sat down with a cup of coffee and wrapped myself in one of the blankets Maureen had left. I had a sense of that cocooned security unique to the English holidaymaker who finds a warm, dry refuge on a wet day.

Just after 9am the rain dwindled to a faint drizzle. There was blue sky out to sea. I put on my boots and waterproof and went out for a walk. The anxiety that had troubled me in Beer yesterday had vanished and I was feeling more like the holidaymaker I purported to be. Within ten minutes of being outside the rain stopped and the sun came out. I spent a pleasant couple of hours wandering around the area idly exploring, dropping into the teashop, and then taking the path toward Kingcombe Vale. I had a look at Undercliff from a distance. There was nobody about. I didn't stay long, thinking there'd be plenty of time for closer observation in the coming days.

Back in Branscombe, I remembered that in the morning I had seen from my caravan window what looked like a roof in the midst of a thicket over the other side of the valley, and I had it in mind to find out what it was. I missed it at first, passing a vast tangle of brambles to the right of the path a little inland.

When I came back down I caught the smallest glimpse of weatherboards washed a faded blue, hiding in the thicket. I walked over for a closer look. Poking around I could see what looked like a large shed. It was completely surrounded by brambles ten feet deep, like the nest of some huge bird. The roof was only visible from a certain angle and an elevated position. I could see it from my caravan and perhaps walkers coming down to Branscombe Mouth from Beer might catch a glimpse of it at a certain point in their descent. But it was almost completely hidden.

I decided to walk up the valley into the village. I went into the Mason's Arms but Paul the barman was nowhere to be seen. Then I walked back down the road toward the farm, wondering if I'd bump into Maureen. There was no sign of her or anyone else at the farmhouse so I carried on across the field of cows back to the caravan. It was past midday by this time. I had a sandwich and opened the book again, lingering at the photo section that had caught my eye in the pub in Hammersmith. Not even 48 hours before, I realised.

After lunch I decided to head off inland, before working my way back to Beer to look at the binoculars I had noticed. To my irritation Hidden Treasure was closed again when I got there, so I went into the shop where I'd bought my provisions the day before and asked when it opened. Mornings only, came the answer.

By then I must have walked more than 15 miles and my legs were feeling it. I decided to have dinner in the pub on the sea front to get my strength up for the walk back to the caravan.

I placed my order and took my drink to a table by a window looking out to sea. I saw a handful of newspapers in a rack and noticed among them yesterday's *Evening Standard*. No doubt a visitor had brought it down with them the night before. I flicked through the pages paying little attention until I came to a headline on page seven. It was a short story at the bottom of the page, two columns each of a single paragraph depth, with a photo between the headline and the story. *Man dies in Nunhead flat fire.* The photo showed my block, with the Olive Grove office on the ground floor, and two floors above the burnt-out, glassless windows of my flat, like black, sightless eyes. The story was brief and factual. A fire overnight. A neighbour had called the fire brigade. Fire confined to one flat. A body found in the bedroom, which appeared to be where the fire had started. The police assume it is the occupant of the flat. Name not released until next of kin located. No other casualties.

I sat staring out of the window. I must have looked odd because when a girl came with my dinner she asked if I was OK. I said I was fine and tried to eat my food, managing only a few mouthfuls. Several scenarios crowded into my imagination, none of them pleasant. I decided to see if the story had featured in any of the day's national papers and took everything I could find in the rack, but there was nothing. That comforted me, though not much. With some effort I pulled myself together and tried to think it through.

I kept coming back to one thing. As far as the police were concerned, I was dead.

CHAPTER 13

Saturday April 14th to Sunday April 15th, 1973

The day after reading the news of my death I went for a walk. It was clear and I could see the long arm of Portland Bill stretching into the sea miles ahead. I needed some more supplies, and I thought I'd have one more try at the binocular shop.

The previous night I had stayed in the pub for two hours. I steeled myself and tried to think things through, my un-eaten food congealing on the plate in front of me. In my mind the *Evening Standard* report confirmed that some people, surely from the Olive Grove, wished me ill, though why exactly I couldn't say. Questions clamoured for atten-tion. Had they noticed my stepping back, my detachment? Did they know I had seen the limp falling woman through the gap in the door? Whose was the body in my flat? How had the fire started?

I thought about going back to London and reporting to the police. Why, they would ask, had I bolted, and whose was the burnt body? Because the Olive Grove is a cult, and maybe they drugged or hypnotised me, because they are suspicious that I am suspicious of them, and they are watching me and I've no idea really who the burnt man is. It might be Harry the plumber, who I knocked out when I was sneaking out the back door in the dead of night. It sounded perilously thin. It sounded downright suspicious. I cursed myself for not calling the police that night when I thought I was being watched, before anything happened.

The waitress took my plate away. I ordered another drink, and then another, and was feeling a little better when I realised nightfall was imminent. I half ran back along the cliff in failing light. By the time I got to the caravan it was dark, and I kept looking behind me even though I knew there was no one there.

I was out of bed before dawn and sitting thinking as the sun came up.

You need to understand my position. With the exception of the men watching my flat that night, and whoever was controlling them, everyone thought I was dead. The police thought I was dead, and might continue doing so for a while yet, maybe forever. There was no DNA profiling in those days. I had no idea how badly the body was burnt, nor of the speed and accuracy of whatever forensic procedures there were to confirm identity, but I reckoned I was clear from police suspicion for a few days at the very least. It would take them that long to trace my dental records. I hadn't registered since moving back to London and hadn't visited the dentist in Leicester since I had my wisdom teeth out a month after arriving. And without the police saying otherwise there was no running story for the press. As far as they were concerned it was just a fatal house fire, worthy of a few column inches. And without press coverage I was safe from zealous, alert members of the public. At least for a little while.

Even if the police did discover that the burnt remains were not mine, what would lead them to search for me here? The car would, eventually. For now it was just a car parked on a side street, nothing unusual about it. But when Oliver returned from Peru and discovered that I was dead he would look for it and eventually, being unable to find it, would report it missing to the police. In time they would locate it, and wonder how it came to be abandoned in Lyme Regis. Then, sooner or later that policeman who'd spoken to me in the café would remember. I needed to attend to that car before long. Then there was Maureen. She had my name and address on her booking form. But unless both were widely published in the national press, which was unlikely, she would not attach any significance to the information.

I reckoned if I kept clear of anyone from the Olive Grove I had a little time. The only problem was I didn't know everyone at the Olive Grove. Who was to say they didn't have people looking for me who I'd never seen before? This bothered me, but the more I thought about it the more certainly I understood that there was little I could do about it apart from keep my distance from anyone who aroused my suspicions, for whatever reason. Unless I ran from everyone. Unless I disappeared.

The thing is, the fire had prodded awake a dormant reporter's curiosity in me. Afraid though I was, I wanted to know what they were doing. What they were hiding. What they wanted from me. Who they were.

I decided to stay in the area for a few days and lie reasonably low without actually going into hiding. I wanted time. Just long enough to think what to do next, and nose around while I was thinking. Then maybe I could start again. Actually, I'd have to, because how could I return to London and explain the fire in my flat, the charred body that wasn't mine?

I began thinking of the funeral, the burying or further burning of that charred body. My funeral. I wondered who would turn up. Would anyone turn up? A few distant relatives, maybe. A couple of people from work. What about Lillian? George would go. Actually, George would probably take the service. What, I wondered, would he say? I briefly entertained a fantasy of turning up myself to hear, but dismissed it. Vanity.

I went to bed that night in a panic but by breakfast I was feeling a lot better. You can tell I wasn't thinking straight. I realise now that the sheer thrill of the adventure was attractive to me, and maybe that upset my judgement. I'd led a pretty mundane life and the threat and the questions were sharpening my senses. So it was with some exhilaration that I set out along the cliff top back toward Beer. I found myself thinking that I could be free to reinvent myself, to start again. I understood then those people you hear about sometimes who vanish, assume new identities, even if they haven't done anything wrong. To start again.

As I turned over all of this in my mind I lost sight for a while of my original purpose for travelling to Devon. Even before the events that had precipitated my departure – my meeting with the Two, the watcher outside my flat – I had been intending to come down to get some space, but primarily to look for Amelia. In fact, even if those events had not taken place I was due to travel down, and would have done so about eight hours later than I eventually did. Quite possibly ending up in the very same caravan. It was with a little effort that I reminded myself that reinvention would not be possible, for a while at least, until I either found Amelia and persuaded her to come with me, or gave up the search. And of course, if I did find her how could I possibly persuade her to come with me if I intended to be someone else? She too would have to know about the burnt body in my flat. She would wonder what was happening, who I was, what I was doing. Would she even begin to consider coming with me? Not a chance. Unless, somehow, absence had made her heart so fond that she became sufficiently devoted to me to brush aside all concerns. More likely she would report me to the police. So if it were almost certain that she wouldn't come with me, what was the point of trying to find her? To warn her. That was the point. If she was with the Olive Grove she was with some strange, dangerous people. That was the only thing I was sure of. As I've said, I wasn't thinking straight. Would you, in my situation?

I was pondering all this when I felt the compulsion that I'd felt the previous night to look behind me. This time there was someone there, a man heading in my direction, gaining on me. I had already seen several other people walking dogs and though I felt some little nervousness each time I encountered someone, wondering if they were from the Olive Grove, there was a safety in knowing there were plenty of ordinary people about. I had been thinking overnight that there were two ways I could conceal myself, and that I'd probably have to alternate between them. The first was to lie low, so no one knew where I was. The second was the safety-in-numbers, hiding-in-plain-sight, lost-in-the-crowd approach. It was this second approach I was relying on as I walked, as even though the scattering of people on the cliffs hardly constituted a crowd, I didn't believe the Olive Grove capable of populating the entire region with innocent-looking dog walkers, twitchers, farmers and holidaymakers.

Anyway, they probably didn't even know I was here. No one apart from Maureen and Paul knew I was here. I was a man on an Easter walking holiday. I would not go to Kingcombe Vale or Undercliff itself, but I would find vantage points near enough to see if I could spot Amelia with the binoculars I had not yet bought. If she was there of her own free will she'd come out of the house at some point. She liked walking in the area. So all I'd have to do is wait and watch. What I'd do if I saw her I hadn't yet worked out. And if she was being kept there against her will and I never saw her? Well, I couldn't yet think my way through that possibility either. I wasn't thinking straight.

I glanced over my shoulder again, as if surveying the view. Though the man was maybe two hundred yards away there was something familiar in his gait, and as he came nearer I recognised the snowy hair of John Muir, who I'd once met in the graveyard at Kingcombe Vale. For a moment I panicked and considered changing course to avoid him, but rapid mental calculation led to the conclusion that even if he had read the *Evening Standard* news story – very unlikely – the chances that he would connect it with me were slim to the point of invisibility. After all, we had met just once, briefly, months earlier, and I don't think I even told him my surname. And anyway the report didn't mention my name. He certainly didn't know I lived in Nunhead, and there was nothing in the report to indicate that the charred occupant of the flat had any connection with the Olive Grove.

At fifty yards the old man, his eyes still keen, raised his arm and called, "I thought it was you."

I stopped walking, called a greeting in response and shook his hand as he drew alongside me.

"Remind me of your name," he said, not at all out of breath.

"Martyn – and you are John, correct?"

"That's right. So you're down at Undercliff again? Nice weather for it."

You can think things through very quickly when you have to. In the few seconds between identifying Muir and shaking his hand I'd decided to trust in my story, adapted for these unexpected circumstances.

"Actually, no. I left the Olive Grove a while back, but I've always loved this part of the world – used to come here as a child with my parents. I had a few days free so I thought I'd come down and do some walking."

"A nice time of year for it. And where are you headed today?"

"I'm going into Beer. I forgot my binoculars and I saw a second-hand pair in a shop there, but it was closed."

"Oh, I know the place, I think, just off the main street? I'm going that way myself. If you don't mind walking at an old man's pace."

An old man's pace turned out to be a brisk one, and he told me he was on one of his 'regular circuits' as I fell into step with him for the descent into Beer. He was good company, droll and witty.

I entertained a brief apprehensive fantasy that he might be connected with the Olive Grove in some way, but his self-evident honesty dispelled it. We talked a little about the Olive Grove, and Muir said that there were two men often there who looked familiar, though he couldn't quite place them. He described them and it was apparent he was talking about the Two.

"No, those names aren't familiar to me," he said when I told him who they were. "Some faces just look familiar, don't they?"

"I guess so, yes. So the house was empty for a while before the Olive Grove took it on?" I asked.

"That's right. And before that it might as well have been empty. After Handley left, which was before the War mind you, a couple of staff stayed to look after the place. A woman who was some kind of housekeeper, I imagine, and her husband who was a gardener and general factotum. The pair of them lived there for some time keeping the place immaculate. No one in the village knew how they managed it, but I suppose there must have been some kind of trust paying them a retainer. Then she died many, many years before her husband and he, who was already getting on by then, stayed on alone. Imagine that, living in a big place like Undercliff on your own. As time went on the house became too much for him and you could tell that it was falling into disrepair, but he wouldn't accept any help. A few of us from the village used to drop in but he would always dismiss us, saying that he was managing very well thank you. He wouldn't let us into the house.

"Once, I went down there after a particularly bad storm had taken a few trees and there was no answer when I rang the bell. I walked around peering in a few windows and saw him lying dead on the kitchen floor. Must have been in his late eighties, I'd have thought. Tall, thin, bald man. Anyway, I went up to the village phone box and called the police. When they turned up and broke down the door they asked me to identify the old man, so I got a little look around the house. I'd been in there a few times when Handley was around and it was exactly the same. All of Handley's books everywhere, a room full of electrical apparatus of some kind, but everything was covered in dust and it was obvious that rain was getting in. Eerie really. Then after that the place was boarded up for years and left empty until your old friends came in."

***

When we got to the village Muir walked with me to the shop. A wispy, distracted woman stood behind the till. Muir knew her, and bargained on my behalf for the binoculars. They were, he told me afterwards, a good brand. He invited me to join him for a coffee, mentioning that he had a book that I might be interested in.

"It's an autobiography by Ambrose Fleming, that scientist buried in Kingcombe Vale. Actually I find a lot of it rather dull, but as he lived out his later years in the area there are quite a few mentions of local landmarks and characters. And going back to what we were talking about earlier, there's a section about a visit he made to Undercliff."

I wondered when he said that if he'd picked up that I was scouting for information.

"I'd like that. I only brought one book with me and I've read that already," I said.

"Well, I've got to dash now. I'm driving to Exeter this afternoon. Why don't you drop in tomorrow? Have a spot of lunch."

I thanked him and he gave me directions to his cottage. It was on the northern outskirts of Kingcombe Vale, inland from Undercliff.

It was getting on for lunchtime when the old man set off back up the hill for home. I was at a loose end and his mention of Exeter prompted me to catch a bus I saw waiting at the end of the street. I got into the city just in time for lunch and then wandered around for a while, before going to the cinema for a late afternoon showing. A couple of times I thought I saw people looking at me across the street, and when I got on the bus back to Branscombe at about 6pm a youth I'd noticed in the cinema foyer got on after me. But he disembarked just outside of Exeter and I thought nothing more of it.

I got back to Branscombe at 7pm and had dinner in the Mason's Arms. This time Paul the barman was serving again. I tried to lead him into a conversation about the Olive Grove to see if he'd picked up any local gossip, but all he said was that he'd heard that the old house was now a retreat centre, and that when he was a boy and it was empty he used to go there with friends and throw stones through some top floor windows that weren't boarded up.

I was in a kind of limbo all that day, suspended between several states of being. I reflected that people I knew might now be finding out that I had died, and I found it oddly liberating. I then felt pangs of guilt about this, and had to fight down a sudden urge to call someone, George maybe, and tell him I was alive after all. On some level I was relishing the notion that my past – the failures, the things I'd done wrong, the mediocrity – had all been washed away. It was an illusion of course, but a powerful one. Then balancing that was the Olive Grove, the fear and intrigue. I remembered back to when I was a keen cub reporter just catching the scent of a story. I felt like that about the Olive Grove. I knew for certain that there was something going on. I kept getting glimpses of things that I thought might connect, but I couldn't yet see the whole picture. It was the moment before meaning. But I really needed to keep looking so I *would* see the whole picture. And then there was Amelia.

The next morning I set off for John Muir's cottage at about 10am. It was a steep walk up out of Branscombe. When I got to the cliff before Kingcombe Vale and Undercliff I turned inland so that I was walking along the opposite side of the valley past the house. I had underestimated the length of the walk and I didn't have time then to stop and observe the place for long, but I paused for a moment and tried out my binoculars. Jenny was pottering about in the garden but there was little else to see. Apart from Tim's Land Rover there were no cars in sight. I walked on, keeping to the high ground above the village, past the church, before bearing left and down for a short while to where I thought I'd find the old man's cottage. I knew it as soon as I saw it. It had the same well-turned out and compact neatness as he did. It was a bungalow that, he told me later, he had built himself back in the 1930s. A covered veranda ran along the whole front of the house, which looked straight down the valley. He was sitting on this in a deckchair as I walked up the path.

John Muir was in a talkative mood. "Serving at early morning Holy Communion this week ... life quiet since my wife died ... don't get too many visitors ... a daughter, son-in-law and teenage granddaughter in Poole ... visit them every couple of months ... going up for Easter actually... but when you get to my age you find you don't have so many contemporaries."

All of this he said matter-of-factly, without a trace of self-pity. He seemed like a man happily reconciled to his circumstances. We ate on the veranda. He then led me into a small room off the hall, which he called the library. Floor-to-ceiling bookcases covered three of the walls. From one of these he pulled out a thick, black hardback book without a dust cover, heavy gold leaf lettering embossed on the spine:

Memories of a Scientific Life by Sir Ambrose Fleming FRS.

"Got this second-hand years ago," he said. "Then years after that I found another shorter book of the same title. Comparing the two I'd guess this was a privately-printed, revised second edition. The other one was published in the 1930s sometime. This one doesn't include any publisher's details, but it does say, here, *printed 1943*. He was well into his 90s by then. Died in 1945."

I took the book and flicked through the pages. More than 300 of them, on that rough, unrefined, yellowish paper books were printed on during wartime. Judging from the contents page the first edition had covered in nine chapters Fleming's childhood and professional life up to retirement. In this second edition he'd added an extended postscript concentrating on the many interests he'd nurtured in retirement in Sidmouth. The new invention of television being one of them. A black-and-white plate section included the usual selection of snaps from a life that had begun not too long after photography itself.

We agreed that I'd return the book early the following afternoon, as Muir was travelling to his daughter's later that day. I had nothing much to do for the rest of the day and wasn't planning to read the whole book anyway. I left at about 2.30pm and retraced my steps back along the east side of the valley toward the coast path. This time I found a vantage point in a copse just off the footpath and sat for 30 minutes watching Undercliff. I didn't see a thing. The Land Rover wasn't where it had been parked earlier and I surmised that most likely only Tim and Jenny were in residence, and had gone out somewhere for the afternoon.

When I got back to the caravan I settled down to the book. For the most part it was dull stuff written in stiffly didactic tones, full of technical detail way over my head. The only section that grabbed me was a mention of Sir Arthur Handley, which I reproduce in full here:

Shortly after arriving at Sidmouth I attended service at the Norman church in nearby Kingcombe Vale. There I met Sir Arthur Handley, a retired businessman with whom

I had exchanged correspondence over a pamphlet that I had published on the subject of the scientific basis for the Genesis account of Creation. I was at the time President of the Victoria Institute, formed sixty years earlier to discuss questions lying on the borderland of Philosophy and Science and Religion. Handley was nominally a member of the Institute, though I do not recall him ever attending meetings. He invited me to lunch the following week at the house that he had built near the Church. This proved to be a somewhat disappointing event. His religious interests were broad, and I detected in him an unhealthy fancy for the esoteric. Similarly, he considered himself a scientific man, but his interests were beyond the fringes of mainstream science and his methods unsound. Knowing my background, he questioned me intently over a theory he had that Life itself was a sort of electrical force, and could be extended and even transmitted through the proper application of electrical current. He intimated that he was close to perfecting an apparatus for this purpose. I formed the view that he was something of a crank and we did not become close friends. Nevertheless we saw each other occasionally thereafter.

On one occasion in 1937, my good friend Lodge came for a visit, and when I happened to mention that I had seen Handley he remarked that he had been in correspondence with him regarding some spiritualist matter. Now, I disagreed sharply with Lodge's views on spiritualism, but we remained close friends and I did not doubt the sincerity of his pursuit of the truth. The poor man had lost a son in the Great War, though his interest in spiritualism predated that unfortunate event by many years. I decided to call Handley on the telephone to see if it would be possible for the three of us to meet. Handley invited us to afternoon tea the next day. Unfortunately, the meeting was not a success. Handley and Lodge found themselves to be *in disagreement over their concepts of what happened to the personality after death, while I myself considered that both held nonsensical views anyway, and kept out of the discussion. Handley had two assistants with him who said little, though their presence contributed to a rather awkward atmosphere. One was a photography enthusiast and we posed for a group portrait, a copy of which Handley sent me the following week, and which I include in these pages. The photographer himself activated the camera's shutter with an electrical switch on the end of a wire long enough to enable him to be part of the portrait. I never saw Handley again after that meeting. He left to go travelling shortly afterwards and, as far as I am aware, has not yet returned.*

After reading those two paragraphs I turned to the plate section to look for the photograph. It was the same portrait I had seen in the folder at Undercliff. Handley seated in the middle of a front row of three, resting his arm on a stick. On either side were two old men, one Oliver Lodge, the physicist and spiritualist, the other Fleming, according to the caption. Behind them stood two younger men, named as Edward Spector and Edmund Talus. Date 1937. I wondered which of them held, out of sight, the electrical switch. I looked at the photo for some time. I had seen it before, of course, but it reminded me of something else, though I couldn't pinpoint quite what.

CHAPTER 14

Monday April 16th, 1973

I slept well that night. All the cliff walking was doing me good. When I woke up in the morning I decided to set off early with a picnic lunch and watch Undercliff for a few hours, before dropping the book off at Muir's. I was in my position in the copse by 11am. It was a warm morning, and shafts of sunlight broke through the leaves in the trees like messages from heaven. I had with me an RSPB pamphlet I'd found in the caravan about rare birds you could sometimes see in the area. If anyone challenged me, though there was no reason they should, I would say I was looking for rare birds.

Of course, no one did challenge me. I sat in the copse for three hours and didn't see anyone at all on the path. I didn't see much at Undercliff either. It seemed clear that only Jenny and Tim were in residence. I observed both busying themselves around the gardens. There was no sign of anyone else. Then Tim drove off in the Land Rover, returning thirty minutes later with a load of fence posts, which he carried around to the back. I could see markers set at regular intervals forming a boundary down one side of the kitchen garden. One by one Tim removed the markers and hammered posts in their place. Every time the long mallet hit a post a sound like a pistol shot echoed across the valley. It was vigorous work and after a while Tim took of his shirt, drank deeply from a bottle, and continued stripped to the waist. He had the physique of a man who had lost a lot of weight in middle age. A sinewy musculature was apparent through loose folds of skin, especially at his stomach, lower back and chest.

By the end of my vigil the idea of watching Undercliff for a sight of Amelia was beginning to seem foolish. I could sit there for months and never see her, for all I knew. There in the peace of that copse watching Tim and Jenny – two gentle, bereaved, middle aged folk music enthusiasts – it was hard to keep alive the idea that the Olive Grove was some malign agency out to do me harm, and that Amelia was entangled in their tendrils. I began to consider other possible explanations for the burnt body in my flat, the men waiting outside that night. I began to wonder if I shouldn't just accept that Amelia had ditched me and forget her. The idea of going back to London and explaining to whoever was interested exactly what had happened once again recommended itself.

At 2pm I set off toward Muir's bungalow. Everywhere birds were singing. Had I been the birdwatcher I claimed to be I could have named them, but as it was their calls came to me like sweet anonymous benedictions. I opened the gate to Muir's garden and saw him sitting on the deckchair on the veranda, where he had been the day before. He seemed to be asleep. Hens were scuffing around in the pen.

As I walked up the path I wondered how I would wake him if he didn't stir at my approach. Would I call out, or touch him gently on the shoulder and say "John?"

At ten feet something made me stop. It may have been the faint yellowish tinge of his skin, or the angle of his head, or a rigidity in his stillness. It took a few seconds for the fear to take hold. In those few seconds I wondered if I should find something to cover the old man's face. Isn't that what you do? Then my heart began to pound and my muscles tighten. I looked around me, expecting to see someone else, but there was no one to see. Just the pretty garden, a bank yellow with daffodils, the hens and the singing birds. My

first instinct, which I just managed to suppress, was to turn
and run. I had never before seen the dead body of someone
I knew. Both my parents had gone before I could get to
them, and I declined the viewings in the chapel of rest. In
my reporter days I'd seen the police fishing suicides out of
the river and prising road traffic casualties from crashed
cars, but that was different.

I was afraid of the body, and oddly embarrassed by it,
as if I'd burst in on a private scene. I think at some level
I was scared, too, that someone may have killed him, an
act somehow connected to me. But I didn't explain that to
myself until a little later. What I did, by act of will, was walk
closer, calling, "John, John," though I knew the old man was
past hearing. A few feet from him I crouched down to look
into his face, finding I could not bear to meet the gaze of
those half-closed, sightless eyes. A coffee cup lay upturned
beside the chair, its contents leaving an expanding stain on
the veranda's boarded floor. There was no blood, no sign
of any injury. The door into the house that I had walked
through yesterday was open. I could hear Radio 4 in the
kitchen. I thought about walking past the body into the
hallway where I had seen the telephone yesterday, and
calling the police. But panic got the better of me and
instead I turned and ran down the path, through the gate
and away from the bungalow and the mortal remains of the
man who'd built it.

I ran for about a quarter of a mile back the way I had
come. The running accelerated my already rapidly-beating
heart until I was gasping for breath. I reached a spot where
I knew I would get a view of the bungalow if I left the path
and climbed a few steps into the adjacent meadow. This I
did, falling down on the grass with my chest heaving and
tears in my eyes. I sat like this for maybe five minutes while

my breathing settled to a bearable rate several notches above normal.

As far as I could tell nobody had seen me, and I remember being relieved at that. I did my best to think through what I should do. I had liked John Muir, and the thought of leaving his body sitting there unattended appalled me. Even if I hadn't known him I would have felt, like anyone, some instinct to treat with respect the body of a fellow human being. The flies would start to settle on him soon. I knew that his daughter was expecting him that evening, and no doubt when he didn't arrive she would call, and when there was no answer she would raise the alarm. But that might not be until past dark, and there were animals that could approach as dusk fell. But if I called the police I would have to tell them who I was, what I was doing in the area, how I knew John. They would ask questions and sooner rather than later connect me to a house fire in Nunhead and a charred body, at which point they would begin to see my report of an old man's death in a different light.

Again, the compulsion to tell all was strong. After all, I had done nothing wrong. But I am not a brave man and the thought of wrongful accusation, misunderstanding, questioning, a trial, prison for crimes I did not commit, terrified me and overpowered the urge to come clean. Nonetheless, I felt wretched at the prospect of leaving him.

I was considering an anonymous telephone call when I saw a car approach. The bungalow was on a large, gently-sloping plot down a drive of about two hundred yards from a lane. The car turned into the drive and pulled up out of sight, on the side of the bungalow opposite to the veranda. I saw writing on the car but I couldn't make it out. I fancied I could hear the tinkle of a doorbell. After a minute a man walked around the side of the bungalow and stopped, looking down the length of the veranda. He had seen the body. Like me he walked toward it tentatively and stopped a few feet in front of it, looking around. Then he did what I had been unable to do and first walked up to the body and touched it on the shoulder, and then stepped into the house.

A minute later he came out and walked back around the house out of sight, presumably returning to his car. With fifteen minutes a police car and then an ambulance had arrived. The man moved his car to make way for the ambulance, and I saw then that it was a taxi. I had assumed John Muir was going to drive to his daughter's, but obviously not. No doubt he had planned to take a taxi to Exeter or Honiton to catch the train. I got up to go, feeling an immense relief that his body would be dealt with respectfully, dutifully.

I walked back to the caravan absorbed in my thoughts. On the one hand I recognised the overwhelming likelihood that John Muir had simply died of natural causes. He was an old man, and old men have a habit of dying. Yet just a day earlier he had seemed so fit, so vigorous, so bright. I couldn't help but speculate that his death might be in some way connected to the Olive Grove's pursuit of me, but how that might be I couldn't work out at all.

I arrived back at the caravan in low spirits. My earlier optimism that there was nothing suspicious going on and that a straightforward conversation with the police would sort things out had abandoned me. The fact was, a body had been found in my flat and I could provide no account of why or how it got there. What's more, I had run from the scene, whatever way you looked at it. The first person to see me after I'd said goodnight to George, Ken the drunk excepted, was the petrol attendant just before Salisbury

Plain. I didn't know exactly what time the fire started but me starting it and driving through the night to that petrol station might be a viable chronology, and if so would seem to the police a plausible explanation. And that would not be good.

It was becoming clear to me that I had two choices: to vanish, or to unmask the Olive Grove for what I thought it was. If I chose the latter course and succeeded, if it was revealed as a cult, then the idea that it might have some involvement in the burnt body would at least seem more reasonable, which would take the heat off me.

I sat down to eat, wishing I had a television to watch to take my mind off my situation. With nothing else to do I flicked though Fleming's book, the pages opening to the photo I had seen in Undercliff. Again, something nagged. Some words of John Muir's came back to me, casual words, uttered in passing: "Some faces just look familiar…"

I reached for Noucquet's book and opened it to the photo I'd noticed in the pub in Hammersmith. A group of fifteen or so men standing in front of what looked like a shepherd's hut on wheels, in a rough semi-circle, two of the men standing slightly apart off to one side. I put the books next to each other on the fold down table and I saw it. The two men standing slightly to one side of the photo in Noucquet's book looked like the two younger men in the photo in Fleming's book – Edward Spector and Edmund Talus. Just like them. Different clothes, different hair, but just like them. Another realisation almost immediately overshadowed the first: the men in both photos also bore a marked resemblance to Simon Hill and Magnus Eves.

There were no names in the caption in Noucquet's book, just this: *A dwindling band – 1919*. Nearly twenty years separated the photo from the one in Fleming's book. If they were the same men they had weathered well, but it was just possible. Middle age started earlier in those days, and young men with their whiskers and stern camera gazes tended to look older than young men now. They could have been in their 20s in Noucquet's photo, their 40s in Fleming's. Just possible, but there was another 36 years between that and the Two. If they were still alive they'd be old men by now. And yet the resemblance was compelling. Fathers and sons, perhaps. Facial features, shape of the head, even something about the way the two men held themselves. I wished I had a photo of the Two in front of me at that moment.

I had no idea what all this might mean, if indeed it meant anything at all, but I felt a renewed sense of a story just out of reach, waiting to be discovered and told. I must have sat and puzzled about this for a while because the next time I looked at my watch it was 9pm and dark outside. I decided to phone George. The opposing compulsions to run away or to go back to London and explain what had happened were pulling me apart, and it seemed like if I told George I could unburden myself without necessarily giving up the option of vanishing. I'd spent too much time on my own thinking and I was so absorbed in myself I didn't immediately consider how a call to George would place him in an uncomfortable position. I just had to speak to someone, and I couldn't think of anyone better.

I made for the telephone outside the Mason's Arms. It was after 9.30pm when I dialled.

"George, it's Martyn. I need to speak."

"Dear Lord. Dear Lord! What is going on? I had a call from the police saying you were dead. A fire. They called me as they saw my name in your address book and thought I might know your next of kin. Are you in trouble, Martyn?

I drove over and saw the burnt-out building. What in the Lord's name is going on?"

"George, I think I might be in trouble, but I swear on God if he exists that I have done nothing wrong. Nothing. I don't know who that person is they found in my flat but I didn't put him there. I don't know how the fire started but I do know I didn't start it. I had nothing to do with it. Those are facts. Facts, I swear. I need to talk to you. Will you listen? Can you help me?"

"Where are you? Martyn, tell me where you are."

"I don't want to just yet, George, as it might put you in a difficult position if you feel you have to report me. At least that way if you do want to report me you won't know where I am. But please, please, hear me out before deciding what to do. Please."

He sighed loudly and I could hear him sitting down. "OK," he said. "This had better be good. I'm confused and I'm tired, so I want it short and clear." So I told him what had happened, starting with his departure from the pub in Hammersmith. I made no attempts at explanations because I didn't have any. I think I spoke for about thirty minutes, feeding coins into the greedy slot.

When I had finished George was silent. "Well?" I asked. Still more silence. Then finally he said he had a few questions. The pips went and I fed in my last coin. "You'll have to call me back," I said to George, giving him the number, aware of the implications of doing so and, when it came to it, just not caring.

After a few moments the phone rang. I was expecting it but it made me jump. George was just starting to speak when there was a bang on the door behind me and I turned to see an indistinct face a foot from the glass, broken into squares by the little window panes. It was a man, overweight and heavily bearded, and he looked angry and impatient. I opened the door while still holding the receiver to my ear and he said he wanted to make an urgent call. I hesitated for a moment and asked George to call me in five minutes. As I vacated the booth the waiting man pushed in past me, impatient and brusque. He had, I think, come from the pub opposite and was probably a little drunk. I walked over the road and sat on the pub wall while he made his call. Twice as he spoke he looked over his shoulder toward the pub. His call took longer than five minutes and I began to worry that George would think I didn't want to speak any more and had taken the phone off the hook and left it dangling while I ran off to hide somewhere. But eventually the man came out. Looking across the road at me he pointed at the phone box and said "all yours," in the tone of someone at the limit of their patience. I mumbled "thank you".

After holding my gaze for a few seconds he turned and walked down the hill into the shadows. As I walked across to the phone box I could hear a ringing inside. Behind me more people came out of the pub. It was getting near closing time.

"George, sorry, someone needed the phone and they took longer than I thought. There's a pub opposite and people are coming out, so someone else might want the phone soon."

"OK, Martyn. Tomorrow is my day off. I will get up early and drive to Devon. You are, I assume, in the vicinity of that Undercliff place that looms so large in your story? Yes, I called directory enquiries with the area code. You are going to have to trust me. Tell me exactly where you are so I don't have to drive around the Devon country lanes looking for you. I promise I will not call the police until I have seen you, but I will not promise that I will not call them after we have met. I want to hear your story face to face, to look you in the eye. If, then, I feel obliged by conscience to report you I will, and if I do, I promise I will not abandon you, I will try to help you. I can just about square it with myself not to report you now, because you are not actually suspected of any wrongdoing. Of course if I did report you, well then you would become a suspect, wouldn't you, but I will allow myself to play a trick on my conscience for the time being. So tell me where to find you. I'm an early riser. I think I can be there by 11am or thereabouts."

I hesitated for a moment. If I met George he could report me and the police would find me within a few hours, I'm sure. Yet I badly wanted to talk to someone. What else could I do?

"OK. Meet me at the Mason's Arms, Branscombe, at 12 noon tomorrow. And please, if you can find one, bring a copy of *New Life!* magazine from about nine months ago. The one with the feature about the Olive Grove in it. I can't explain now but when you come you'll see."

"OK, Martyn. See you tomorrow. Take care until then."

I put down the phone and walked out into the street. There were a few people getting into cars in the car park behind the pub.

I stood for a moment looking at the sky, feeling something of the relief of confession even though I knew I had done nothing wrong.

"Nice evening," came a voice from the direction of the pub. I couldn't see anyone at first, until an orange spot of light drew me to Paul the barman. He was leaning against the side of the porch, smoking a cigarette.

"Yes. Have you closed?" I asked, thinking that a drink was a very good idea indeed.

"We have, but the clock might be a little fast. It often is."

I took his meaning with gratitude and we walked into the empty bar. I ordered a whiskey, for which he refused payment. He poured one himself and said "cheers".

"Enjoying your break?" he asked. I think he was grateful of the opportunity to unwind after a long evening's work. He said he'd been on his own since 9pm because his parents were tired and had clocked off early.

I said I was and answered vaguely when he asked me what I'd been doing. Wanting to steer the conversation onto neutral ground I asked if he had many people in on a weekday evening. He busied himself behind the bar as he spoke:

"More than usual tonight. There are a few people around here thinking of starting a regular folk night and they were in tonight to discuss it. Seems to me that that's all they'll ever do, because they've been in here discussing it every week for the past couple of months, I hear. Actually, a couple of them are from that Undercliff place we were talking about the other day. Nice people, but there seemed to be some sort of disagreement and this other guy got angry and stormed out. Do you like folk music? I do, but they're terrible pedants, these enthusiasts. I go up to Cecil Sharp House sometimes when I'm in London. It's great when the singing starts, but all of the agonising about the tradition … bet that's what they argued about tonight."

As he talked I thanked my good fortune. I had missed Tim and Jenny only by chance. I shuddered when I speculated on the encounter that might so easily have taken place minutes before.

"So they haven't actually set a date to meet yet?" I said, hoping to find if they were due back any time soon.

"Course not, no. Probably never will. Won't be until after you've left I'm sure. The Undercliff people were saying they had a big group coming down for Easter. Good for business. They might all come over here for lunch one day."

CHAPTER 15

Tuesday April 17th, 1973

I got to the Mason's Arms fifteen minutes early but George was already there, sitting on the wall at the front. The same wall I had sat on the previous evening. I was shocked at how drawn and spent he seemed. Maybe this showed in my face, as his greeting was prefaced with "up at 5am and after your call I didn't sleep much." He was quiet and watchful. There was none of the usual conviviality. We sat side by side on the wall, mostly in silence, until the pub opened. We ordered and I led George to a table in the back garden. Though the sun was shining he was cold and had to get a jacket from the car.

"Have you got the magazine?" I asked.

"It's here," he said, tapping a briefcase, "but we'll come to that later.

"I've been thinking on the way down, and I want to say my piece first. Are you ready? I will speak plainly. There are two ways to look at this. The first is that you joined a cult led by two shady characters who somehow seem to have been around for decades without getting any older. You fell for a girl there and when she disappeared you became suspicious. You went to speak to said shady characters and they drugged you, or hypnotised you – or both. They then decide to – what? – kidnap you, do away with you? We don't know, but we do know that they plant people to watch your flat – which, conveniently for them, is in the same building as the church office. You escape, in doing so accidentally giving one of the watchers a bad knock on the head. Next thing you know your flat has burned out with someone, generally assumed to be you, charred to a cinder inside. Who was that person? Maybe the man you bumped on the head. We don't know, but that's what you think."

"Yes, that's about it," I responded. "And when the Two find me they can do to me what they will, without fear, as everyone thinks I'm already dead."

"Is that what you think? Really think?"

Despite his evident exhaustion, there was a command in George's voice, a manner that I had not encountered in him before.

"I don't know … you said there were two ways of looking at it?"

"Actually, let me correct myself. I think there are three, though I've discounted the third. My money's on the second, which is that you joined a church that may or may not be a bit weird, but is essentially harmless. You met a girl there. She liked you but you liked her more, and in the end she backed off. She decided the best way to make the break was not to see you at all, at least for a while, and maybe she got a few people at the church to cover for her while you licked your wounds. You went to see the Two in a heightened emotional state and had some sort of intense spiritual or hysterical experience, the sort of thing that happens routinely in that church anyway. The people you saw outside your flat were nothing more than common burglars. The man you hit – Harry, was it? – was one of them. You said yourself you never trusted him anyway."

"Yes, but what about the fire in the flat?"

"Well, how about this? One or more of the burglars broke into the flat after your escape. After all, they knew it was empty. They somehow started a fire – a discarded cigarette end, for example. And one of them, possibly the one you bumped on the head who was already a bit groggy, was overcome by fumes and then consumed by the flames.

The others, if there were others, made a run for it."

"Sounds far-fetched to me."

"And your preferred version doesn't? You've spent a lot of time on your own sharpening your emotions to a fine point. Easy to get funny ideas."

"Look at these," I said, taking two books from my bag. "Here's Adam's book. Look at this photo here – those two on the end. 1919. Now, look at this photo here. 1937. Now, give me the magazine. There are the Two, Simon Hill and Magnus Eves. Take a good look. George."

George stared at the three photos in turn, saying nothing. I watched him but his face was expressionless. The food came and we ate in silence. George picked at his. Then I asked:

"Well, what about the photos? You've seen them yourself."

George paused for some time before replying:

"Just coincidence. A couple of people in an old photo who happen to look like a couple of people in another old photo who happen to look somewhat like the pair who run the church you went to. Two pretty ordinary-looking blokes in two old photos; two pretty ordinary-looking blokes at the Olive Grove."

Then he paused again:

"The thing is, Martyn ... well ... I expect you've come across people who dismiss us believers with the argument that we just see random unconnected things in the chaos and arrange them into some semblance of order to make the chaos bearable. We persuade ourselves that there's a pattern, meaning, sense, to comfort ourselves. Maybe we do. I've always thought, though, that everyone does that some of the time, religious or not – most of the time, maybe. If there is no meaning, if it is just a void out there, who really looks it in the eye? We all see things we want to see. Maybe, old fellow, things with Amelia, in your life in general, became, um, chaotic and you ..."

"I'm imagining things to make myself feel better. Is that what you are trying to say, George? Yes, I thought so. And I must confess I have wondered just that myself. Which is why I wanted to talk to you. You said there were three ways of looking at it. What's the third?"

George paused again, then, not quite catching my eye, said:

"You are not telling me the truth. Something happened – I don't know what – that you want to keep quiet, and you are in some way responsible for the fire and the charred body. You ran and you are hiding."

"Do you believe that?"

George turned his head a fraction so that he was looking at me face on, his baggy eyes holding my gaze, then said:

"No, Martyn, I don't think I do."

"Why not?"

"Because we've been friends for years, and I think you are a fundamentally decent man. And if you had done something wrong why would you call me?"

"Because you're a good-natured innocent, easily manipulated into providing cover for me."

"And is that true?"

"No. Well, I suppose you are good-natured, and if not an innocent then possibly more trusting than some. But am I manipulating you? No."

We sat in silence for a while longer, then George walked into the pub and ordered some coffee.

On his return, as he sat down he said:

"The Two – what are they called, Simon and Magnus? What are they like?"

"I've been thinking about that a lot recently. On the one hand there is absolutely nothing odd about them, unless being normal is odd. They are friendly, they seem conventional. Simon is more extrovert, Magnus a little intense. They are hard to place socially. I mean, you get no sense of whether their parents were rich or poor, what sorts of houses they grew up in, what schools they went to. I suppose at a push you'd assume they had some kind of education and professional background. The speaking in unison thing does seem a little strange at first, but come on, you dress up in robes every Sunday and I don't think you're odd. But the thing is, when I try to summon them in my memory now there's a space there. I needed that photo. There is something blank about them. Like outlines not coloured in. You know when you meet a lawyer or accountant or someone like that, and they are friendly and they ask you how you are and you talk, and yet you leave with the sense that you have never quite engaged with them as people, just their professional personas? It's a little like that."

"I know exactly what you mean, Martyn, but when you're a church leader you have to keep something back. You can't have close personal relationships with everyone in your flock. It would be impossibly draining. That blankness you're describing is probably just them keeping a safe distance. Necessary self-preservation." George paused again as if weighing what he wanted to say next.

"The thing that I don't get is this. If there is something sinister going on, what on earth is it? What in heaven's name could their motive be to spirit off Amelia and goodness knows who else? What would drive them to go so far as to kill someone and leave them burnt to a cinder in your bedroom? Just to frame you?"

It was at that point that my argument, if I had one, felt most flimsy. It reminded me of when I was a junior reporter and I'd go to the editor with what I thought was a great idea and he'd bark at me through a cloud of Woodbine smoke, "where's the story?" And the truth was that I didn't have a story. I had a lot of events that seemed strange to me, and felt like they were part of a story, but I couldn't see the end of it. There was no punchline. Or rather the only punchline I could imagine to fit the facts seemed incredible, beyond implausible. So incredible that I had not even voiced it to myself until that moment.

"In Fleming's book he talks about Handley believing in a sort of life force and thinking, just before he went missing, that he was close to harnessing it. What if the Two are onto something like that? What if they've found a way of extending their lives by, I don't know, feeding on people's souls?"

I regretted saying it immediately. For the first time George looked disturbed, alarmed, panicked even.

"Martyn. Come on. You can't believe that, can you?" He had abandoned the forthright manner and now spoke gently and slowly. It was not a manner of speech natural to him. Something, I'm sure, he had picked up in some counselling training.

"I'm not saying I do, but think for a minute what you believe, George. Take all the tradition and culture out of it, and just look at the raw essence of your beliefs. You believe in a God who is simultaneously three beings and one, and one of those three died to save everyone (who, incidentally, he'd created in the first place) and then rose from the dead. You'd defend that to the death and many have before you. But does it not seem far-fetched when expressed like that?"

George said nothing and I had the sense of having taken

the conversation down a wrong turning. I cast around for a new tack to take and said: "Don't you think there's something suspicious about John Muir's death? I suppose you're going to tell me that's a coincidence, too."

"The man was well into his 80s, you say."

"But he seemed so fit and healthy."

"I've known many apparently robust octogenarian parishioners go to sleep and never wake up. Happened in one of my sermons once. Not a bad end. Martyn, why don't you come back with me now? We'll walk down to this caravan you've rented and get your things and drive back this afternoon. You can sort out your car another time. I will go with you to the police and support you when you try to explain to them what's happened. I do not believe you have done anything wrong, but I think you might have got confused."

I very nearly agreed. You hear sometimes of people who have maintained deceptions for years abruptly confess, suddenly overcome with weariness about it all. I felt a bit like that, though any deception I was perpetuating was not because I was covering up a wrong. But I said no.

"If I go back I will immediately get caught up in a whirl of questions. If people don't think I've done anything wrong they'll think I'm ill – which is what you think, isn't it? I might never get to the end of those questions. They might define the rest of my life. I could end up in a mental hospital or in prison. And even if I did I still wouldn't lose the fear that something else was going on. I'm not saying now that I won't ever go back, but I don't want to yet. I want to try to find out more. I think there's something going on and if I discover what it is I'll not only be revealing a wrong for what it is, I'll also be clearing myself. Do you see? What will you do, George? Will you report me?"

George sipped at his coffee. Then he spoke slowly and deliberately, as if the words were occurring to him for the first time just moments before he spoke them.

"I've got a few loose ends to tie up. Let me go back for a day or so and sort them out then come down and join you for a week. We'll take a look at Undercliff while we're at it, we'll talk about things. Is there room in the caravan?"

"Surely you're on duty at Easter," I said. "Busiest time of the year and all that."

Again he paused. When he spoke his voice was quiet and resolute.

"I'm on sick leave. The day after we met in Hammersmith I went for my routine check up and mentioned a few twinges. The consultant had me under an X-ray machine that very day. Commendable efficiency but it was too late. The cancer is back and it has spread. Nothing they can do about it. I have six months at the most. They've given me tablets and I'm not yet in any real pain, but I tire easily. Maybe that accounts for me driving down here rather than phoning the police as soon as you contacted me, which is what I probably should have done."

Briefly I forgot my own predicament. I was filled with pity for George but could find no adequate way to express it. I think I said I was sorry. But George was not demonstrative and neither am I.

"Who else have you told?"

"Only the people I have to tell. The PCC, the Archdeacon, the Bishop. And Annabel."

"Your mother, too?"

"No. We talked about that, my sister and I, and decided it was kindest not to. She's in a home now and her memory has gone. I'm not sure she could take it in, and if she did she'd be very distressed, of course, but would forget it five minutes later. Then I'd have to remind her, and distress her again."

He broke off the conversation at this point on some pretext or other.

I could tell he didn't want to talk about his illness any more. He asked me what I thought of his proposal to join me.

"It appeals, yes, but now you've heard me out, do you have some sort of duty to report me? Can I trust you not to report me?"

"That's a good question. At the moment I believe that you have done nothing wrong. The more sinister explanation you are suggesting for recent events is, I think, absurd and certainly incorrect, though I concede it does fit the facts as you've relayed them to me. I believe in the law and the police and doing the right thing, but I believe the duty of friendship is stronger. I could do with a bit of an adventure, even though there probably won't be one. I could certainly do with a holiday. I don't believe you're guilty of anything and anyway at the moment you're not suspected of anything so I wouldn't be harbouring a criminal. I have a slight twinge that burglars are out and about unchallenged in Nunhead, but I suppose they are anyway. I won't lie and say I haven't seen you if asked; I won't falsely identify the body in your flat if asked; but no, I won't report you. Yet."

The tension eased and for half an hour we could just about persuade ourselves we were simply two old friends having lunch in a country pub. George said he'd been to the area many times as a child, and had stayed in one of the chalets on Branscombe Beach with his parents and sister, the summer before war broke out. He was, I think, reviewing his life as the dying do. He said he'd drive back to London that afternoon after having a sleep in his car, and would come back down the day after next – Maundy Thursday. At about 2pm we shook hands and I left him, comforted, relieved and saddened in equal measure.

That afternoon I was at a loose end. Over the previous few days there had been an ebb and flow in my own convictions about what was happening, and at that moment, after speaking to George, I was doubting myself again. But even so, in the absence of anything else to do I decided to walk over to watch Undercliff for a few hours. I had begun to think that if I wanted to find out more I had to get inside the building and observe and listen unheeded, but that seemed impossible. I had to return to the caravan first to pick up my binoculars and as I walked from it down toward the beach café and chalets at Branscombe Mouth I thought of George as a young boy throwing stones into the sea, half a lifetime ago.

I got to my place in the copse opposite Undercliff at about 4pm. The day had started bright and fresh but it was now heavy and hazy. I put the binoculars to my eyes with little expectation, and indeed all I saw was Jenny planting something in the back garden that I had once helped to clear of weeds. I decided to give it until 5pm. Fifteen minutes before my planned departure a vehicle drew up on the gravel drive in front of the house. I recognised it at once as the Olive Grove minibus. In the stillness the engine and the crunch of tyres on gravel were clearly audible across the valley. The minibus stopped in front of the main door into the house. I could see through its windows the sliding doors on the far side of the minibus open, and people starting to spill out into a group in front of the house. I counted eight women and one man, the driver. My binoculars were good but the light was not. My view was impeded, with people bustling around the minibus taking bags out, sometimes stepping from behind it onto the open drive, at other times partially visible through its windows.

It was through this obscure frame that I first saw her. Short, neat hair, short jacket, in contrast to the others. It was only a glimpse but I think it was her. Getting up from the back bench-seat of the minibus and stepping down onto the drive. There she stood almost completely out of view until the driver, who was handing suitcases down, passed a bag to her that she took, immediately stepping to one side to make room for someone else. At that point I got a clear sight of her from the waist up for a second or two, standing in front of the minibus's short stubby bonnet with her back to me. Then she walked back behind it and, I presume, into the now open door of the house. Glimpses, partially obscured, a few seconds, but I thought it was her. In my time at the Olive Grove she alone among all the women with their long curls had short neat hair, she alone among the lace and cheesecloth and denim wore tailored jackets.

I waited there for another two hours, hoping for another glimpse, but no one came out of the house. Having yearned for so long to see her I now felt flat. I realised that if it had been Amelia I'd glimpsed then it became much more likely that my fears about the Olive Grove were overheated imaginings. That George's more prosaic explanation – or something like it – was the truth. She had simply been avoiding me. So though I could still hang around and intercept her when she went out for a walk, I'd then have to explain to her what I was doing there. She would have heard about the fire in my flat and the body, and thought it were mine. She would be mourning me (at least I hoped she would) but if I suddenly appeared from behind a hedge as she was out walking she'd think I was a ghost. Then she'd think I was a murderer on the run.

I walked back to the caravan that evening in the blackest of moods. As I reached Branscombe Mouth I decided to go up to the telephone box to call George. He had just arrived home, having had to stop several times to rest on the journey back. He didn't feel like a long conversation.

"Well, it might have been her, but you saw her for a second or two at a distance of what, half a mile? So it might not have been her. Surely she can't be the only woman with hair like that. But if she is there that's good news, isn't it? She's OK, and the idea of some kind of sinister plot looks ever thinner."

I said I supposed so, and we agreed to talk more when George returned. I realised with some shame as I walked back down the valley to the caravan that I had considered the possible sighting only in the context of my fears about the Olive Grove. The fact that it might confirm that Amelia was OK was secondary. George's assertion that I had spent too much time on my own, thinking, seemed ever more reasonable. But there were questions unanswered. Harry in the yard, the South American student, the note in my flat. Most of all, the burnt body.

As I walked up the steps to the caravan, isolated heavy drops of rain began to fall. The sun hadn't yet gone down but the cloud was now so thick it seemed like it had. By the time I reached the caravan door the rain had built to a steady patter, which, once I was inside, beat a regular tattoo on the roof that continued all night. I prepared some food with little enthusiasm and sat down to look at the photos again. I had taken George's copy of *New Life!* so I could now line up all three alongside each other.

Although Simon seemed to be a white European, Magnus's ethnic origin was unclear to me. I'd always thought he might have been mixed race. Part Tunisian,

maybe. But this was less apparent in the men who I thought
corresponded to Magnus in the two older photos. Though
both pictures were of course black and white, and a little
blurred by time, the faces that might have been Magnus's
could just have been dark-haired and olive-skinned. In
truth the resemblance between Magnus and his lookalikes
in the earlier photos was not as pronounced as I had first
thought. He was thinner now. But in both older photos his
posture was identical. Standing upright with his hands
crossed in front of him, rather like a footballer in a wall,
left hand over right. As I considered this I saw in the earlier
photo, the 1919 one, a thick ring on the little finger of his
left hand. Passing on to the 1937 photo, which was a closer
shot, there again was a ring on the same finger, same hand,
just visible between the shoulders of the older, august
gentlemen sitting in the front row. Without the benefit of
considerable magnification it was impossible to tell if it
were the same ring, but it could have been. I turned to look
at the *New Life!* photo with a feeling of inevitability, as I
knew what I would see. I recalled that I had noticed once
before Magnus's ring, a gold signet with letters engraved
on its large face. And there it was.

CHAPTER 16

Wednesday April 18th, 1973

It gives you an idea of my state of mind that noticing the ring in the three photos gave me some comfort. George, of course, would say that it didn't prove anything at all. Many men wore signet rings on the fifth finger of their left hand. But it did reassure me that there were at the very least some curious coincidences. I was starting to worry about my sanity after speaking to George, who clearly doubted it. Anything that demonstrated some oddness was welcome, even if it didn't prove a thing.

I slept heavily, lulled by the repetitive sound of the continuing rain. I woke at about 7am just as it was easing off. Looking out of the caravan I saw breaks in the cloud above, though far out to sea it gathered in dark, ominous banks. I decided on a morning's watching from the copse. I knew that Amelia often walked after breakfast when staying at Undercliff. I wasn't at all sure that I would confront her if I saw her outside the house, but I wanted to confirm her presence if I could.

I took the quick inland route and was in position shortly after 9am, by which time the dark clouds I'd seen out to sea had advanced almost overhead. The rain began about thirty minutes later. I had my waterproof on and I thought at first that it and the trees would keep me from the worst of the weather. But after about ten minutes the deluge became so heavy that it was apparent I would be soaked if I stayed uncovered for much longer. I had noticed, about fifty yards down the hill to the left, just outside the copse, some kind of small farm building at the top of a sloping meadow. I decided to shelter there until the rain passed.

It was ramshackle but watertight, about 20 feet by ten feet, three windowless brick walls with a low corrugated iron roof and a compacted earth floor. The front was open, giving what would have been an excellent view down the valley and across to Undercliff. There was nothing in the building apart from a plastic beer crate. I sat on the crate and settled down for what looked like a long wait. The rain was so heavy I could barely see the house.

Shortly after 10am I heard voices and laughter behind me. The only way I could look to see who was there was to brave the rain and step out of the building, peeping around first one front corner, then the other. Huddled under a tree in the copse back up the slope were two men and a woman. They looked as if they were deciding what to do. It would not have been possible to leave the building and go back through the copse unnoticed. So I retreated into the barn and surveyed the sodden meadow in front of me, wondering if I could make the hundred yards or so down the slope over open ground to a hedge without being seen. I was about to give it a go when the murmur of voices behind me became running footsteps, shouts and shrieks of laughter. They were making a dash for the barn and if I made my way across the meadow now it would look like I was running from them. There was nothing for it but to stay put, hope to God they weren't people I knew from the Olive Grove, and trust to my story.

Seconds later they were careering round the corner in front of the barn. A young, blond woman, still a teenager probably, wearing a fawn duffel coat already heavy with rain. Two slightly older men: one bearded and longhaired, the other with a ginger comb-over pasted wet and flat on his head. The bearded man was wearing an army surplus combat jacket, while his friend was coatless, a soaking, baggy, hand-knitted jumper hanging about his skinny upper body.

I had retreated toward the back of the building and when I stepped forward to say hello, just as they came to a skidding halt, they actually jumped back.

"Sorry to surprise you. Looks like we had the same idea," I said, heady with relief that I didn't recognise any of them.

"Oh, hello! Sorry, yes, we're soaked!" said the girl, laughing. She shook off her duffel coat and held it out at arm's length in front of her. "Look at that," she said, as the coat dripped onto the floor. They were in high spirits, simultaneously introducing themselves, slicking wet hair back from rosy faces and teasing the inadequately dressed man, called Clive. After a few minutes they calmed down.

"I'm so sorry to disturb you," the girl, Claire, said. "We were out for a walk when the rain started and we saw this building and just ran for it. Do you work here?"

"Oh no, I'm on holiday down the coast. I was birdwatching in the copse and took shelter here."

"We're on holiday too. Over there, though you can hardly see it at the moment," she said, pointing across the valley. I saw an opportunity:

"The big house? I noticed it earlier. Is it a hotel or hostel or something?"

"No. Well, I suppose you could say it is a sort of hostel. A church in London called the Olive Grove, where we all go, owns it. Church members come and stay most weekends, and as it's Easter there's a whole crowd of us there at the moment."

"OK," I replied, with what I hoped passed as polite interest. "What sort of church is it?"

"It's great," said Clive, who in spite of his thinning hair couldn't have been more than in his mid-twenties.

"Nothing traditional about it at all. Loads of young people. Rock music. Do you know The Flock? We're independent."

The other man, John, who looked like the oldest of the group, interjected in a more measured tone that sounded rehearsed:

"The church has been going for a few years but we're all new to it. This is our first time here. It's very friendly and welcoming. Completely non-judgmental. We've got a guest service tomorrow. Open air if the weather allows. It's Maundy Thursday and we're going to take some things from different traditions and do something contemporary. That's what we're about. If you are staying nearby you would be most welcome. It's in the afternoon, at 3.30pm, and afterwards we're having tea. Just turn up if you feel like it."

I thanked him and said I'd think about it, inventing another arrangement that I would have to cancel. I tried to probe with a few further questions that Clive, Claire and John, sensing an evangelistic opportunity, answered with alacrity. But I didn't find out anything more than I already knew.

The downpour continued for some time and conversation dwindled. I began to feel claustrophobic in that dark building with three strangers, about whom I knew virtually nothing except that they went to the Olive Grove. I was much relieved when the skies lightened around 11am, and the rain faded to drizzle. I announced my departure and John said they'd be off shortly too.

We shook hands and I walked back up the slope through the copse, while they called after me: "God bless. Hopefully see you tomorrow."

I felt I couldn't hang around in the copse pretending to look for birds so I gave up on the idea of watching Undercliff for the morning, thinking I might come back later that afternoon. I got back to the caravan and after lunch, feeling tired, decided to stretch out for a snooze. I had been asleep for 20 minutes when I awoke to the sound of the little gate at the top of the steps swinging shut. I sat up to see who it was and immediately lay down again. A mass of coppery curls, unmistakably Pam's. Flattening myself into the bed as best I could I pulled the covers over me. She stepped up the two wooden stairs to the caravan's door and knocked. After a pause I heard her lean against the door and I thought she was going to turn the handle. It was unlocked. Instead I heard her slide something under the door and retreat down the steps, the gate swinging shut behind her.

I lay motionless for several minutes. Had she opened the door or looked through a window she'd have seen me. I peeled the covers back. From where I was lying I could see a piece of paper on the floor by the door. I sat up and stole a glance around the side of the window. Reassured that there was no one about I crawled over to pick up the paper and then back to the bed, making sure I kept below the window just in case.

It was an invite to the Maundy Thursday service that the people I'd encountered earlier had mentioned. It was actually a photocopy of a handwritten document on Olive Grove headed paper, with the intertwined leaves logo. On one side were these words:

The Olive Grove is a church that meets in Nunhead, London and Kingcombe Vale, Devon. You are warmly invited to our Maundy Thursday service at 3.30pm, followed by tea.

On the other side was the address and a rather skilfully-done map showing how to get to Undercliff by road and on foot. Tim's work, probably. Handwritten underneath this, in pencil, were the words *sorry to miss you, will call again.*

I turned over the paper several times. I felt deeply uneasy at the thought of Pam coming to the door of my refuge, but as the initial shock subsided I reflected that she could not have known I was inside. If she suspected anything she'd have tried the handle and peered through the windows. I could imagine all too easily her shrill, forced cheerfulness as she called my name. The most likely scenario was that she and others from Undercliff were conducting a leafleting campaign in the district. This was in character. The Olive Grove was proselytising by nature.

If my assumption was correct then Pam and maybe others would have delivered leaflets to all the neighbouring caravans and chalets. I locked the door and pulled the curtains, and waited for a while. I was bothered by the note about calling again, but I reasoned that the call, if it came, would be later in the day or the following morning, rather than just after the first visit. My plan was to give it a decent interval and then wander around the network of tracks in search of an opportunity to strike up conversation with any fellow holidaymakers I might come across. When it wasn't raining there were always people sitting out in deckchairs taking in the view. I could then chat discursively about this and that, dropping in a reference to the flyer, which was bound to lead people to say they'd got one too. If they had. If it was just me I'd have to forget my leafleting campaign explanation.

After a further 30 minutes I locked up the caravan and walked to the gate. My terrace was the highest location in Haven Holidays, and afforded a decent view of most of the other dwellings. The main track through the area ran down past the bottom of my steps and continued for another

50 yards or so. It ended at a cramped turning circle, with steps down to the beach. All along this main track were parking spaces from which paths or flights of steps led to caravans or chalets. Many of these I could see clearly, neat lawns in front with picnic tables and deck-chairs, maybe washing lines too, or children's garden toys. Others were partially hidden from me, with only a roof and a back wall visible, or maybe a side view and part of the garden. The drizzle that had continued intermittently until after I'd returned to the caravan had stopped and the sun was out. Everywhere doors were opened and people were settling into deckchairs or getting things from their cars. I could see two men chatting further down the track. If I strolled around for 20 minutes it would be easy enough to get into conversation with someone or other.

The risk was that I'd bump into Pam. I tried to work out how long it would have taken her to deliver flyers to all the dwellings. I counted 28, though there might have been a few more tucked away. Even allowing for all the steps and paths, and factoring in the conversations she was bound to have with unsuspecting cornered residents it wouldn't have been more than a 45-minute job for one person, surely. And that was assuming she was alone, which she probably wasn't. When it came to this sort of low-level evangelism the Olive Grove encouraged people to go out in pairs. But I couldn't risk seeing her. She would know about the fire and the body in my flat. There would be no chance of explaining anything to her, or talking her out of going straight back to Undercliff and telling everyone there, loudly, that she had seen me. I waited, wondering what to do next. Then I saw my opportunity.

Walking down the track from the gate into Haven Holidays was a Dutch couple I'd spoken to before. Recent and improbably young retirees, they were on an extended trip around England to celebrate their new freedom. Their VW campervan was in a garage for repairs and, like me, they'd chanced upon Haven Holidays and decided to stay for a week. They were a sociable pair, speaking almost perfect, accent-less English. Only the mild formality of their phrasing gave them away as foreigners. I walked down the steps and invited them up for a drink. They said they were returning from a ten-mile walk during which they had got soaked, so they wanted to go home and change. But why didn't I come and join them in 20 minutes for some cold beers they had in the fridge? I agreed. I'd seen their place before, a large chalet just two plots down the lane from me. Pam would have got to them minutes before or after coming to my caravan, which she had done an hour ago now. Even so, I was looking over my shoulder as I walked the few yards down the lane.

The chalet was a more substantial proposition than most of the other dwellings, with a decked area extending in front of the double doors that led into the main room. These were open, and as I stood on the threshold and called in I saw an Olive Grove flyer on a chair.

The Dutch couple appeared together from a door at the rear of the main room, clothes changed and grey hair combed back into order. They suggested we take the chairs to sit outside, which gave me the opportunity to pick up the one with the Olive Grove leaflet and say that I had received one of those earlier too. The woman – I don't recall either of their names – said that they'd been given it the night before.

"Four women from the, what is it? – the Olive Grove, are staying in a place further down. Apparently there are so many of them they could not all fit into their big house and this was the only place they could find to stay. They walk along the cliff path every morning and spend the day there, then come back late at night. They are good people, but we will not go. We do not believe. Do you?"

The woman must have noticed my discomfort and attributed it to British reserve about being asked about my beliefs. She apologised for asking a personal question and the man changed the subject. We sat drinking cold lager and chatted about walking in the area. It would have been pleasant in other circumstances. After what I hoped was a decently sociable interval I made my excuses and returned to my caravan, running the few yards up the lane to my steps. Just as I reached my caravan the rain started again.

I locked the door behind me, shut all the windows and drew the curtains. The lingering mustiness became more apparent. I made a cup of coffee and sat down to think. I felt confined in what had been my refuge. There was only one way in and out, so if anyone came up the steps I was trapped. This had occurred to me before, but up to that point I had trusted in my anonymity. No one walking past down the lane would have the slightest idea that I, or anyone for that matter, was in the caravan. There was no car in the parking space. On reflection I realised this was still the case. They surely didn't know I was here. Pam didn't know I was here, probably just a few hundred yards from her. I was OK for now, but there was the promise of a follow-up call. I had to get away and find somewhere else to hide. At least until George came back.

When I'd called him the night before we'd agreed to meet outside the Mason's Arms at 10am on Thursday. He said he wasn't sleeping and might as well set off early when there was no traffic. I had to make sure no one saw me until then. I wasn't exactly clear what George and I would do when we met – we would have to talk about that – but I was thinking along the lines of finding somewhere else to stay further away from what now felt like occupied territory. I considered booking in at the pub for the night. Then I recalled Paul the barman mentioning that people from the Olive Grove might be coming for dinner one night over Easter. The thought of skulking in an upstairs bedroom with dozens of them making merry below didn't appeal. And if there were so many Olive Grove members in the area that they couldn't all be accommodated at Undercliff there was a risk I'd find them in any other hotel or bed and breakfast. For that reason the safety in numbers approach no longer worked for me. I needed to hide. Sleeping rough had its merits, if I found the right spot. I thought of packing up my rucksack and curling up in some hollow along by the cliff path. I'd seen plenty of them, overhung with hawthorn. A flurry of rain changed my mind.

I got up to make more coffee and, feeling light-headed, remembered that I had not eaten since breakfast. I picked up the squashed, damp sandwiches I'd carried over to the copse and back that morning. They didn't appeal and I went to throw them into the pedal bin. It was already crammed full and contributing to the musty smell, so I pulled on my waterproof and took it and the picnic to the bigger bin around the back of the caravan. Next to it was the locked chest of garden tools.

Just before 9pm, after the sun had set but before it was completely dark I stepped out of the caravan, locked the door and put the key in my money belt. I realised I wouldn't be able to give it back to Maureen but she was bound to have a spare. My rucksack was fully packed. In one hand I was carrying an electric torch with a feeble beam, in the other a pair of secateurs from the garden chest. There was enough light to negotiate the steep steps so I turned the torch off. Just before I reached the track I stopped and stood stock still for a full five minutes, listening. Hearing no human sounds I stepped onto the track and made my way out of Haven Holidays.

By the time I reached the teashop, locked and shuttered for the night, the last traces of evening light had gone. That didn't bother me. I'd done the walk enough times to know where I was going. It was just a short stretch up the path. When I came to it the thicket surrounding the derelict hut appeared like a looming, impenetrable black mass. I began to doubt the wisdom of my plan. While I was preparing it in the relative comfort of the caravan I bolstered my confidence by reminding myself of my National Service training, which involved many nights in less favourable conditions. But that was a long time ago. I was a young man with a crowd of other young men. Now I was on my own, closing in on middle age. I almost turned around and went straight back to the caravan, but as the rain was holding off for a while I decided to press on. It wasn't late and I could easily turn back if it didn't work out.

Walking around to the side of the thicket furthest from the path I stopped and looked around. The light had gone but as far as I could see there was no one about. I turned on my torch, knelt in the damp grass and got out the secateurs. They were sharp and effective. I made better progress than I was expecting. The density of the vegetation gave me two advantages. It kept the ground underneath dry once I got inside. And anything I cut I could move to one side while I edged forward, then leave to spring back into place behind me, entangled and supported as it was by all the growth around it.

Within a few minutes I was well inside the thicket with, I hoped, little visible sign of my entrance point. I shone the torch through in front of me and caught glimpses of the wooden structure I was aiming for.

I was about to start cutting again when I heard a noise outside, some yards distant. Probably an animal. But it got louder and closer, and there was something about its heaviness and regularity that didn't sound like any animal. I knelt still and silent. I almost prayed.

Then a voice, urgent, familiar, sibilant, whispered: "Martyn! Martyn! It's Pam. I know you're in there."

CHAPTER 17

Wednesday April 18th to Maundy Thursday, 1973

I turned off the torch. I didn't move. I didn't say a word. But it was no use. Pam would not stop.

"Martyn, I know it's you. I saw your face when you turned the torch on. Come on. Please! I'm on my own. I promise I'm on my own."

Still I didn't respond. In increasing cramped discomfort I waited. Five minutes, ten minutes. Willing her to stop, to go away. But still she kept talking: "Martyn! Please! Tell me you are not a ghost. Tell me what happened." I tried to run through all possible scenarios but the only one I could think of was Pam going back to her chalet and saying she'd seen me. That man from church who died in a fire. If she did I'd have to leave the thicket and find somewhere else to hide all night. Or who was to say she wouldn't just pretend to go and get her friends, then stand a few yards off waiting for me to come out?

After ten minutes of increasingly intense pleading, similar thoughts seemed to occur to her. She fell quiet, though I could hear her breathing. She was only a few feet from me. I heard her unscrew a bottle top and take a swig. Then she spoke again, calmer this time, sadder.

"Listen. Consider your position. I don't know how far you've got into that tangle but I was watching you for about ten minutes so I don't think you can get out in an instant. There is nothing to stop me running back to my chalet and telling the rest of them that I've seen you, our dear deceased brother who apparently perished in a fire in his flat, hiding in a den up the hill. There is nothing to stop me running to the phone box in the village and calling the police and saying the same thing. You might get away in the meantime but you wouldn't get far. Even if they thought I was a crank they'd be obliged to do some nosing around and they'd soon discover the body in the flat wasn't yours, if they haven't already. Then you'd be wanted for murder. I don't know what happened and I don't know what you are doing in a big bush but I'd like to know. I can't say you owe me an explanation, but maybe if you give me one it might be better for you."

She paused for a while and I heard her put the bottle to her lips again. Then she continued.

"When I first joined the Olive Grove it seemed like the answer to all my problems. I felt like I'd found my niche at last. But after a while something changed. I can't put my finger on it but I began to feel ever so slightly uneasy. You must have noticed how so many people there are damaged. Grieving, recovering, in pieces. People who've lost something. At first I liked that because that's me, isn't it? – and I felt at home. But gradually I began to feel different to everyone. They all seemed to experience something that I couldn't quite get. All those people in The Flock, they've come from a similar place to me and they talk about being completely transformed but I didn't feel transformed. I felt like someone just about hanging on. I was trying all the time but it just wasn't there. You seemed different, I noticed that. You weren't the only one with your eyes open looking around the room, you know. And Amelia seemed different too, at first. More thoughtful, though not later. More normal, both of you. But when she left and I heard you'd died I felt even more unsettled. You probably didn't know you were an ally of mine but you were. I came down here to give it one more go, but I feel so claustrophobic I had to get out. The leafleting was the final straw. I realised I was trying to persuade people to join in with something I didn't believe in anymore. I told the others I was going to see a cousin in Lyme Regis and would be back late. I've been sitting up here watching the sky grow dark, having a drink. The closest I'll get to peace at the moment."

After that there was silence for a full five minutes. I kept thinking. It began to seem to me that the risk of explaining was less than the risk of running. From what she'd said, it sounded like she might sympathise with my fears about the Olive Grove.

"When did you last see Amelia?" I asked.

"So you are there. What a relief. Thank God the bottle isn't making me see things already."

We talked like that for a few minutes, me still sitting in the thicket. The absurdity of it occurred to us both simultaneously. Pam started giggling and I couldn't help but smile to myself.

"So whose was the body in the flat?" she asked.

"Doesn't that worry you? Whoever it was, maybe I killed them and started the fire to make it look like accidental death, and then ran."

"Don't think that hasn't occurred to me since I saw you cutting your way in there. That's why I sat watching for a while rather than calling to you straight away. If I hear you coming out I'll run like hell. But as I said just now, I don't think you can get out in a hurry. So why don't you stay there and I'll stay here, and you can tell me your story? Then I'll decide what to do."

I thought for a little longer and realised she had me where she wanted me. If I told her everything and she didn't believe my story she'd run. If I refused to tell her she'd run soon enough anyway. My guess was back to the chalet in both scenarios, because if she went straight to the phone box she'd be on her own and I might be able to catch up with her. My one chance of stopping her running was to tell all and hope she believed me. Anyway, if I kept her talking I might find out more about Amelia.

So I told her my story, much the same way I'd told George on the phone. I told her I'd been in the caravan when she'd delivered the leaflet. Apart from laughing at that detail she listened in silence. When I'd finished she remained silent for several minutes longer, then she said:

"Come on, you fool. What have you got in there anyway? A burrow? A sett? A den? Let me in and show me around. The rain's starting again."

I retreated the few feet back to my hidden entrance and pushed the cut branches aside. She was standing looking down at me, a bottle of vodka in her hand, velvet bell-bottoms wet around her boots.

"Room for two?" she asked, and got down on her hands and knees. I picked up the secateurs and went to work again.

Within 15 minutes we had reached the hut. A door led into a small side porch, which in turn led into the hut's one room. From this a big glazed door, glass intact, faced down the hill, though even in daylight all you could have seen from it was snarled-up branches. There was a window on the wall opposite the porch but it had been boarded up. It seemed a robust structure, the boards and beams thick and for the most part solid, though a part of the floor had rotted away in one corner. I wondered what it had been used for. Not a holiday chalet. There were no signs of any kitchen or bathroom facilities. Maybe a coastguard lookout.

Whatever it was, it hadn't been used for years. Cobwebs

and dust aside it was empty. When the rain got heavy again I heard a drip in the corner where the floor had rotted through, but there was enough room for us to make ourselves almost comfortable without risk of getting wet. We sat huddled against the hut's back wall.

The torch was fading so I lit two candles. Then I got a sleeping bag and blanket out of my bag and we pulled them over us. Pam handed me the bottle.

"Got this in Beer," she said. "First drink for 11 months. Funny how destruction feels better than salvation."

"So you don't believe?" I said.

"Actually, I think I do, I just don't want to do it the Olive Grove way."

Then she said: "I don't know what to make of a lot of what you've said – the photos, for example – but obviously my presence here in this shack confirms that I don't believe you killed someone and set fire to your flat."

"Why not?"

"Well. For a start you are no fool. If you did kill someone I think you'd have thought of a better way to cover your tracks. Starting a fire and then running is too risky. Drawing attention to the scene of the crime. If you left before the fire took hold there'd be no guarantee it would consume the body. It might go out of its own accord, or someone might raise the alarm and the fire brigade put it out while the body was still readily identifiable. And if you stayed until it *had* taken hold you'd be running the risk of being overcome by smoke. Or of someone seeing the flames, raising the alarm, and the fire brigade getting there before you got out. No, you'd have dragged the body out in the dead of night or something like that. Or maybe you'd just have left it and banked on getting out of the country before it was discovered.

"Maybe there was some accident and you panicked. That would be more your style, I'd say. But even so I can't see you holding out here for so long before giving in and telling all.

"Sometimes you just have to trust your judgment. I can't see you as a killer. I just can't. Despite appearances to the contrary I'm pretty thoughtful myself; pretty observant, too, and you just don't strike me as the type. I think you are honest, at root. Besides, a lot of what you said ... I can't say it rings true, but some of it ..."

"What?" I asked.

"Well, that speaking in unison thing the Two do is pretty weird, isn't it? You get used to it after a while, but imagine if you heard it in any other context – at work, for example. And what you say about them seeming distant, I'd say it was more than that. It's as if they've got the outward trappings of personalities but inside there's nothing there at all. I've noticed Magnus, the way he talks to people like there's no one else in the world, then when it's over it's like he's been switched off. And there's this thing of people who seem very involved suddenly stopping coming. Amelia, for instance. Who was keener than her? Then next I know the word is she's gone back to Belgium."

"Really?"

"Yes, that's what people were saying. There was an implication that it would be kind not to tell you. Some people even thought you'd committed suicide in your grief, you know. I heard that Simon gave a statement to the police suggesting that."

"So you haven't seen her?"

"No, not for quite a few weeks now."

"I thought I might have seen her at Undercliff."

"What, in the last day or two? I don't think so. I haven't

seen her there anyway." She paused for a moment. "Most of all, though, I had an experience that sounds a little like part of your story.

"About two months ago I went to see the Two for a telling. There were a few others there. Yes, Harry was there, definitely. It all started off well enough but then I gradually faded out, and next I knew it was several hours later. Angie, that woman who sings in The Flock, was sitting with me but everyone else had gone. She said I'd been slain. I didn't like it. Loss of control. It reminded me of waking up after a night's drinking and not remembering where I'd been or what I'd done. Then a few days later I was getting some money from my purse and I noticed a little card there that I hadn't seen before. That same verse about the eyes of God was written on it. Nothing else. I never found out who put it there. I tried to take it as reassurance, but I think that's when I started to feel hemmed in. For a few days after I kept bumping into people as well – the Two, people from The Flock, others – on the tube, the bus, in shops, everywhere. Then it stopped. Ever since then I've had the feeling of no longer being part of the in-crowd. Of being very subtly excluded. A couple of times the last few days I've walked into rooms and conversations have stopped. And Magnus and Simon barely speak to me now, yet leading up to that telling they took every opportunity to declare that I had some kind of unique calling."

"What was it?"

"They got vague when it came to detail, but there was always stuff about sacrifice."

"Take a look at the photos," I said, taking the books and magazine from the rucksack.

She stared for some minutes in the combined light of dying torch and flickering candle.

"Well, as much as I can see in this light I can't deny there's a strong resemblance. I'd go as far as saying uncanny."

"What do you make of it?"

"Haven't a clue. I can hardly accept that they're like vampires sucking out souls rather than blood, but put it this way – I've heard nothing to reassure me that the Olive Grove is my continuing spiritual home."

We sat in silence for a while after that. I asked her about the psoriasis healing. She didn't answer for some time. "I don't know. It was pretty bad – backs of my hands, arms, back, and over most of my chest and stomach. They didn't actually pray for healing but one evening, after they'd prayed for me and laid hands on me I went home and as I got undressed I saw the skin on my arms was smooth. I took off all my clothes and looked at myself in the mirror. Not a trace. That morning when I'd had a shower it had been all over me. Not a sign of it since then until, well, until this morning I saw that it was back. Not as bad, but still... Feel."

She took my hand and slipped it under her blouse. I could feel the skin at the top of her breast rough, angry and flaky. I left my hand there for a moment and withdrew it. "What do you make of that?" I asked.

"Don't know," she said. "Maybe miracles wear off when your faith dies."

Then she lent her head against my shoulder and in a few more minutes she was asleep. I looked at my watch. It was just after midnight. I liked this version of Pam much more than the Olive Grove version.

My plan was to leave before dawn, so I could find some hiding place near the Mason's Arms before anyone was about. I don't think I slept at all that night, though Pam did. I was so stiff and uncomfortable by about 4am that I had to get up, at which point she woke. We had some coffee from a flask I'd made and then I packed up my rucksack. After some deliberation, I decided to leave it in the hut for the time being. I needed to be able to move fast if I had to. I just kept the money belt. We scrambled back out into the field shortly before dawn.

"What are you going to do now?" I said.

"I think I'll sneak back into the chalet before the others wake up. They're sharing a room in the back and I'm on the couch in the main room so I won't disturb them. When they get up I'll tell them my cousin in Lyme Regis is ill, which is why I was so late back, and that I'm going to go and look after her for a few days. Then that'll be the end of me and the Olive Grove."

"Will you tell anyone?" I asked.

"Tell them what, that I've seen a ghost? Bye, Martyn. Look me up when you've sorted yourself out. God bless us all." And with that she kissed me on the cheek and walked off down the hill.

I watched her for a few moments then turned and made off toward the village, doing my best to keep clear of paths and houses.

***

I couldn't find anywhere safe to hide near the Mason's Arms. Knowing which way George would drive in, I found a spot about quarter of a mile up the road, behind a hedge. From there I could see cars approaching through a gate a few yards further up. I settled down to wait. Four hours later I stepped out into the road and flagged down the car. George leant over to open the passenger door and began to speak. I ignored him and got in.

"Drive straight through the village and up that steep hill

next to the pub. Only stop when you are at least a mile clear of the houses. Now!"

There must have been authority in my voice. We drove through the village. There were a few people about and I looked down as if studying a map, my left hand half covering my face. We then climbed up a steep, winding lane inland out of the village. I hadn't been that way before. Soon we were driving through open country and the occasional small wooded area. After five minutes George pulled in next to a gate and said "Will this do?" We were high above the village, looking down on the thatch and cob.

"You look awful," said George, switching off the engine and winding down his window.

"So do you," I replied.

"Obviously there have been developments and I want to hear about them, but give me ten minutes," he said, taking from his shirt pocket a packet of pills. He pushed one from its blister and popped it into his mouth. Then he closed his eyes and sat perfectly still. I could see the pulse slowing in his neck. After a while – it seemed longer than ten minutes to me – he spoke again, without opening his eyes.

"OK. What's happened?"

As I told him he interjected with a few questions. When I had finished he fell silent again for a few minutes more, eyes still closed.

"I think we should go back to the caravan," he said.

"We can't. They're right on our doorstep there. I was thinking you could go and pick up all my stuff from the hut and we'd find somewhere a few miles away, out of their orbit."

"Do you trust Pam? It all hinges on that, as far as I can see. If you do, it is as safe as anywhere. Safer, actually, because if we check into a hotel you'd have to give a name and ID.

She's the only person from the Olive Grove who knows you are there, and if she doesn't tell anyone and does what she told you she was going to do and leaves anyway, then you're OK. So do you trust her?"

"I think I do, yes, but why risk being so close to them? I'm sure there are plenty of other places we could stay."

"Maybe. It is Easter weekend, mind you. But I thought you *wanted* to get close. Isn't that the point? We want to find out what's going on. If anything is. You've got me as cover, remember. I can answer the door if anyone comes calling. No one will have a clue that I'm connected to you."

"Pam will. I told her you were coming."

"OK, but she's on your side."

We went on like that for some time. Again I was divided. The impulse to run and the compulsion to find out more. Eventually, fortified by George's confidence, I agreed. We drove off, George with my keys to the caravan and instructions for where to park. He dropped me off before we reached the village and I walked cross-country, avoiding paths until I reached the gate to Haven Holidays. The car was where it was meant to be. I ran the few yards down to it and climbed the steps to find George sitting on a sun lounger in front of the caravan drinking a cup of tea. He looked much better, like he was on holiday. I got another lounger, poured myself a cup of tea and sat down next to him.

"I've been thinking," he said. "I'm going to go to the Olive Grove Maundy Thursday service." Then, anticipating my objections: "Wait, wait – hear me out. Why not? You would love to get up that close yourself, wouldn't you? The whole point of me being here is to help you find out if there's anything going on, if there's anything sinister about them. Seeing them in action seems like the best way to do that. I'll be perfectly safe. There'll be other guests there. What are they going to do – get us all? I can say a flyer was pushed under the door of the caravan I'm staying at – quite true – and as a vicar on sick leave it seemed like a good way to spend the afternoon. I've looked at the map. I can find it easily enough. I'll drive over and you can watch from your wood."

I could see the sense in it, though it made me uneasy. "OK," I said. "Just come straight back." George assured me he'd be careful. Then we made an early lunch. George had brought a few things to supplement my dwindling supplies. It started drizzling so we ate inside. George positioned himself where he would have a clear view of anyone appearing at the gate, while insisting I sat where I wouldn't be seen from outside. Either he was taking it all seriously or humouring me.

As we ate he began to talk again:

"I bumped into Adam when I was back at home. I told him I'd read his book and asked him what he was doing next. He said he was planning a follow-up, trying to solve the mystery of the murder in 1919, and the two men from New Dawn who were accused and then disappeared mysteriously. It was a famous episode at the time. Research is at an early stage but he has located some press reports and police archives. Interestingly, this information indicates that the two men featured in the 1919 photo in his first book – the ones you think look like the Two – could, *could* mind you, be the suspected murderers."

"How on earth did you get him onto that? You didn't give anything away did you?"

"No. Just casual questioning. He's never happier than when talking about his enthusiasms and I saw an opening. There's a New Dawn archive in a university somewhere that has ledgers with membership details. After the men went missing the police produced wanted notices with their names and photos. Adam says those photos look like the two men standing to the side in the one in his book, but he can't be absolutely certain. But the police published their names and he cross-referenced them against the New Dawn membership ledger. I scribbled down what I could remember of what he said afterwards. I could hardly take notes when he was talking."

George got up, bumping the table as he went. He was too big for the caravan. He opened the suitcase he'd put on one of the bunks at the back and got out an opened envelope. He began reading from it as he walked back to the settee.

"John Hooper, aged 29. Joined New Dawn in 1916. Teacher by profession. Excused war service on account of a weak chest. That means consumption, according to Adam. And Henry Arthur, aged 27. Librarian. Injured in France in 1915 and invalided out of the Army. Also joined New Dawn in 1916, after John Hooper."

"Anything else?"

"That's all Adam said."

"Any indication they knew each other before joining New Dawn?'

"Adam didn't say either way."

I took a bite of my sandwich. "It sounds to me like you're starting to take this seriously, George."

"Just trying to understand where you're coming from old boy, that's all. If the two suspected murderers are the two men in the 1919 photo, who look like the two in the 1937 photo with Handley ... well, that isn't stretching things too far in my mind. A couple of rogues preying on vulnerable people in a fringe sect commit murder for whatever motives. Probably money or sex – always seems

to boil down to those two. Anyway, they escape and turn
up later as Edward Spector and Edmund Talus, assistants
to Handley – himself a cranky, wealthy type, ripe for
exploitation. Who, let's not forget, goes away not long after
and is never heard of again. I'm not saying that *did* happen,
just that I can believe that it *might* have. It seems possible.
But I simply cannot extend that narrative another 35 years.
That makes no sense. Anyway, time's getting on. I'd like to
have a rest before I drive over to Undercliff. You, my friend,
look like you could do with a wash and shave."

I had to agree. When I stepped out of the bathroom 20
minutes later George was sitting on the settee.

Pointing at his dog collar he said:

"Thought I might as well go in uniform."

That seemed like a good idea, though I couldn't say why.
We discussed whether there was anything in particular
he should watch out for. I described Amelia and Harry the
plumber as best I could.

Then I said: "Just watch the Two closely. See if you
can engage them in conversation. You've never met them
before. I'm interested to know what you make of them."

We left together just after 1.30pm. The rain had stopped
again and the sun was shining. George drove me part of the
way. I got out in Weston and picked up my cross-country
route. As I was walking I recalled John Muir saying that the
Two looked familiar to him. Must mention that to George,
I thought.

I reached the copse at about 2.15pm. I could see his car
parked to one side of the house and a crowd of people on the
lawn. Tim was setting up speakers and microphone stands,
and a few others were putting blankets on the ground. A
cable trailed from the house. There were chairs set out in
two rows. It took me a few minutes to locate George in the

throng, but there he was, holding a cup and chatting to two young women. He looked like he was enjoying himself. I noticed several other people I recognised and many new faces – guests, probably. As I sat there waiting for something to happen I remembered my rucksack. I'll go over to the hut when it's dark and collect it, I thought. I settled down to watch the service with anticipation, as if a curtain was about to go up.

CHAPTER 18

Maundy Thursday, 1973

After ten minutes people began to settle in ranks on the chairs and blankets. By my reckoning there were about 150 there. I expect someone had announced that the service was about to start, but as I couldn't hear individual voices, just a background hum, it was as if the crowd moved of its own volition like a single entity. Two men from The Flock appeared with acoustic guitars and stood flanking a microphone while Angie stood at another, a tambourine in her hand. The PA just about lifted her voice over the valley.

"Welcome to the Olive Grove, everybody," she said. "Let's raise our voices to the Great Choirmaster."

They sang for about 15 minutes, a mixture of familiar Olive Grove songs and a couple of traditional hymns. By the time the music reached me it was fragmented. The scratchy acoustic guitars and Angie's voice were clear yet disembodied, disconnected from each other and the communal singing, which sounded like a distant murmur. Some people were raising their hands as they sang. George had got one of the chairs and was standing stiffly in front of it, arms behind his back. I saw him look around the crowd a few times.

When the singing stopped Simon and Magnus stepped up to the microphones. The two guitarists stood behind them like a guard while Angie walked into the crowd. The Two spoke separately, taking turns welcoming people. There was no unison speaking. I could hear most of what they said, though not all. It was so light and inconsequential, so conversational it hardly amounted to a sermon. Then they announced a "new take on a traditional Maundy

Thursday ceremony", which would take about ten minutes. It would, they said, be a time for people to reflect. At this the two guitarists started again at one of the microphones. I expect their playing was gentle and ruminative. I'd often heard them do that sort of thing as an aid to meditation in services. But from where I was sitting it sounded like an irregular sequence of metallic pings. Like running a key along a wire fence. Tim walked on and moved the other microphone to one side, creating a space. In this space he put two chairs on which the Two sat. He then placed an earthenware bowl, quite large, between their feet. I noticed then that Simon and Magnus were both barefoot, and I saw sandals beneath their chairs.

They sat like that for a while as the guitarists continued playing. As far as I could tell the crowd was sitting still, in silence, apart from a small group gathered off to one side behind a clump of trees and shrubs. They would have been out of sight of everyone else. Bunched up together, they were unwinding a huge strip of white cloth. Tim and Jenny were there; Neil and Kath, too. And others: a few familiar faces, a few unfamiliar.

This group formed themselves into a line and processed out from behind the trees, joined at the waist, one with another, by the white cloth. It looked like a bandage for the deepest of wounds. Tim led, with the cloth running a few feet from his belt to the waistband of Jenny's dress, and so on through the entire group. There were twelve of them. They looked like passengers escaping a sinking liner, lashed together. Or prisoners on a chain gang.

Tim led the line out in front of the crowd, walking slowly, head bowed. When he reached the Two he crouched on the ground between them and dipped his hands in the bowl. As far as I could see he then splashed water onto their feet, one at a time, and rubbed them dry with the slack of the sheet that joined him to Jenny. When he had finished he stood up and moved a little to the right, while Jenny took up position between the Two. It went on like this through the whole line. Through the binoculars I could just about see that Simon and Magnus's eyes were open, I think, but apart from that I couldn't tell anything from their expressions. They just sat impassively.

When the ritual had finished the line of twelve walked back the way they came, this time with Tim at the rear. Simon and Magnus then stood up and gestured with their hands for people to rise. As the guitarists broke into a strum Angie stepped up to her microphone and began singing, and everyone joined in. It was not a song I knew.

After that the service ended. It had been short. Under an hour. The mingling and talking started up again, and Jenny and a few others began circulating with trays. A few men carried out two trestle tables, followed by women carrying plates of food. I couldn't make up my mind whether to scan the group for Amelia and Harry or keep my eyes on George. I tried to do both until I saw George making his way through the crowd toward Simon and Magnus, who were standing in front of the chairs where they'd sat to have their feet washed. They were wearing their sandals again.

George ambled toward them arm outstretched, a broad smile on his face. He was a picture of good cheer. No one would have suspected any ulterior motive, even if he had one. And I wasn't sure that he had. For all I knew the service might have convinced him of the Olive Grove's orthodoxy, and he was just one church leader extending warm greetings to colleagues. Talking business. Magnus and Simon responded in kind, shaking George's hand in turn with their apparent relaxed cordiality. The three of them spoke for some time, with much laughter. They all looked at ease, George, the tallest, bending slightly to listen when one or the other spoke. After about fifteen minutes George looked at his watch, said something, and turned and walked toward his car. The Two walked with him. When George reached the car he shook hands with Simon and Magnus, got in the car and reversed out of his parking place, while they went back toward the house.

I could see other people drifting away by then. The Two went into Undercliff. There was nothing else to see and I was bursting with anticipation to hear what George had made of it all. I left the copse and half-walked, half-ran back along my shortest cross-country route. I was at Haven Holidays in a little over an hour. George's car was parked in its space. I took the steps as briskly as I could, walking through the gate at the top, which was propped open with a stone. The caravan door was open too, and George was standing in the doorway side on. I would have called out if I wasn't out of breath.

George was standing at the kitchenette. There were three cups by the kettle. He was talking. I could see the backs of two familiar heads through the side window in the caravan's main room. George walked out of sight saying "here you are, you two," in his cheeriest voice.

All of this happened in a fragment of time, but it was time slowed down. I turned and ran down the steps, back up the lane out onto the coast path. There were quite a few people about. An old woman sitting on a bench was staring at me. Her face was lined, thin brown legs bare between baggy shorts and clumpy walking boots. She looked concerned. I expect I looked a bit wild. I hesitated, unsure which direction to go, fearful she was about to ask after my well-being. I decided to walk uphill toward Beer.

I reached the top of the ascent. Sitting on the grass a few feet from the path I did my best to look like a holidaymaker taking a rest. I could see down to the beach café and the beach. Though there was the promise of more rain it was warm and sunny. The tables in front of the café were full of people eating ice creams. Children played on the pebbly beach. I could hear the cries of a few brave souls tiptoeing into the water, mingled delight and pain. There was a man on the beach standing at a table set up near a boat. A small group gathered around him. I'd seen him before, selling fish he'd just caught. You selected the one you wanted from a big bucket of sea water and he pulled it out alive and cracked its head on the table. Then he filleted it, chucked the offal into a sack, and wrapped the flesh in paper and gave it to you. Seagulls circled him expectantly. A parking area behind the café was full of cars. People walked past me along the path, nodding and saying "lovely day" if they came from Beer, breathing hard and red-faced if they'd just made the ascent from Branscombe Mouth.

It was useless trying to think things through. George had the Two in my caravan. That much I knew. And that knowledge made linear thought impossible. I got up to walk toward Beer with a sense, rather than an idea, of putting distance between them and me. But within a few paces I turned and stood looking back down the way I'd come. I'd rested at this spot before, on my first walk to Beer on the day I arrived. The path ran close to the cliff edge, which was marked with a flimsy barbed wire fence.

Defying instinct I walked toward the edge. I knew the caravan was down there somewhere. One foot forward, hand on a fence post, bracing my body as if against the push of an invisible hand, I compelled myself to look over the edge.

The cliff descended vertically for only a few feet to a
ledge about six feet deep, from there angling out into a
steep grassy bank. I knew beyond this there must be other
sheer drops, but I was OK if I couldn't see them. There was
evidence of recent picnicking on the ledge. To my right I
could see, far below me, about a third of the roof of the
caravan and the part of the clearing between it and the gate
from the steps. I lay down at the top of the cliff and looked
through my binoculars. I didn't need them but it made me
look like a patient birdwatcher rather than a potential
suicide.

Mercifully I didn't have to wait long. First Simon, then
Magnus and finally George emerged from the caravan
and walked toward the gate. They stopped there for a
while looking down to Branscombe Beach. George pointed
something out. Then he shook hands with them both and
Simon and Magnus walked down the steps out of sight.
George remained standing there for a minute looking
around, then went back inside. I turned my attention to the
gate into Haven Holidays and, sure enough, within a few
minutes the Two walked through it and back down the hill
toward the café.

I watched them descend into the crowd, lost them for
a few minutes, then picked them up again sitting on a low
wall in front of the café, eating ice creams. When they'd
finished they set off up the coast path in the direction of
Undercliff, walking with intent. They were in good shape.
A few minutes more and they were out of sight.

I waited a little longer in an agony of indecision. I wanted
to confront George, to challenge him, to ask him what the
hell he was doing. But what happened if they came back?
I didn't really believe George could be in league with them
against me. But given his previous frankly-expressed

doubts about my judgment I could believe he believed ever more strongly that I was misguided. Confused. With my passport and wallet in my money belt I considered the idea of walking on to Beer and catching a bus ... Where? ... It didn't matter. Anywhere a long way away.

Then George came out of the caravan again and stood at the top of the steps, scanning the tracks of Haven Holidays, the beach and the crowd in front of the café, as if looking for something in particular. After a couple of minutes of this he descended the steps out of sight. Like the Two before him he appeared a little later at the gate to Haven Holidays. He leant against the gatepost for a rest, striking up conversation with the old woman I'd seen earlier who was still sitting on the bench. Then he turned as if to walk toward Beer. He was about fifty yards from me. I stood up and walked back from the edge of the cliff to the path, then down toward him.

There were a group of hikers coming along behind me, walking at a brisk pace and joking among themselves. They overtook me just as George and I met, and we had to let them step around us and continue down the hill before we spoke.

In those brief moments we stood in silence ten feet apart, staring at each other. I looked straight into his bloodshot eyes. He spoke first.

"I saw you out the corner of my eye when you got to the top of the steps. I'd propped the gate open so it wouldn't make a noise and made sure they sat on the sofa with their backs to the gate. I thought that if I stood facing them with the caravan door open then I would see you and somehow be able to give you a sign. But thank the Lord I didn't have to."

"You didn't have to invite them back, George!"

"I didn't invite them back, you fool. I said goodbye to them after the service and drove back to the caravan. I'd been sitting outside dozing for about 20 minutes when I heard footsteps. I walked to the gate thinking it was you and there they were. They said they'd decided to drive over to see the chalet where Pam and the others were staying, though they didn't mention her name. Said they're thinking of buying one as auxiliary accommodation, because the Olive Grove has grown so much there isn't always room at Undercliff. They'd seen my car and decided to pay me a call. What could I do?"

"Told them you felt tired and politely dispatched them."

"I did say I was tired, but they said an idea had occurred to them that they wanted to discuss, and I thought I was safe for a while. I was almost certain you wouldn't get back so quickly but I set things up so I'd see you approach if you did, and they wouldn't. I thought you said it was a two-hour walk. I thought I'd keep them for fifteen minutes. They didn't see you, Martyn."

He spoke rapidly, short of breath and needing to get the words out. I was above him on the steep path and though he was much taller than me he had to look up to meet my gaze. At that angle his imploring face looked childlike. We stood in silence for a while longer. George didn't flinch from my stare.

"Let's sit down here by the path for a bit," I said, suddenly weary. "What was their idea?"

"They want me to take a part in leading a Good Friday service tomorrow."

"Tell me you said no."

"I said yes."

"So you're in with them?"

"No. I'm doing what we agreed, which is snooping

around on your behalf. I'm your man on the inside... Let me explain."

"I think you'd better," I said.

Sitting on the grass looking out to sea, George described his attendance at the Maundy Thursday service. He hadn't seen anyone who looked at all like Harry. He did approach a woman who fitted my description of Amelia – or at least was about the right age and had short hair – but she turned out to be a French Canadian in England for three months with her fiancé. Who, George said, soon appeared and put a proprietorial arm around her. The service itself seemed to puzzle him:

"Much of it was neither here nor there. Some of the terminology was a little unorthodox. The music wasn't my sort of thing but I wasn't expecting an organ and choristers. But the ceremonial feet washing ... well, the thing is that feet-washing *is* a Maundy Thursday tradition in lots of Christian denominations. It springs from Jesus washing the disciples' feet the night before the crucifixion. So far, all well and good. But it was the wrong way round. The whole point of it is that power serves, rather than is served. Jesus serves his disciples. Usually Holy Thursday feet washing is either communal, or the priest washes the feet of 12 people chosen to represent the disciples. But here it was the other way round. The twelve disciples washed the priests' feet. And the long cloth that linked them all together. That was meant to represent the linen Jesus was wrapped in after death, though the symbolism was muddled."

The more George spoke the more he relaxed, and the tautness between us slackened. "So what's your gut feeling?" I asked.

"I *felt* mildly uncomfortable, but that is probably down to the style of the event not being my style, and not knowing anyone. But never trust your inner feelings, old boy. That's what an Anglican theological education teaches you. In my experience feelings are too easily swayed by how well you slept the night before, or whether you've got enough money in the bank – things like that. And God knows I've got enough to make me feel uncomfortable now. Use the brain God gave you, that's how I try to do it. So on that basis the correct question is, what do I think? And the answer is that I am inclined to think they are probably not quite right, because that foot-washing was the wrong way round, and they must have known that because I can tell they know their Bibles. But I doubt there is anything seriously amiss. By my reckoning they started out OK but have drifted a little off course, probably a little too pleased with their own positions, which is attributable to having no one to answer to. They got in a position of power, and power can go two ways – it can give or take. My guess is they're drifting down the latter route. It's happened before and it will happen again. As I said to you, there's no chain of command to keep them in check. But I haven't seen any evidence that they are some malign cult feeding on vulnerable acolytes. Personally they seemed harmless enough – friendly, interested in me."

"But what if that's their cover?" I said, noticing a shrillness in my voice. "Isn't the best way to disguise something bad to make it look as closely as possible like something good? Almost the same, yet not quite?"

"Well yes, but then you could go round suspecting anyone or anything appearing basically good as being a particularly persuasive counterfeit. You'd doubt everyone and everything then."

"OK, so what if there is something amiss, as you say, but that it is far more amiss than you realise? Remember, I didn't start to doubt them for months. You've only met them once and you doubt them a little already. Assume that they are worse than you think they are, that there is something deceitful and predatory and manipulative about them. Then what about everyone else? What about Amelia, Neil and Kath, Tim and Jenny, Angie, all of them? Are they a part of it too, or have they been taken in? Are they simply damaged people looking for solace who've been duped, and if so what does that say about the God they believe in?"

George looked at the ground for a while, pulling up stalks of grass.

"There are a lot of questions there, Martyn. Yes, I can see that if I have mild reservations based on one meeting, then there is a distinct chance they might grow with continued exposure. Equally, they might not, or it might go the other way and my initial unease might evaporate as I get to know them. Remember, I approached them from a position of bias, courtesy of you. Despite my best efforts I couldn't put out of my mind all you'd said. Maybe if I got to know them better my own impressions would gradually outweigh yours.

"What about the others? Well, my guess is that the Olive Grove meets their needs to some extent, whether it is orthodox or not. I doubt very much they are knowingly a part of some sinister secret cult because I doubt very much such a cult exists. And what does that say about their God? If He's the same as mine then He'll look at their hearts, not the trappings of their religious expression. They want comfort, and comfort comes in many forms. Even if it has some falsehood in it, doesn't necessarily mean you can call it false comfort. We all make mistakes."

"What, you mean God too?" I replied, and then regretted it.

George didn't answer for a while, then said:

"No, I mean sincere faith doesn't insure you against bad judgment – your own or anyone else's. In my book it is perfectly possible for people to believe sincerely and do the wrong thing. History is littered with people who did bad things, silly things, misguided things while thinking what they were doing was exactly what God had told them to do. I do sometimes think that faith is healthier, stronger even, if it is tempered with a measure of critical detachment. A standing back, a wondering, a questioning."

I had the sense then that there was little point in pursuing the conversation any further. At least he had some doubts about the Olive Grove, even if they weren't the same as mine.

"So what about this service tomorrow, then? What are you going to do? And more to the point, why are you doing anything at all?"

"As I said, my purpose for being here is to help you find out more about the Olive Grove. The closer I get to them the more I'll find out. Also, if I'm right and they are going a little off course perhaps I can help put them back on the straight and narrow. A little old-fashioned Gospel truth never did anyone any harm. They plan to go down to that Devil's Field place you've mentioned in the morning and have an open-air service. They've asked me to preach."

"What will you say?"

"Oh, I'll think of something. I've got a few tried and trusted old favourites up my sleeve. Shall we go back to the caravan for some food?"

"What if they come back?" I said.

"They won't, trust me," George replied. And I did. Or at least I had to.

George was once again exhausted by the time we got

back to the caravan. He slept for 30 minutes on the couch while I sat outside and after that seemed much better. His conviviality revived and we spent a pleasant enough evening eating a meal improvised out of the bits and pieces we had lying about. I recalled that I intended to mention to him that John Muir said the Two looked familiar to him, but when I raised it he cheerfully brushed me aside:

"I know where this is going. The Two are that pair in the photo with Handley, who may be the vanished suspected murderers from New Dawn. Forget it, Martyn – not possible. They'd be in their 80s."

I didn't have the energy to pursue it. And he was right, of course. A little later I asked him what he was planning to do after the service. I had a sense that the story was approaching its conclusion, though what that might be I couldn't tell. He said he'd wait until after the event and consider it then, but that at the moment he still thought I should go back to London.

"You assume that the fire incriminates you, but maybe that isn't the case at all. Maybe the police can identify when it started. Just suppose it started an hour after you left the building. You can prove you were at that service station before Salisbury Plain at a particular time. Couldn't you demonstrate that it would be impossible to get there at that time if you had started the fire? Maybe they already know the body isn't you. Maybe they know it is some serial burglar from southeast London who got out of prison two days before and returned to his old ways. Maybe what you say will prompt them to nose around the Olive Grove a bit, and ask where Amelia is, and they'll find something."

"There are a lot of maybes in that," I said.

"Which add up to a lot less than the maybe of running," George replied. "If you are innocent surely the best way to prove that is to put yourself into the hands of the law, rather than run from it?"

"You said 'if' then, George."

"I know you haven't done anything wrong, old boy, but running makes you look guilty."

I knew he had a point. I think if he had said there and then "let's go back tonight", I would have gone. But he didn't.

Halfway through the evening I remembered my rucksack. I waited until twilight and set out even though it was raining lightly. George stayed in the caravan. As I walked down the hill toward Branscombe Mouth in the failing light I heard a helicopter in the distance, though I couldn't see it. I made my way through the thicket easily enough and found the rucksack where I'd left it. Back in the caravan I unpacked it, thinking that I'd get George to look at the photos in the books again. At the bottom I noticed a scrap of paper. I reached in to pick it up.

It was folded in half and a little crumpled. On it, in pencil, were written the words:

The eyes of the LORD are in every place, beholding the evil and the good.

Without speaking I showed it to George. "Proverbs 15, I believe," he said.

CHAPTER 19

Good Friday, 1973

I went to bed exhausted on account of sitting awake the previous night in the hut with Pam. But I woke the next morning feeling that I'd barely slept at all. My mind would not settle. My conversation with George about the note the previous evening had been unsatisfactory.

"Perhaps someone preached on that verse while you were staying at Undercliff before, and you scribbled it down and then forgot about it."

"But it's not my writing."

"It's in capitals. How do you know it isn't yours?"

"It just isn't."

Then George began to surmise that the note had been put there at the same time that the other note had been left on my coffee table in London. I agreed that was a possibility, though doubtful because I was sure I would have noticed it before. Anyway, there was little comfort there. The discovery of a second note, even if it had been placed at the same time, simply doubled the unease I already felt about the first.

"Perhaps Pam put it there," George said.

"But we were in the hut together. One room. I was awake the whole time. She had no chance. I would have seen it. Anyway, what if she did? Does that mean she's on their side, playing their game?"

"Perhaps it was a word of encouragement."

"Some encouragement! What I'm worried about is that they got in there sometime after I left the rucksack. Just a friendly reminder that they're keeping track of me. That they know where I am."

We continued like that for some time, me getting increasingly anxious, George exasperated. Eventually he said he'd had enough. He was tired and sick and he wanted to rest. His illness and my fretting were too much even for his placid good nature. I was tired too, and I conceded that there was no point in discussing the note any more. We couldn't find out who put it there by talking about it. And if they knew where I was, what was the point of running? They'd only follow.

It was about 11pm. I persuaded George to take the sofa bed in the main room. It was the biggest in the caravan, and not uncomfortable. I moved to the smaller room at the end, separated by a plastic concertina door. In it were two bunks, more like hammocks than beds. I took the lower one. I could just about stretch out without my head and toes touching the walls.

Though it afforded some privacy the concertina door was completely ineffective when it came to keeping out sound. At about 11.30pm I got into my sleeping bag. I think I fell asleep immediately, but woke when George went to the bathroom. I looked at my watch. It wasn't yet midnight.

The whole night passed like that. Short bursts of sleep interrupted by George's regular visits to the bathroom and, on three occasions, the sound of the kettle boiling. He must have been up all night. On top of that the rain fell constantly, and ever heavier. After each interruption I lay awake for a while, thinking about the note. I thought a lot about Amelia, too. There had been a shift in my attitude. When it all started I had wanted to know where she was because I wanted her back. Now I wanted to know where she was because her absence was part of a mystery that threatened me. I was dimly aware of that change at the time. With hindsight it became much clearer. Sometimes in those periods of wakefulness I could hear George muttering rhythmically to himself, very quietly. I think he was praying.

I recall looking at my watch at 6.15am, noticing that the rain had stopped, and wondering if I might as well get up. But I must have drifted off again, into my longest spell of sleep that night. The sound of George opening the front door woke me. I looked at my watch again. It was 7.30am. I was about to call out "morning, George" when I heard him speak.

"That's quite alright. I was already up and about. How can I help you?"

A wind was blowing, rendering the voice that answered less distinct. A short conversation ensued, of which I heard enough to realise that the caller was a policeman. After a few minutes I heard George say: "Yes, I'm here with a friend. He's still asleep."

The caller must have asked if George wouldn't mind waking me, and I heard him walk the few steps toward the concertina door.

"Martyn," George said through the door. "There's a policeman here. He needs to have a quick word with you."

I hesitated only for a moment. When I opened the insubstantial door it was with some relief. It was out of my hands. They'd found me. There was nowhere to run and I didn't have any more difficult decisions to make.

George was standing there, blocking my view. He looked like he'd shrivelled overnight. I could have believed he was an inch shorter and half a stone lighter. His shoulders were drooping and his thin hair stuck up, revealing a flaky scalp. He mouthed the words "it's OK, don't worry".

I got out of bed, pulled on my jeans and a t-shirt, then walked to the door of the caravan. The policeman standing outside wore a waterproof cape that was blowing in the wind, though the rain had stopped.

"Good morning, sir. Sorry to disturb you. Just a routine call. I was saying to your friend that the body of a woman was found at the bottom of the cliffs near Beer late yesterday evening. We are speaking to everyone in the area to check if anyone is missing. Is it just the two of you staying here, sir?"

"Yes, it is," I replied.

"Were you on the cliffs over toward Beer yesterday evening, sir?"

"No, I wasn't. I haven't been over that way for a few days."

He asked me a few more questions, none of them uncomfortable, which I was able to answer truthfully. He jotted notes in his pocket book. Then he said.

"We think the woman was somewhere in her mid-thirties. She had curly auburn hair. Have you seen anyone matching that description in the area acting erratically in the past few days?"

I can only believe that at this I must have shown some kind of reaction but he didn't seem to notice. In fact he looked bored. He'd probably asked the same question 20 times already.

"No, I don't think so," I replied.

"Thank you, sir. I think that's all. And it's Martin?"

He'd heard George call me. I had no choice.

"Hope. Martyn Hope," I replied.

"Is that Martin with an 'i', sir?"

"No, a 'y', actually."

"Thank you. I always ask that because my brother is called Martyn with a 'y' too. Thank you. Good day."

I watched as he walked off to the gate and disappeared

down the steps. Then, closing the door, I turned to George: "It's Pam."

"We don't know that. It might be, but who can say there aren't other women around here answering that description?"

"It's Pam, George. It all fits."

I wasn't in the mood to reason with George, I just had a deep conviction that, yes, of course it was Pam. It was obvious, and just short of predictable. All at once I was overcome with a petulant, childish irritation that I had got myself caught up in a sequence of events over which I had no control. "That's two unexplained deaths in this little drama. Three if you count John Muir," I said, as if the most significant thing was the inconvenience it caused me.

George tried to maintain a position of reasonable doubt but it looked like his heart wasn't in it. Maybe he was just worn down by a sleepless night.

"Even if it is Pam, and we don't know that, chances are the explanation is straightforward. If very sad. The path runs close to some very steep cliffs. If she'd left the chalet early yesterday morning as she told you she would, she'd still have had most of a bottle of vodka in her system. Easy to see how she could lose her footing and go over the edge, especially with all the rain we've been having."

I just looked at him.

"Well, all I can say is just don't jump to conclusions. It might not be her. And even if it is her, the chances are it was just a terrible accident."

"Yes. If you take it in isolation, an accident might seem the most plausible explanation. Drunken woman walking along a cliff early one morning, grass still wet, slips over the edge. Yes, I can see that. But if you see it as the latest in a sequence of unexplained events …"

I tailed off. Even after everything that happened over the past few weeks I still wasn't convinced. Sometimes, when I set it all out in my mind's eye it seemed like proof – though proof of what I couldn't say. At other times it just seemed like a jumble of unconnected events. I tried to express this to George. It came out muddled and I suspect he took it as further evidence of paranoia. He looked at me for a moment then looked at the floor for a moment longer.

"As I said in the pub the other day, it's like faith," he said. "We see lots of things that seem like a pattern pointing to something bigger. Signposts. Other times, though, they just seem like evidence of their own haphazardness. There comes a point when you just have to decide to believe or not believe."

"And what do you see at the moment? A pattern or nothing?" I asked.

He didn't answer directly, but said:

"I think we should continue with our chosen course. What else can we do? I will go to the Olive Grove's Good Friday service and I will say my piece and we'll see what happens. I suppose soon enough we'll know if that poor woman at the bottom of the cliff was Pam, but we might never know for sure how she got there. We need to get a move on. I have to be at the house at 10am."

I shrugged agreement and George set about making breakfast. I reflected with renewed irritation that there were now two police notebooks, a few miles apart, with my name in them.

We set off in the car at about 9am. The rain was holding off, though it looked like it might start again at any moment. I had with me my small bag with provisions and the binoculars, and around my waist the money belt with passport and wallet. I didn't feel safe leaving anything of value in the caravan. I was wearing my waterproof. George was wearing corduroy trousers and a crew neck jumper beneath which his dog collar was visible. All his clothes were too big for him. He dropped me at Weston and I walked down to pick up the coast path. Undercliff beach, which was private, was only accessible from the cliff staircase. Devil's Field separated it from Kingcombe beach, which was open to the public. I judged it would be possible to get up onto Devil's Field from Kingcombe beach and find a spot from which I could observe proceedings without having to stray onto Undercliff beach itself. The service was due to start at 11am.

I set off from Weston at a pace. I needed to get onto Kingcombe beach as soon as I could. The steps down to it were not much more than half a mile from the Undercliff staircase and I didn't want to risk running into anyone from the Olive Grove. By about 10.15am I was on the shingle heading west along the deserted beach toward Devil's Field. I had never explored it from this side before, and as I approached I could see things weren't going to be straightforward. The tide was in. This side of Devil's Field was about 20 feet above the beach, but unlike the Undercliff side there was no way to get up there. From cliff to sea ran an unbroken bank of red earth, worn smooth and almost vertical. I stood staring at its blank, forbidding face. The end, around which the sea was breaking, was rock, a little lower and just as impassable.

The cliff face itself was irregular and pitted, where chunks had fallen out onto the beach from time to time. The only way I could see was to climb straight up it and then over to Devil's Field. I've already mentioned my fear of heights. On account of that, climbing had always seemed to me a singularly unattractive activity. My experience extended no further than wall bars in a school gym and the assault course in National Service basic training. So though I had to climb just 20 feet it felt perilous. The hardest part was getting from my tenuous foothold on the cliff over to Devil's Field. It was more a leap than a step that got me over.

Once on the level ground of Devil's Field it was all thicket, and I could see no sign of the network of paths accessible from the Undercliff side. About fifty yards in front of me toward the sea was a slightly raised area topped by a rocky outcrop. When I reached this I could see down into the hollow and the main clearing, where I was certain the service would take place. It was probably another 30 yards away, maybe less. Above it, a little above the height of my lookout, was the smaller clearing where Amelia and I had once sheltered under the overhanging cliff. That seemed a long time ago. I settled into a cleft amidst the rocks and lifted my binoculars to my eyes. I realised I might be seen if anyone looked up, but there was no reason that they should. They'd all have their eyes closed anyway.

It was now past 10.45am, and as I scanned the field and the beach beyond I could see people already making their way to the clearing. I focused on the staircase and saw a steady procession descending single file to the shingle below. It took me a while to pick out George, but eventually I saw him walking down holding the rail. Behind walked Tim, carrying quite a big piece of wooden apparatus. I couldn't see what it was at first.

Within a few minutes people began spilling out of the various paths onto the clearing. With the noise of the wind and the waves I couldn't hear any voices, but I had the impression that no one was talking anyway. They assembled of their own accord in loose ranks, facing the cliff. Looking to the staircase again I could see the end of the descending line of people. It was now nearly 11am. They were running a little late. George and Tim were on the beach somewhere, out of sight. Soon they would be making their way through one of the tunnel-like paths on Devil's Field, the branches of trees meeting over their heads.

Shortly after 11am I saw them appear on the main clearing and walk toward the path that led up to the smaller, higher clearing. George seemed to stumble, and Tim took him by the arm. He handed the wooden apparatus to another man I didn't recognise, then walked on with George. I couldn't tell if he was propelling or supporting him. They were moving slowly. My attention was fixed on them and the mass of people on the clearing, and I hadn't looked up to the higher clearing for a few minutes. When I did I saw that Simon and Magnus were there. The front of the clearing was bordered by dense shrubbery about five feet high. They were standing in front of this natural barrier, staring impassively down at the people below them. A few minutes later George and Tim appeared next to them, followed by the other man. Tim walked to a spot roughly in the middle of the clearing near the front, and set up the apparatus that this other man had been carrying. I saw then that it was the wooden stepladder. The one I had seen Simon standing on early one morning, in the library that was out of bounds.

Tim left the ladder standing there and disappeared with the other man back down the path into the crowd below.

When the service started it was close to 11.30am. Simon ascended the ladder and spoke. Through the binoculars I could see his lips moving, but I could hear no words. He must have projected his voice, shouted even, because though the mass of people was much closer to him than I was, the wind was blowing hard. While he spoke George and Magnus stood just behind him at the foot of the stepladder. They were probably below the crowd's line of vision. Then I heard, carried on the wind and almost a part of it, the cascading voices of the sacrifice chant we had sung at Undercliff on my first visit. This went on for a long time – ten minutes maybe – after which Magnus climbed the ladder and mouthed silently to the hundred or so upturned faces. There came a point when he appeared to stop speaking and just stood there, looking ahead. Everyone in the crowd below was standing with their eyes closed. Some had their hands held out. While I was looking at them Magnus descended the ladder and when I trained the binoculars on it again George was climbing it. As he got to the top he seemed to sway slightly, side to side, like a tree on a hill in a storm. He was taller than Magnus and Simon and was perhaps standing on a higher rung, so that a greater part of him was visible above the top of the ladder. They were at the bottom, Magnus to George's right, Simon to his left. He held on to steady himself, leaning down, and looked at the people beneath him. I saw his mouth move and then their eyes opened. At that moment the first drops of rain began to fall.

I zipped up my waterproof then put the binoculars to my eyes again. The sky grew darker. Something moved at the limit of my field of vision and I noticed, far distant, a solitary cow on the sloping field beyond the staircase. It kept turning around, backward and forward close to the edge. Then it tried to ascend the slope, but seemed to slip and slide back to the drop and over it, all the while moving its head urgently as if looking for help that didn't come.

When it hit the beach below it bounced and split open across its belly. George was still speaking. I didn't look at my watch but I think he continued for no more than ten minutes. The Two just stood there, their expressions betraying nothing. The rain got heavier and I could see people in the crowd huddling into coats, putting up hoods, but no one made for the shelter of the trees surrounding the clearing.

Then it happened. Like the experiences of childhood my recollections of the next few moments are etched indelibly on my memory, though how accurate a record they are I am now not sure. This, I think, is what I saw:

George stopped speaking, let go of the ladder and straightened up. Stretching out his arms, palms turned upward, he looked to the sky. Did I see a smile on his face? I think I did. The cloud was so thick it was almost like night. A solitary fork of lightning split the gloom and there was a noise like thunder, amplified a thousand times. Then a piece of the overhanging cliff about the size of a man's head fell off and plunged to the floor behind the ladder. I saw both Magnus and Simon turn to look at it, but George didn't move. Magnus, who was nearest to the track that led back down to the main clearing made a move in that direction, but he was too late. With a grating roar the entire overhang broke free from the cliff and slid down onto the upper clearing, breaking into pieces as it fell. I saw Magnus engulfed just before he reached the path. Simon seemed mesmerised, and stood there looking up at the falling rocks as they thundered toward him. George was the last to fall. Standing arms outstretched, not once did he turn to look at the landslide about to overtake him, nor did he attempt to escape.

Below, on the main clearing, the crowd fell back in disarray. People stumbled, and while some bent to help others just pushed by and trampled over them. I could hear screams above the cacophony of the fall. The whole scene became hellish and vague behind a cloud of red sandstone dust that the rain, heavy though it fell, could not dampen.

CHAPTER 20

After the Fall

From the first rock to the last it took no more than 30 seconds for the cliff to collapse. This I learned over the following days from newspaper accounts, but at the time I had no sense of the duration of the catastrophe. It was as if time was abolished on that part of Devil's Field, events taking place concurrently in a preternatural chaos, with me outside looking on. Like a helpless god.

My first reaction, purely instinctive, was to shout for help – a useless, unheard cry. Then I hovered indecisively, one moment considering climbing down to the clearing, the next making to retrace my steps to call for aid. In the end I did nothing but sit and wait and watch.

What had been the higher clearing had caught the section of overhanging cliff that had broken free. All formerly level ground there was covered with a ragged heap of earth and rock, sloping back from the shrubs that had marked the clearing's boundary to the main cliff behind. The bank of compacted shrubbery that stretched down to the bigger main clearing in the hollow below looked much as it had before. Just a few stray fragments had spilled over into it, most caught in the roots and branches before they could fall far. Consequently the main clearing remained free of debris. Had the people grouped there held their positions no one would have been hurt, but they had scattered like a panicking army. Already I could see some sprinting across Undercliff beach toward the staircase. Others formed a ragged semicircle at the very back of the clearing.

When the fall ground to a halt, a sense of stillness hung in the air, though the rain was still falling and the wind still blowing. I saw a thin figure, bald head wet and shiny, break free from the semicircle and run toward the path up to what had been the upper clearing. It was Tim, brave Tim. A few other younger men followed, disappearing behind him into the tunnel through the shrubs. How far they got I couldn't see, but after they had moved out of sight the cliff above started to discharge rocks. It was not another landslip; just chunks losing their hold in the raw, newly uncovered face. Like a giant spitting out pips. Some of these fell directly into the bank of green, driving Tim and the others out. He emerged holding a handkerchief to his temple, blood running down the side of his face onto his shirt.

I realised then that the rain was easing, and the wind subsiding. Time returned, or rather I recovered my sense of it. I could see people ascending the staircase now. It would take the fastest runner about 15 minutes to get to Undercliff, but there was no telephone in the house so they would need to go further into the village to call for help. An image flashed through my mind of the conversation that would take place. Between a wet, breathless, wild-haired hippy and a suspicious local.

It must have been about 40 minutes after the landslide when a helicopter came buzzing along the coast from the east. It made several sweeping circles over Devil's Field and Undercliff beach as if looking for a place to land, before coming to a hovering halt above the cliff like a curious insect. Then I heard the sound of another engine mingling with the helicopter's, and saw an inshore lifeboat speeding toward us from the west, close to the cliffs. It was followed a few minutes later by a larger, slower-moving motor launch. The lifeboat pulled in close to Undercliff beach and lowered a dinghy into the water. Into this, four policemen climbed. Two of them began rowing. When they reached the shore a fretful gaggle of Olive Grove members surrounded them, like shipwrecked mariners greeting rescuers. After a short encounter the policemen ran toward Devil's Field. By the time they appeared in the clearing the bigger launch had moored next to the lifeboat and was discharging at least a dozen more men. As these landed I could see still more descending the staircase onto the beach, and gathering at the top of the cliff looking down at the vast gash left by the fall. Mixed with the dark police uniforms was fireman's yellow. There were people carrying stretchers and boxes and other equipment. Then soldiers arrived, on land and from the sea.

Before long the rescuers outnumbered the bedraggled crowd that had made up the Olive Grove's Good Friday congregation. It looked as if the Army was in charge. Soldiers in pairs ushered people away from the clearing, down from Devil's Field, and into a group at the foot of the staircase. They were taking a roll call, a pointless exercise as some had already run for help and there was certainly no comprehensive list of who had gathered that morning anyway.

In the hollow a group of soldiers, police, firemen and paramedics assembled, with ropes, ladders and shovels. The equipment was palpably inadequate in the face of the landslip, as high as a house. By now the wind and rain had ceased. The acoustics of the clearing in the hollow allowed me to catch fragments of barked orders above the helicopter's drone. Debris was still dropping from the cliff from time to time.

A smaller group at the top of the cliff dropped a rope over the edge. A man began inching down it, walking backwards down the precipitous escarpment, stopping every few paces. Even the thought of standing at the top looking down made me lurch inside. He descended some distance until he reached a shrub, which must have grown on the small tussocked level area at the top of what had been the overhang. It now clung to the sheer face, sticking out at a crazy angle. The climber stayed there for a while looking around, holding onto the rope with one hand while tapping at the cliff face with some kind of implement. Then he began the climb back. When he got to the top he stood there for some time, in conversation with the others. While this was going on the people on the clearing were keeping their distance, some looking up with binoculars at the cliff face. The helicopter flew off, returned about 30 minutes later, and then disappeared again. At the very back of the clearing soldiers set up a camp, centred on a large, open-fronted tent.

I learned later that it wasn't until Sunday morning, after much watching of the cliff and assessment by geologists, mining engineers and assorted other experts that the soldiers were allowed to commence what was quite obviously a recovery operation, not a rescue.

I stayed watching until about 1.30pm that Good Friday. I was reluctant to leave. George was dead and the most I could hope for was to see soldiers dig out his pulped remains. Even so, I felt some obligation I can't explain to keep a vigil. In the end, though, self-preservation overrode my impotent loyalty. Somebody would see me if I stayed up in those rocks much longer.

By the time I left the tide was receding. I was able to make my way down to the seaward edge of Devil's Field, and scramble down a much less demanding slope onto slippery, seaweedy rocks. I made my way around onto Kingcombe beach and walked towards the steps up to the cliff path. I came across a hiking group at the foot of the steps. They had been attempting to walk westward down into Sidmouth. Police just beyond the top of the steps were blocking the coast path. They'd seen me emerge from the rocky foot of Devil's Field and asked what was going on. I fell back on my birdwatching story and said there'd been some kind of cliff fall, though I hadn't seen it from where I was sitting. They had some idea of making their way along beaches and rocks until they could pick up the coast path further west. When I explained this was impossible they decided to walk back to Seaton, from where they'd started that morning. I fell in with them, thinking that I might avoid awkward questions from the police. As it was, once we reached the top the police, standing about fifty yards to our left toward Undercliff, just nodded acknowledgement. I left the hiking group a few hundred yards further on to pick up my inland route back to Branscombe. The thought of company, cheerful company, was intolerable.

That walk back to the caravan was a weary one. Though I was now conditioned to the physical effort my legs felt like the trunks of fallen trees. It wasn't just sleep deprivation. I'd been stretched taught for days, undecided between running and returning, with the Olive Grove's ambiguous threat growing around me. The cliff fall, shocking though it was in its abrupt violence, cut me free. With that sudden release of tension a slackness came over me. I confess that although I did grieve for George then, and much more later, I was mostly thinking about myself. The Two had perished with him. The Olive Grove had been severed clean through at the root. Within hours its leaves would start to wilt, its branches droop. The thing was dead, though it might retain some appearance of life for a short while. Whatever its constricting menace had been, I was free from it.

It was probably about 3pm when I got back to the

caravan. The sun was out and there were plenty of people about, eating ice creams, drinking tea, skimming stones, writing postcards home. As I climbed the steps to the caravan for the last time a fear came over me that I would see the Two standing there as I walked through the gate. But of course there was no one. I would have preferred not to come back but I had to get my rucksack. It was clear to me now that I was going. The Olive Grove couldn't touch me now, and the police probably weren't yet looking for me. Now was my chance.

As I opened the door and stepped inside I saw George's suitcase open on the bed. Yesterday's clothes, shaving kit. When I looked through the caravan there was nothing else of his anywhere. He had packed it all away but in his haste had neglected to zip up the case. It was the act of a man expecting to leave that day. The thought came to me that George might have written some account of the last few days for his own purposes, and that it might be in the case. But I was reluctant to root through his things to check. I felt like I'd felt when I came across John Muir's body. I hesitated for a while before forcing myself to lift up the first layer of clothes. There was nothing there. It was at that moment that grief and loss hit me hardest, and a sense of shame at my meanness of spirit.

I packed everything I had into my rucksack so that when I left the caravan only George's open suitcase remained. I was due to return the keys to Maureen on Easter Monday. I left them in the caravan, with the door unlocked. No doubt when I failed to appear she'd come up to see what was going on. That gave me a few days. If the police traced George to the caravan before then I'd just have to hope they'd assume he was staying on his own.

Avoiding paths and roads where possible I walked

inland until I picked up the A3052. There wasn't a great deal of traffic about and it was early evening before I got a lift. The lorry driver said he was running late and had to step on it. "Diversions further back because of a landslide," he said. As we approached Lyme Regis I considered asking him to drop me there so I could pick up the Herald, but then thought better of it. The car sometimes didn't start if it had been left standing. We arrived in Portsmouth at about 9.30pm. The ferry was due to sail an hour later.

The lorry driver pulled into the line of vehicles waiting to board. I thanked him, and taking my rucksack climbed down from the cab. Though I longed for privacy and a bed I decided to book the cheapest ticket I could, as money was short. I was tempted to pay by cheque but reflected that if anyone came looking it would be another footprint in my trail, so I dipped into my shrinking cash reserves.

The ferry wasn't particularly busy, mainly commercial traffic and a few low-budget travellers like me. I chose a seat in a corner of a near-deserted saloon on the top deck. There I spent the six-hour crossing fitfully dozing on a hard plastic seat, leaning against my rucksack. Sailing away from England, from the Olive Grove, from myself. It was getting on for 7am in Caen when I stepped off the ferry. I wanted to book into a hotel there and then, but I knew I had to keep moving. In spells of wakefulness through the night I had made my plan.

After reviving myself with caustically strong coffee in a café near the harbour I prepared to walk to the train station. I nearly cried when the barman I was paying told me it was almost 20 kilometres away, but I recovered myself and asked where I could pick up a bus. At least my grammar school French was good enough to understand. Once at the train station I found a bathroom with shower cubicles you could book for 30 minutes at a time. In one of these I washed off days of anxiety, tension, fear and grief. When I stepped from the shower, rented towel over my shoulders, I caught a glimpse of myself naked in the full-length mirror on the back of the door into the cubicle. I had changed. With the repeated cliff walks, the strain, the irregular sleep and the missed meals I had lost weight. My face was weathered brownish-red like the Devon soil. I had tried shaving in the caravan but had given up after a day, so I'd grown the beginnings of a beard. When I shaved it off my jawline was sharper than it had been since the Army days.

I selected the most presentable outfit I could muster from the limited options in my rucksack, and walked over to the ticket office. There I flicked through the timetables mounted on hinges on the wall. I was looking for the train that would take me furthest in a day. Where it went I didn't care at all. When I found what looked like the best bet I bought a second-class ticket and, with 20 minutes to spare, went off in search of food. In the shop I noticed a rack of French newspapers and made a show of idly flicking through them, but of course there was no mention of a cliff-fall in Devon the day before. While doing this I noticed the date: April 21st. For a second I couldn't attach any significance to it, though I thought there was some. Then I realised that it was the day before my 37th birthday.

That was the start of years of wandering. I arrived at my destination – I won't tell you where – at just after 7pm that evening. Though I had slept a little on the train I was exhausted, and I booked into the first cheap-looking hotel I could find. I was asleep before 9pm.

I woke as dawn was breaking and walked over to the window. The town square seemed insubstantial in the mist and half-light. There was no one around. I sat in a chair and watched for a while, then I must have fallen asleep. In my dream, two figures walked into the square from opposite sides, toward a statue in the centre. There was a four-sided bench surrounding the base of the statue. The two figures sat on this bench. As the mist cleared and the light grew I could see that it was George and Amelia. They were talking and laughing. George looked better, more like how I remembered him from the old days. Amelia seemed happy and bright, like she did when we first met. I watched them for some time until they arose, shook hands, and exited the square in different directions. I awoke with a lingering sense of the anguish I had felt at being unable to follow them.

The sun was up and there were a few people in the square. I went downstairs and ate a big breakfast, a solitary birthday celebration, while listening to the Easter Sunday church bells ringing in the Resurrection.

I checked my money and reckoned I'd be able to eke it out for another week. I asked the proprietor if he knew anywhere I might find work. He was obviously used to travellers seeking casual labour, and suggested a large farm about ten kilometres away. I hitched over there later in the day and after a night in a barn at 6am the following morning was out in the fields helping the farmer mend a fence.

So began a peripatetic career. A few weeks here, two months there, on farms, vineyards, building sites, in bars, garages, holiday camps. Cash in hand, no questions asked. Staying in farm buildings, caravans, tents, hostels. On the surface it seemed like an insecure life, but I found a sort of peace in the mostly hard physical work, in not owning anything apart from the contents of my rucksack, and not looking more than a few weeks ahead. There was a whole shifting community of people like me. Probably still is. British, Australian, American, Irish, German, Dutch, aged between about 18 and 35 mostly. At the first job I told them I was five years younger than I was and nobody batted an eyelid. At the next place I shaved another five years off and everyone accepted that too, so I settled on 27. It wasn't just my age I changed. I chose a new name, another homeland, an alternative history, a different hairstyle and clothes. All the while I kept my passport hidden in my money belt, which I only took off when in the bath or shower, and even then kept in sight and reach. Sometimes I'd get it out and look at the photo of the person I used to be.

After about four months I found myself washing up in a seafront hotel in the South, long evening shifts in sweltering heat. Working with me were two Americans, probably somewhere in their mid-20s. After work we'd sit outside drinking cold lager. They said they were brothers, though they didn't look alike. They also said they were draft dodgers. This may have been true, though there was something about them that made me think the tale might be more complicated than that. By then I had worked up a cover story, which I used when necessary. I was running from a failed marriage to a woman with family connections to organised crime. I needed to find myself new identification. The two Americans told me of a trustworthy man in the town who, for a fee, would produce sufficiently-realistic papers for anyone wanting to start again. They had used his services themselves.

I was wary, but knew that I had to find what would pass as formal confirmation of my new identity. And surely the only way to get that would be from a forger in a back street of an unfamiliar town. If not this one, then another.

So after a few days' indecision I went to see him. I found a chuckling old man who said he'd learned his trade in the resistance during the war. My passport had some value, and augmented with cash I'd accrued in the money belt I was able to buy my new identity. He said it would take two days. I was nervous about paying him up front, though reassured when he agreed he'd only take my passport when I picked up the new papers. Two days later I turned up three hours early and watched his house from a café down the road. Not a soul came or went during that time, and when I knocked on his door the old man answered with a wink and said "you've been watching me, my friend."

In his little kitchen at the back of the house he laid the new papers out on the table for my inspection. They seemed OK, and indeed they serve me still. I gave him my passport, picked up my new papers, shook his hand and left.

And that was the last of Martyn Hope.

Taking leave of myself unlocked something. From that day on I started writing again, and for the next 18 months or so my rucksack became progressively heavier with notebooks. Nearly two years after leaving England I found myself in a pleasant small city where it was cheap to live. I leased a flat, bought a typewriter and typed up my notebooks. People say it is hard getting a book published but I found it easy. The first agent I sent my novella to agreed to take me on, and the first publisher she sent it to signed the book. So I became a writer, and in time a creative writing tutor.

Actually after that first surge of inspiration I ran dry, but I learned discipline and methods that, along with a natural curiosity, have served me well enough. I am not famous, but if you follow a certain genre of fiction, chances are you'll know my name. It's been a good life. I'm not going to tell you any more about it in case you decide to come looking for me.

***

In the first weeks of my wandering I tried to keep up with the Undercliff story, but information was patchy. Remember, there was no internet then, no 24-hour news, just newspaper reports that I'd usually see a day or two late. It seems that George's body was recovered on Easter Sunday, my birthday, but I couldn't find any mention of the Two. There were a few stories in the tabloids skirting around a sensation, but they had little of substance to say. A photo of Tim bleeding from the head was syndicated and appeared in most reports, along with photos of George and quotes from his sister, and an aerial shot of the cliff. Within a week the story had fallen out of the news. It was the time of Watergate and burgeoning IRA troubles, against which a cliff-fall in Devon paled. Nearly two years after leaving, shortly before I settled where I still am, I met an Englishman in the bar I was serving at. He had a South London accent, and when I asked him where he came from he said Nunhead. I said I'd visited friends there once about three years ago, who went to a church in an old bingo hall. "I remember that," he said. "They left a while back. It's boarded up now."

I was to find out later that the police did track Martyn Hope to the caravan, but I could not confirm if he was wanted for questioning about an unexplained death. I suspect he was.

I never went back. It was Martyn's home, not mine. Even though I could not forget the Olive Grove and all that happened, I was in time able to put it away in the back of my mind. Then when we got a decent broadband connection here I took to snooping around remotely. As you get older you look back. I've said before there isn't a single Google mention of the Olive Grove or the Two. Streetview revealed that the old bingo hall was gone, a block of flats in its place, whatever secrets it held buried forever in the foundations. Apart from a birth certificate on a genealogy website and some university records, there's no trace of Amelia. I couldn't locate a death certificate. There's no trace of The Flock either. Nowhere can I find a copy of their cassette, or the Olive Grove book. Not on eBay, not anywhere. It looks like the sea has taken Devil's Field. I've included a map so you can see how it was. Or at least how I remember it. Two years ago I was rather aimlessly googling 'Kingcombe Vale' when I noticed adverts for a luxury holiday lodge. It turned out to be a two-bedroom wooden cabin with a hot tub on the porch, one of a group of six. The advert said it was three years old. As I scrolled through the estate agent's photos there was something about the slope of the land that looked familiar. Then I saw a photo of a shared residents' garden, benches situated around the paved flower design that I had helped uncover 40 years earlier. It was clear that the house was no longer standing. I wondered if Tim and Jenny had stayed there into old age, keeping the house ready, ever the faithful retainers. Waiting.

I said just now that when I stopped being Martyn Hope something was unlocked and I wrote freely. Now I find in coming back to Martyn I am writing freely again.

I am almost at the end of my account now. That is just as well because time is short. Six months ago the doctors told me the bloating in my stomach was not, after all, indigestion, but cancer. They gave me a year at the most. The way things are going I think that was optimistic. I've heard people say it's a shame I'm dying relatively young, that I would have had a few more books in me. But really I'm 78 not 68, so I can hardly complain.

There is just one more thing I want to say. The day following my 38th birthday, just over a year after the cliff-fall, I came across a story in one of the less reliable newspapers. It had been published three days earlier. Most of it was nothing new. The same photos of Tim and George and the cliff. But one section caught my eye, which I will copy out here. Make of it what you will:

THE MYSTERY OF UNDERCLIFF

It wasn't until Easter Sunday that the cliff was deemed stable, and the Army and emergency services were permitted to begin their grim work. Within three hours of digging they had recovered the body of the Reverend George Parsons. The following day his car was located in nearby Branscombe where, it appears, he had been staying in a caravan that a friend of his, Martyn Hope, a one-time member of the Olive Grove, had rented some days before. There was no sign of Hope at the caravan and no trace of him has been found since. There has been speculation that he perished in the cliff-fall, though his body was never found and no witnesses placed him at the scene. A few days before the events described in this report charred human remains had been found in Hope's burnt-out flat in London, their identity not yet established.

Digging continued throughout that day and the following day. Dozens of witnesses confirm that the leaders of the Olive Grove, Magnus Eves and Simon Hill, were standing next to Parsons when the overhanging cliff broke away and that they must have perished with him. However, their bodies were never recovered and no one could bear witness to their actual demise. Experts believe that the force of the impact could have opened up cracks in the ground many feet deep into which the men may have fallen before being buried.

A year on, the Olive Grove has broken up, but a remnant remain at the big house called Undercliff, convinced that their leaders somehow escaped and will one day return.

The day after Parsons' body was recovered, two sets of skeletal remains were found. Judging by the condition of the bones, the fragments of clothing clinging to them and a few coins scattered in the vicinity, they had been lying there for between 50 and 60 years. Although a number of personal possessions were found with the bodies, including a watch, and a signet ring engraved with the initials 'ND', those bodies remain unidentified. The police believe they were buried in an earlier fall, decades before, and had lain undiscovered until Good Friday last year.

The End

Epilogue
October 31st, 2015

Adam Noucquet read those last words and paused. There were five more pages in the manuscript. The first was a hand-drawn map. He turned to the next. It was a scan of a photo very familiar to him. A group of men from New Dawn standing in a rough semi-circle, two off to one side, a little apart. On the next page was a scan of another photo. Three older men seated, with a pair of younger men standing behind them. Adam knew what the next page would be before he turned to it. Another scan, colour this time: two men, one bearded, with longish silvery hair. Then, on the last page, this:

Dear Adam

Do you remember me? We only met the once, in that pub near the river in Hammersmith. I can't remember its name but you probably can because you lived nearby. One evening in Spring 1973. You'll remember George of course. I expect you went to his funeral.

For decades I never thought I'd write this. But after the doctors told me I had a year I sat in my car in the hospital car park and knew, just knew, that I had to make a record of these events before it was too late. Why? I'm not sure really. I'll leave that one to the psychologists.

I think of this as a memorial to George. A memorial to Martyn Hope. A memorial to Amelia, whose memory, I found, had faded most with time. I've thought about sending it to my agent as my final novel, and I might yet do that. There is still time. In the meantime I'm sending it to you because you are the one person I could trace who had

any connection to these events. And because if my story is
a mystery, a part of it is your mystery too.

Best wishes, and don't be fooled by the postmark.

Adam read this last page through three times. Then he
looked at each photo in turn. Yes, there was a likeness.
There really was a likeness.

He sat back thinking for several minutes, then looked
at his watch. It was nearly midnight. He had opened the
package containing the manuscript on returning home late
that afternoon. After he sat down to scan it, wondering
what it was, he ended up reading it in one sitting, breaking
off now and then for food and drink.

Adam went to the fridge and poured a glass of milk.
Sitting back in his chair he looked out of the open window
into the night. It was still quite warm. When he had first
moved to New Zealand with Rebecca over thirty years
ago he was struck often with a momentary sense of, not
homesickness exactly, but the vast distance between where
he was and where he'd come from. As the years passed
and children were born, and house extensions built, and he
climbed the academic ladder, those moments became less
frequent until eventually they stopped altogether. But now
the feeling came back to him. Of London, many thousands
of miles distant, and the past, even further away.

He had only the faintest recollection of Martyn Hope.
A wraith in the corner of a memory. More than the man
himself he recalled the handful of odd newspaper accounts
that appeared in the days after George's death. The ones
reporting that George had been staying with Martyn in
a caravan in Branscombe, and that Martyn had not been
found. Of a charred body found in Martyn's burnt-out flat,

that wasn't Martyn's body. He remembered George well, though, and sometimes thought of him still. They had been planning to meet that Easter Monday. The funeral had been a desolate affair. George's sister ushering their mother to the front of the church to mourn the son whose loss she could not comprehend.

Adam sat for a while longer, then got up and closed the window. He walked upstairs and took from a cupboard the pole that opened the hatch into the attic. He pulled down the ladder, which he hadn't climbed for nearly a year now. When Rebecca died, not unexpectedly, he was matter-of-fact about tidying up her things, packing her clothes into boxes for a proposed trip to a charity shop. But then he found he couldn't do it. He had put the boxes in the attic and ever since avoided going up there.

Adam paused for a minute at the foot of the ladder, went to get a torch, came back and paused again, before stepping on to the second rung and pulling himself up. The boxes were nearest the hatch on the right, next to the light switch. It wasn't so bad when he saw them. Behind were dusty collections of their children's toys kept for the grandchildren who hadn't yet arrived. It was a family joke that Adam couldn't let things go, that he was a hoarder.

To the left was his archive. Lidded plastic storage boxes filled with ring binders, folders and loose papers. They stretched back into the gloom of the attic like strata of history waiting to be uncovered in an archaeological dig. The bare light bulb was inadequate but Adam could see well enough with the torch on. There wasn't enough headroom to stand up so he crawled along the boards until he found what he was looking for. 1973. There were three boxes for that year. Though he hadn't looked in any of them for at least 20 years he could recall the one he needed. Pulling the box out he put it behind him on the boards, turned around, and pushed it back toward the hatch. It was always a difficult manoeuvre taking one of the boxes down the ladder but over the years Adam had perfected a technique, balancing the box on a shoulder and steadying it with one hand as he descended. And anyway, this particular box was light as there wasn't much in it.

Back downstairs, Adam spread out the contents of the box on the kitchen table. There was a manila folder containing maybe 30 pages of jottings, typed notes and inky old photocopies. That was as far as he'd got with his second book. It had seemed like a great story. An unsolved crime. The two accused men escaping in curious circumstances and vanishing without trace. But the trail had gone cold and he could not continue. He had put names to the two men who vanished, and found another photo of them in a cache of New Dawn papers that confirmed that they were, almost certainly, the pair standing slightly aside from the group in the 1919 photo in his first book. The official police account of their escape suggested mesmerism – the guards hypnotised into unlocking the cell doors. But from that point Adam could proceed no further.

Next to the folder Adam placed a plastic wallet containing a single sheet of A4 paper. It was a copy of a handwritten note:

> *Hello Adam*
> *I'm going down to Devon for a few days to see a friend who is unwell. I don't think I'll be able to make our drink on Monday. Hopefully another time. Was intending to call but am leaving early so didn't want to disturb you, and I expect phone boxes are few and far between where I'm heading.*
> *As Ever, George.*

The note had arrived on Easter Saturday 1973. Adam handed it to the police when he heard about George's death, taking this copy before doing so. He heard nothing more about it.

Next to the note was a cassette. *Lost Sheep Found* by The Flock. He turned the cassette box over in his hands. The back gave little away, just the song titles. Irritated with himself, he realised that his cassette deck was in the attic where it had been consigned a decade earlier. Though, as far as Adam could remember, it still worked perfectly well. Again he climbed the stairs and then the ladder. The cassette deck was in its original box, with even the polystyrene packaging still intact.

Downstairs, Adam disconnected his CD player and used the leads to rig up the cassette deck. His amplifier was old enough to have a tape button. He switched the power on and saw with a flicker of pleasure the lights blink on in the machine's display, as he knew they would. He looked at the buttons beneath the cassette door, needing a moment to remind himself what each symbol meant. He pressed one and the door opened. He'd forgotten they did it in slow motion. He put the cassette tape in, pushed the door closed, and pressed play.

From the speakers came a swelling organ chord, and a woman singing wordlessly as drums, guitar and flute joined in. Then the music began to slur, one moment a muffled groan, then a frenzied babble. Then it stopped, and all you could hear was the motor of the cassette player turning. Adam pressed 'stop' and 'eject' and pulled out the cassette, trailing behind it a tangle of broken tape.

The Author

Mark Brend is a writer and a musician based in Devon. He has written several non-fiction books including *The Sound of Tomorrow*, which explores early commercial electronic music.

Undercliff is Mark's first novel.

Thanks to David Roberts, Bob Young and everyone at Hornet Books. Also to Lucy Panes, for drawing the map, and to Kevin Pocklington, for his helpful comments on early drafts of the manuscript.

Dedicated with love to Madeleine, Georgia and Gideon.

Also from Hornet Books

SING TO SILENT STONES
Violet's War / Frank's War
David Snell

This two-volume emotional Word War II saga explores the
changing attitudes to the roles of men and women and the
issues of illegitimacy. It begs the question as to how and
why friendships across the divides of nationality, race and
religion can survive in a world in conflict. And it weaves
these stories within the context of the true happenings of
the period.

Also from Horret Books

THE CHANT
Carl Mason

This brave, bold, and compelling legal thriller is the story of Will Taylor, a 35-year-old college lecturer. His rather ordinary working and private life is thrown into turmoil when an unbelievably beautiful new female recruit joins the teaching staff. What follows is a mixture of erotic pleasure and pain, a serious crime that has more than one devastating consequence and a courtroom climax full of twists and turns.

Also from Hornet Books

THE TAPES OF WRATH
Barry Cain

Music writer Barry Cain's debut novel is about gangsters, perverts, decapitation and dreams coming true with deadly consequences. And about Adam Tate, once critically-acclaimed author, now hopeless husband and fair-weather father, whose infatuation with the extraordinary Kate Lyle destroys his life and then his soul.

Also from Hornet Books

FLORIDA KEY
Neil Watson

When Oliver Markland buys an old prison key from a
Florida flea market, his casual purchase sets off a train
of events surrounding a brutal, decades-old murder.
Feeling empathy for the young cyclist who may have been
wrongly incarcerated for the notorious crime, Oliver finds
himself drawn into unravelling a mystery that ends up
threatening his own life.
Can the budding Essex journalist, dubbed by the American
press 'The British Young Sherlock', solve a puzzle left
dormant since dental assistant Sandy Beach was beaten to
death in 1981?
Only Oliver Markland has the key...

Also from Hornet Books

REMIND ME TO SMILE
Martin Downham

Back in 1977, Martin Downham was turning into the
archetypal, stroppy, know-it-all teenager – angry for
no good reason, rude, insolent, indolent, bone-idle and
rebellious. A lengthy spell of destructive adolescence
beckoned, but 'life' had other plans. In the wider world
of work, marriage and kids, Martin eventually tackles
life's grown-up problems with some aplomb. *Remind Me
To Smile* is his mostly hilarious and often touching tale in
which British electro-pop star Gary Numan looms over the
story as an ever-present and strangely reassuring spectre.

Also from Hornet Books

FRACK!
Mark Wesley

James Stack is forced to sell his only asset to any villain in
the Caribbean who won't kill him for it.
His second big problem is how to guarantee that a shale
gas drilling operation in the UK doesn't fail. At first
it's only about money. Then it becomes deadly. Deep
underground, the directional drilling systems have been
hacked - saboteurs have a new, hidden target! Dormant
for hundreds of years, a massive geological fault is about
to get a catastrophic wake-up call, sending powerful
seismic shock waves towards a nearby major city.
The countdown has begun. In 25 days they start to frack!

*All Hornet Books' titles are
also available as ebooks*